COVE

A captivating historical mystery

PAULINE ROWSON

Inspector Ryga Historical Mysteries Book 1

JOFFE BOOKS

Revised edition 2023
Joffe Books, London
www.joffebooks.com

First published by Fathom in Great Britain in 2019

This paperback edition was first published in Great Britain in 2023

Cover art by Dee Dee Book Covers

ISBN: 978-1-80405-972-2

CHAPTER ONE

Wednesday 13 September 1950

'Inspector Ryga?'

'Yes.'

'Sergeant Jack Daniels. Like the whisky, I'm an acquired taste.'

Daniels' handshake was firm and dry. Ryga returned the smile. 'I bet you've said that a few times.'

'Hundreds. I don't mind. It helps to break the ice.' Daniels opened the boot of the Wolseley and Ryga placed his holdall and the brown briefcase inside.

'Where to, skipper? Sorry, sir.'

'RAF?'

'Yes. Not for long though, the war was over before I could do much damage. You?'

'Prisoner of war, Germany.'

'Oh. Sorry.'

'Why? You didn't start the war, did you?'

'No, but . . . Sorry, sir, I didn't mean . . .'

'Forget it, and you can call me skipper if you prefer. Although your superintendent might not like that.'

'He's laid up with a broken ankle.'

'I know.' Ryga climbed in.

'Of course, sorry. There I go again, apologizing.'

'Do I make you nervous?' Ryga swivelled to study Daniels.

'Not really. Well, a bit, yes. Never had Scotland Yard down here on a case. In fact, I've never met a detective from Scotland Yard before and neither has anyone else around these parts.'

'And you wouldn't be meeting one now if it wasn't for your unusual corpse in Church Ope Cove.' Ryga didn't say that he had never been out of London on an investigation before and that he'd only recently been promoted to inspector. Nor did he mention that he was just as nervous and as keen as Daniels to prove his worth. Maybe he should have done — it might have helped to put them both at ease. But he said nothing.

It wasn't that he was afraid to show weakness, or that he was too proud or cocky to admit it, it was just his way. Years working at sea and then the long years of imprisonment during the war had made him watchful and thoughtful. But the war was over. Not that you thought it sometimes — the bombs had stopped, but the hardship, heartache and memories remained, more torturous for some than others. For him? It had happened and that was it. He had moved on. And he was in a much better place now than he had been before it started.

'The mortuary or the Church Ope Cove, sir?'

Ryga wished Daniels would return to calling him skipper. On the train from Waterloo to Weymouth, he had decided it would be the mortuary, but when he had alighted from the London express at Weymouth and walked the couple of hundred yards south along King Street to Melcombe Regis Station for the branch line to Portland, he'd begun to reconsider. He'd already requested that he be met at Easton Station on Portland instead of at Weymouth, where Daniels was stationed, so as to get an initial feel for the island, alone. As the small train had chugged and puffed its way across Ferry

Bridge, on to the rugged, rock-strewn and hilly Portland, and then up the incline towards the south-east of the island, the sight of the sea and the quarry-scarred landscape had made him itch to see where this unusual body had ended up.

'Church Ope Cove. Is it far?'

'Nothing's far on this island.' Daniels put the car into gear. 'It's only four miles long and just over one and a half miles wide. We should be at the top of the cove within four minutes.'

Daniels pulled out into what was probably considered a busy thoroughfare here, but to Ryga, having lived and worked in London for the last five years, it was almost a deserted lane. As they skirted the square with its public gardens and clock tower, Ryga noted the mothers with prams and the elderly people sitting on benches enjoying the late afternoon sun. What little traffic there was practically vanished as Daniels drove south-eastwards along a wide road with attractive white-stone cottages on either side. From their design and mullioned windows they were clearly centuries old. A couple of women stood on their doorsteps, talking, their eyes following the car as it travelled past.

Everything looked as though it was being acted out in slow motion. The world seemed so peaceful and calm, yet Ryga knew that was an illusion. Perhaps to these few scattered pedestrians and cyclists the war in Korea was an alien concept. And yet some of them must have sons doing their national service and must be as concerned as he was over the extension of that national service from eighteen months to two years. Did it mean the Korean War was going to escalate into another world war?

He let down the window, as though a blast of fresh air could disperse such a terrifying thought, and caught the grinding and clanging of the workings of the quarries in the distance, which, from his limited knowledge of the island, were numerous. Portland was famous for its white stone, which had been used on the construction of many renowned buildings, St Paul's Cathedral and Buckingham Palace among them, as well as in the building of the large breakwaters arching into the sea protecting Portland Harbour, home to the Royal Navy and the dockyard. Before the war he had put in by cargo boat at Castletown to the north of the island twice but had never alighted. Aside from that he knew the island had two prisons — Verne, which had only opened a year ago, and Portland, which had become a borstal in 1921. He didn't know if any of the criminals he'd apprehended and who had been sentenced had been sent to either.

He would ask Sergeant Daniels to get him an Ordnance Survey map of the island. He hadn't had time to buy one at Waterloo. He'd only had an hour to catch the train after his boss, Detective Chief Superintendent Street, had told him of his assignment. He'd been driven to his small flat in Pimlico, had thrown some things into his grip, then climbed back into the waiting police car for the railway station, where by the skin of his teeth and a shove from the guard he'd managed to stumble rather than leap into the second-class carriage as the train had chugged its way out of the station.

'Why is it called Church Ope Cove and not Church Hope Cove?' he asked, breaking the silence. 'Was the H left off by mistake centuries ago?'

'"Ope" is local dialect for an opening in the cliff that leads down to the water's edge. The cove was famous for smugglers in the last century.'

'Was?'

'Maybe still is,' Daniels corrected, flashing him a glance and narrowly avoiding a cyclist. 'Perhaps that's why the body has ended up there. He doesn't look much like a smuggler though, not if you expect them to be dressed in woollen pullovers and patched grubby trousers, as in old books and photos. Maybe they've become more fashion-conscious. And thieves and crooks come in all guises, as you'd know all too well, sir.'

Ryga did. While working for the Thames River Police he'd been called upon to assist the Port of London in helping to uncover two highly notable and profitable drug-smuggling rings. It had been because of his background in the merchant navy, and his knowledge of ships, their loading and unloading operations and their crew mentality that he'd been asked to assist. The success of the operations had catapulted him from the River Police into the Metropolitan Police and into the Criminal Investigations Department of Scotland Yard with such breathtaking speed that he had hardly realized what was happening. Now he was being called upon to once again utilize his knowledge of the sea to discover why a man dressed in a pinstriped suit had been stabbed in the neck and ended up dead on the beach of a small cove on Portland on the Dorset coast.

Daniels indicated left at a slight bend and turned into a narrow lane. The handful of cottages gave way to rocks and grass verges, and a stone bridge spanning the lane.

'Where does that go?' Ryga asked.

'Rufus Castle, also known as Bow and Arrow Castle. It's just a ruin. All that's left of it is the keep.'

'Can we get up to it from the cove?'

'Not sure.' Daniels drew the car to halt and silenced the engine. 'This, as you can see, sir, is as far as the road goes.' There were no other vehicles parked and no bicycles. 'We have to walk from here. The only way to the cove is on foot. Or by boat. And as we haven't got the latter we'd better start walking.'

Ryga climbed out and retrieved the brown briefcase from the rear of the car. They set off along the rough track through the rocks, rubble, grass and the remains of rusting machinery that had once extracted stone from the quarries surrounding this part of the coast. Ryga could hear the sea washing onto the shore below, and he thought he could taste the bitter tang of salt on his lips but that was just a figment of his imagination. He was too far away. It was a sensory perception that he'd conjured up many times in the prison-of-war camp, initially as a source of comfort and hope to remind him of what lay beyond captivity — the prospect of liberation. But as the months and years had dragged on without any hope of being freed it had become a form of torture. On his return to England he'd been grateful that the tang of the Thames hadn't been anything like he'd asked his memory to recall. The smell of the river, too, was nothing like that of the sea. It had its own scent: of mud, smoke and fog. But now, as he was reunited with the taste and smell of the wide ocean, the memories of incarceration returned. This time, though, he noted with relief and optimism that they were not as powerful as they had once been. Maybe, finally, after five years he was beginning to forget.

They began the steep descent to the cove.

'Have any of the nearby residents been questioned?' he asked. The sound of the waves washing onto the shore of the small bay beneath them grew louder. Now he had a full view of the endless grey-blue sea with only a sailboat in the distance.

'No. Superintendent Meredith's accident put all that on hold and the Chief Constable told us to wait for the man from the Yard to arrive. He ordered me to meet you and told me I'd been assigned to assist you. I didn't arrange for the constable who was first on the scene to meet us because I wasn't sure where you wanted to go.'

Ryga nodded. If the dead man had arrived on foot, would anyone have seen him? Did he park a car where Daniels had left the police vehicle? If so, his killer must have driven it away. Had anyone in the handful of cottages at the top of the road seen a car or indeed a stranger go past? The deceased must have been one, but then Ryga revised that opinion. The island, although small as Daniels had said, had a fairly widespread community in the pockets of villages scattered around it, so although he might not have been known in this immediate area he could have been known elsewhere.

Three-quarters of the way down to the cove, Ryga halted at an abandoned pillbox, its brick and concrete crumbling to ruins. It must have been a difficult task constructing this during the war, he thought. And cold and lonely being stationed in one in the depths of winter with a gun aimed at goodness knows what — an invading German army? Spies alighting on the beach? The men inside this would have had no hope of shooting down an enemy aeroplane.

Down in the bay on the far left was a handful of beach huts and three fishing boats on the shore above the tideline. Across the sea to the west stretched the cliffs of Dorset. The sea shimmered as the sun's rays caught the top of the small waves. He turned his attention back to the pillbox and peered inside. It was possible the dead man or his killer could have hidden here, but there was no obvious evidence of that, just weeds, brick dust, spiders and mud.

'There's another pillbox on the beach not far from the water's edge,' Daniels said. 'It gets flooded at spring tides. The area behind the cove was mined. It's OK, they were all cleared a couple of years ago.'

'Glad to hear it.'

They continued down and soon were in the sheltered cove. Ryga surveyed the rock-strewn shore. There were some rusting fishing implements and a handful of broken nets by the three wooden fishing boats. Had the dead man come ashore on one of them with his killer? 'Have you a list of who owns the boats and the beach huts?'

'I can get one. The local police will have it.' Daniels jotted this down in his notebook. Ryga suppressed a smile — the younger man was very eager to make a good impression. His usual sergeant in London, Jacobs, wouldn't have needed to be told, but then Jacobs had many more years' experience than either him or Daniels.

'They'll need to be interviewed.' For that he would need the full cooperation of the Portland police — he and Daniels couldn't cover all the ground. He'd been told that the local inspector was called Crispin and he'd find the police station at Fortuneswell to the north of the island. Crispin would have been alerted as to his arrival. Ryga wondered what kind of reception he would get, messing about on an investigation on Crispin's patch.

'Some of the beach huts are probably unlocked,' Daniels said. 'Would you like me to take a look?'

'Yes, but don't go inside. Just see if there is anything unusual.' He didn't say what and Daniels had the sense not to ask him what he meant.

Ryga removed his hat and ran a hand through his hair, squinting up at the cliffs that surrounded him on all three sides, sheltering the small cove from what little breeze there was. In the afternoon sunshine it felt hot. He peeled off his mackintosh and put it down on a large quarried boulder. Being mid-September, there were no sunbathers or swimmers, although it was hot enough for both, and the sea temperature would still be warm. There were also no hikers on the clifftop. They were alone.

Picking up his briefcase, he made for the remains of the pillbox, a forlorn-looking structure of brick, concrete and corrugated iron, and peered inside: only seaweed, seagull droppings, stones and grass growing at the top and up the side of the walls. He didn't think this was the murder scene — in fact, he'd be surprised if it was — but the killer could have been waiting inside for the pinstriped man to arrive, or perhaps the pinstriped man himself had been waiting here for his killer.

Ryga bent down, opened the small case and removed a pair of rubber gloves. He put them on and took a small, slim steel object from the case and poked around in the shingle above the most recent tideline. He couldn't see any bloodstained stones but after a few moments he unearthed a cigarette end. It could have been washed up by the tide, but he placed it in a small brown paper envelope taken from his case, sealed it and put the envelope in a compartment on the inside of the lid.

Daniels returned. 'Three of the huts were unlocked,' he said. 'Nothing inside except some ripped deckchairs, old china, a burner and a kettle.'

'Tell me what happened.'

'The dead man was found over there.' Daniels pointed to an area about three yards from where they were standing. Ryga picked up his hat and coat and headed towards it as

Daniels, beside him, hurriedly continued, 'He was lying on his back, with his arms by his side.'

Ryga reached the location and studied the ground. There was nothing to see except stones. 'He was above the high-water mark?'

'Just. His clothes were dry, including his shoes. But they could have dried out since the previous high tide.'

'Which was when?'

Daniels consulted his notebook. '23.41 p.m.'

'So he could have come in by boat on the high tide?'

'Possibly. It's a fairly treacherous coast, though.'

'But an experienced sailor with a sturdy and shallow draft boat could have done it.'

'I guess so. Low tide was 4.50 a.m. and the body was found this morning at 6.42 a.m.'

'An analysis of his clothes will tell us if the sea covered him or part of him. Who found him?'

'A woman. Miss Eva Paisley.'

Ryga raised his eyebrows. 'What was she doing here that early?' Maybe she was an insomniac or a dog walker or an early morning swimmer.

Daniels scotched those ideas. 'She said she came to the cove early to take some photographs of the morning sun rising over the sea. When she reached the beach she saw the body.'

Ryga looked up at the cliffs. 'Surely she must have seen the body before then?'

Daniels shrugged. 'She told Inspector Crispin that she could see instantly that the man was dead but she checked for a pulse before taking some photographs of the body.'

Ryga was even more intrigued. 'That took some presence of mind. Not easily scared, then.'

'She said she'd seen much worse. I don't know what she meant by that. I only spoke to her very briefly by the car at the top of the cove because Superintendent Meredith was keen to get down here.'

'Too keen, it seems, hence the broken ankle.'

Daniels' lips twitched in the ghost of a smile as though he wasn't quite sure if he should take pleasure at his superior officer's misfortune. 'He was a bit short with her. When she said she had taken some photographs he told her the death of a man was hardly the subject for holiday snaps. Nice party, tall, not what you'd call pretty but attractive in a sort of no-nonsense way. Inspector Crispin and the local constable were with us. They'd already been down to the cove and verified the woman's story before calling CID at Weymouth, but with the Superintendent breaking his ankle and the cove being difficult to access by ambulance, plus the tide coming in, Inspector Crispin said to move the body. We couldn't keep it here.'

'So the police doctor wasn't called to examine the body in situ?'

'No.'

'And there was nothing on the dead man to tell you who he was?'

'Not unless it's sewn in his underwear. Inspector Crispin said he went through the pockets of the victim's jacket and trousers and there wasn't a single thing in them, not even a handkerchief. And no one fitting his description has been reported missing.'

Ryga replaced his hat and pulled on his coat. There was nothing more they could do here. 'Let's go to the mortuary.'

CHAPTER TWO

Ryga couldn't say that he ever got used to the stench of the mortuary but he'd learned how to handle it — with a very deep breath. Best to take it in in one go. Daniels swallowed hard and made a pretence of blowing his nose.

It had taken them some time to be escorted there. This being a military hospital, there were certain protocols to observe even for police officers. They had been introduced to Captain Surgeon Kit Wakefield, a tall man in his early forties with fair, slightly thinning hair, intelligent, light blue-grey eyes and a sharp-featured, face. He led them across the clinical, echoing room to a large refrigeration cabinet, where he slid open a steel drawer that creaked a little, much like the filing cabinet in his office in the Yard, reflected Ryga.

He studied the face of the dead man with interest. Death no longer had the power to shock him. He'd seen too much of it over the last ten years. That didn't mean to say he didn't feel sorrow, pity, anger or despair, or sometimes all four emotions in such a swift succession that they became one. This time he felt none of these, only professional curiosity.

The dead man looked to be at peace. There were no visible signs of a brutal end to his life — there wasn't even a speck of blood on the suit — but a few tiny spots dotted the shirt collar. He was of medium height and build, with dark brown hair flecked with grey, a wide nose, a strong, square jawline and heavy, dark eyebrows under a prominent brow.

'Can I see the stab wound?' he asked Wakefield.

'He's your corpse.' But as Ryga hesitated, Wakefield obliged by moving the corpse's head.

Ryga peered at the left-hand side of the neck. 'I thought the wound would be larger than that.' He was looking at a small incision about an inch in length.

'Not if it was made by a narrow-bladed knife. I've seen plenty this small, some even smaller but just as deadly.'

'Would it have killed him instantly?'

'Difficult to say without doing a post-mortem. I understand you have a GP pathologist to conduct that?'

Daniels answered, 'Doctor Tremaine. He's based in Weymouth. I need to ask him when he can conduct it.'

Ryga would have preferred a Home Office forensic pathologist but they were few and far between, and as his chief had already said it was unlikely he would get one of them they'd have to be content with the local GP.

'I'd be happy to oblige tomorrow if Doctor Tremaine is unavailable,' Wakefield volunteered. 'I have some experience of forensic examination. I was with the British War Crimes Group after the war, involved in the examination of members of the armed forces, mainly air crew shot down over Germany, but also some soldiers who had been shot in the back of the head and others bayonetted, some after being forced to dig their own graves.'

Daniels cleared his throat. Ryga stiffened and hastily pushed away the memories of what he had witnessed when some of his fellow inmates had attempted escape.

'I appreciate that, sir,' he answered. 'Either I or Sergeant Daniels will let you know as soon as possible. But perhaps you can help us now. I have just a few questions.'

'Fire away.'

'Wouldn't there have been blood both on his clothes and where his body was found?'

'Not necessarily. The bleeding looks to have been internal, and probably extensive, meaning death would have been rapid. That doesn't mean that he was killed where you found him, though,' he added. 'It's possible that after being stabbed he lived for a few minutes and staggered to where he fell. But he wouldn't have gone far.'

'So he couldn't have made it down the path from the clifftop?' asked Daniels.

'No. I'd also say he didn't put up a struggle. There are no signs on his hands that he defended himself or that he took a beating, although it's difficult to be certain because bruises look very much like lividity, which you can see by the blueish-pink colour of his face. There might very well be bruises on his chest or abdomen.'

'Any thoughts on the time of death?' asked Ryga.

'His body needs to be fully examined to determine that, but from the lividity in his face and neck I'd say he's been dead for at least twelve hours, probably more, so sometime during the early hours of this morning or possibly even late Tuesday night.'

'Is there anything else you can tell us, Doctor, or should I say Captain?'

'Doctor is fine. By the ravages of his skin, I'd put him down as late forties, although he could be younger and experienced a hard life.'

'A manual worker?'

'Judging by the size and condition of the hands, yes.' Wakefield lifted one and in doing so Ryga glimpsed the sleeve of the dead man's shirt. It was the cufflink that caught his eye. It was square, made of some kind of metal and contained a stone in the middle. He made no mention of it but studied the hands, noting they were large and strong, the skin roughened, the fingers stubby, the nails clipped and clean. There were no rings on the fingers of either hand.

'Was he a smoker?' Ryga asked, thinking of that cigarette end he'd found in the shoreside pillbox.

'From the fingers I'd say no, but that's just a guess because the lividity makes it difficult to see any nicotine stains. An examination of his lungs will give you more information on that. I can't smell any nicotine on his clothes, can you?'

'I can't smell a damn thing in here so it's no good asking me.'

Wakefield smiled.

'Was there a hat with the body?'

Wakefield picked up a clipboard and consulted the paperwork on it. 'Not when he was brought in, according to this.'

'And I didn't see one on the shore,' Daniels added. 'It could have blown away.'

'Was it windy here last night?'

'No, but if he came ashore by boat there could have been enough wind to snatch it away.'

Ryga peered more closely at the dead man's forehead and hairline. He couldn't see any indentation or line where he would have worn a hat but any mark could be hidden by the lividity. He addressed Wakefield. 'Do you think you could get someone to undress him while we wait? I'd like to get his shoes and clothes to the lab for testing.'

'Of course.'

'We'll also need something to wrap them in — brown paper will do.'

Wakefield walked briskly to a door on the far right and after a few moments reappeared with two men dressed in mortuary garb, one of whom was carrying a large pile of brown paper. Ryga and Daniels stepped back while the attendants moved the victim onto the slab.

Wakefield said, 'He was wearing dentures. Do you need them?'

'No. Leave them for the pathologist to examine, unless you can tell us anything about them.'

'Not my field of expertise.'

Ryga instructed Daniels to make a note of the clothes as they were removed. The shoes were first and handed to

Wakefield, who briefly examined them before passing them across to Ryga. They were smooth, black leather lace-ups with a slightly elongated toe. 'The sole shows wear but it's not worn down. And neither has it been repaired.' Ryga peered inside. 'No maker's name.' Although there was some very faint lettering.

Wakefield said, 'They look to be handmade to me. Perhaps he specifically asked not to have any maker's name placed inside.'

'But that doesn't mean they can't be identified. We can check with all the shoemakers.'

'In the UK, yes, but if they were made abroad . . .' Wakefield let the words hang on the chill mortuary air.

If that were the case then Ryga knew they would most probably be unable to trace them. He continued his examination of the shoes. 'The right shoe is worn down more heavily on the heel than the left.'

'Which suggests your victim walked more pronounced on that side, but not enough to indicate he had a limp. Your pathologist will measure the body to see how much shorter the right leg is to the left. It's not uncommon — we all have one side of our body shorter than the other, some people more so. I'd say the shoes were a very good fit, because as you can see from the feet—' he pointed to them, the socks having been placed on the trolley to the side of the body — 'there is no pressure on the toes, no corns or bunions and no hard skin on the soles of the feet.'

Ryga turned to Daniels. 'They're clean and polished, Sergeant, and no saltwater marks on them.' He wrapped them in the brown paper. 'The socks look as though they are silk.'

Wakefield agreed that they were.

Next came the trousers. Ryga noted there was no belt and no braces. There was also no maker's label in them or in the jacket. The quality was very good. He wrapped them up and turned his attention to the geometric-patterned and brightly coloured silk tie. 'It's got a label in it. Van Heusen.'

Wakefield peered at it. 'So it has. Mean anything to you?'

'No.'

'Me neither.'

Daniels also shook his head.

Ryga took the cufflinks from the mortuary attendant who had removed them from the shirt. He turned them over. The weight felt good. Pewter perhaps, square, with a pale pink stone in the centre.

'Unusual,' Wakefield commented.

Ryga agreed. Certainly not run-of-the-mill shop cufflinks. He slipped them into a small brown envelope, which he had removed from the inside pocket of his coat. There was no other jewellery on the victim. The shirt was a good-quality cotton with a soft collar. It was clean, as was the white silk vest. The underpants were cotton, and like the vest looked to be new.

Wakefield asked if he could examine the now-naked body. Ryga was only too keen for him to do so. Wakefield scrutinized it, nodding to the mortuary attendants to turn it on one side then the other and then to lay the corpse on its stomach.

'No tattoos, so he probably wasn't navy or ex-navy. This is a naval hospital, Inspector, and I am a naval officer, so I know that the first thing most seamen do when they finish their basic training is get themselves a tattoo.'

Some merchant seamen too, thought Ryga, although he had never indulged. He had a morbid fear of needles.

'There's an interesting scar on his chest — see here,' Wakefield said as the body was once again turned over.

Ryga peered at it. It was about five inches long and just below the right rib, with jagged edges. 'An operation?'

'I'd say a knife wound, stitched up not very expertly, possibly in a hurry or in a field hospital. It's old — could have been incurred during the war or inflicted in a street fight. The dead can tell us a great deal and I think you're going to need all the help you can get with this one, Inspector. Not like our other corpse over there.' Wakefield nodded in the direction of the body of another naked man lying on a slab. 'Sadly he died on the operating table, cardiac arrest during surgery. It can happen. No relatives and no mystery surrounding him.'

Ryga put his attention back on the man that did concern them. He was eager to hear why Wakefield thought they had their work cut out.

'For a start,' Wakefield said, 'he has no identification on him. Secondly, he was found in an unusual location only accessible by foot or boat. Thirdly, all the evidence about his body points at a hard life but his clothes are of excellent quality and I'd say expensive, including his shoes, which are handmade. His clothes have no laundry marks or labels and he's not exactly dressed for a stroll along the shore or for a walk along the clifftop. Neither is he dressed for boating, so what was he doing there?'

'That's what we need to find out,' Ryga answered.

But as he and Daniels were shown out of the hospital there was another question running through his mind. In the car on the way to Portland police station he expressed it to Daniels. 'How could someone creep up and stab a man in the neck without making a noise on the stones?'

'Maybe he was hard of hearing or deaf.'

That hadn't struck Ryga as a possibility but it was a good point. 'I don't think even a post-mortem will be able to confirm that.' Or could it? Would there be some damage to the inner ear that a pathologist would see? He made a mental note to ask whoever conducted the post-mortem to be aware of it and hoped that Wakefield would be that person. He seemed very skilled in these matters, far more than an ordinary GP, particularly given his recent experience with the British War Crimes Group.

'If the victim wasn't deaf then he must have arranged to meet his killer on the beach and not thought he had anything to fear from him. The killer would have chosen the moment to strike when the victim least expected it. I take it there was no sign of anything around the body that could remotely resemble the murder weapon?'

Daniels shook his head. 'I would have thought the killer would have taken it with him or ditched it in the sea.'

Ryga agreed but said they would need to conduct a full search just to be sure, and it might throw up something further, though what, he couldn't say. 'So we have a man who was likely once a manual worker and possibly injured in a fight or in the war, who made it good and became quite wealthy.'

'Pity the clothes don't tell us much.' Daniels drew up outside the police station.

But Ryga thought they'd already told them a fair amount, or rather had thrown up several questions. Now all he needed were the answers.

CHAPTER THREE

They entered the police station, a large, two-storey building that adjoined the courtroom and faced the sea.

'We need photographs of the victim,' Ryga said. 'You said Miss Paisley took some. Would she have dropped them off here?'

'Nobody asked her to so she probably hasn't. I'll check.' Daniels crossed to the desk, where he introduced Ryga to Sergeant Braybourne, a burly man with thinning, grizzled grey hair in his early fifties. He said that no pictures of the victim had been left at the desk. Ryga asked him to find out if Miss Paisley had a phone number.

'She does,' came the prompt reply. 'And I can give you her address, sir. She's taken over the cottage in Wakeham, just outside Easton, which belonged to her aunt, Prudence Paisley. She died three weeks ago and left it to her niece.'

Ryga instructed the sergeant to telephone Miss Paisley and ask if it was possible for them to have some of her photographs of the victim tomorrow. To Daniels, he said, 'They might not be up to much — probably fuzzy and too distant to help with any possible identification, and if that's the case then you'll have to get over to the mortuary tomorrow with a camera. I'll talk to Inspector Crispin about detailing his officers to search the cove and we need that list of beach hut and boat owners. Perhaps Sergeant Braybourne can help with that?'

'Be glad to, sir.'

Ryga opened his case and extracted the envelope with the cigarette end. 'Get this and the clothes and shoes up to the lab in London by police motorbike.'

'We don't have a motorbike, sir,' Braybourne said.

Daniels quickly interjected, 'I'll telephone Weymouth and ask for an officer to come over.'

Ryga glanced up at the large clock on the wall. It was getting late. 'No, on second thoughts, take this back to Weymouth.' The clothes and shoes were still in the boot of the Wolseley. 'See that it and the other items are sent up the lab tonight, then get off home.'

Daniels looked set to protest.

'There's nothing more we can do tonight, Sergeant. But call Doctor Tremaine before you go off duty and ask if he can do the post-mortem tomorrow. If you can't speak to him tonight, make sure you get hold of him first thing in the morning. Have you booked somewhere for me to stay?'

'I've reserved two places, The Royal Breakwater Hotel in Castletown, within walking distance from here, and The Quarryman's Arms at Easton, closer to where the victim was found. I wasn't sure which you would prefer.'

'I'll take the latter. How far is it from here?'

Braybourne answered. 'About a mile and a half.'

'Then I can walk it.'

'Inspector Crispin's still in his office, sir. He might drop you off.' But Braybourne didn't sound too sure of that.

'I can pick you up from The Quarryman's Arms in the morning,' Daniels added.

With that agreed, Ryga asked Braybourne for directions to Crispin's office.

'I'll get someone to show you up to it, sir. It's on the first floor.'

'That's all right, I can find it.' Ryga was certain that Crispin would have his name on the door.

He did, and the door was slightly ajar. Ryga got the sense both from Braybourne's remark and tone and from the glance that Crispin gave him as he stepped inside the spartanly furnished office, which carried the smell of furniture polish and disinfectant, that the inspector had been waiting for him to arrive and to update him. Fine. Ryga saw no problem with that. But he found himself curious about the man who greeted him, who resembled his name in many respects. Crisp by name and crisp by nature, he thought, taking the thin hand in his and returning the vice-like grip while holding the inspector's steely blue-grey eye contact.

If this man hadn't been in the army, a master sergeant or warrant officer during the war, then Ryga thought he'd give up detecting. But he rapidly scolded himself. It was foolish to make assumptions — he'd learned long ago both at sea and especially in the camp not to label people. They weren't always what they seemed. In fact, they were often very different. The quiet, thoughtful ones weren't cowards but were often courageous beyond belief while the brash, devil-may-care types crumpled at the first real test of character, and there had been many. Besides, Crispin's background was immaterial. It was how good and how cooperative a fellow officer he was that mattered.

Crispin gestured him into the wooden chair across his immaculately tidy desk. Two baskets, one an in tray and one an out tray, were lined up to precision. The in tray was empty, a fact that made Ryga envious and conjured up the picture of Sergeant Jacobs wading his way through his own in tray at New Scotland Yard while chain-smoking, something Ryga didn't permit in his office, but which in his absence Jacobs was bound to have resumed.

It was growing dark. A streetlight flickered on and continued to blink at him behind Crispin's upright figure and narrow head as if it wasn't quite sure the blackout of the war years was really over. Sometimes Ryga wondered that himself. Petrol was no longer on the ration but meat, eggs, cream, butter, cheese, margarine, cooking fats and sweets all still were and people were getting tired of the shortages, never mind weary of the deprivations of homelessness, hardship and poverty. Many were finding it difficult to adjust to life after the war. He'd been lucky getting a recommendation for the Thames River Police by a former fellow prisoner and, since his promotion, in securing a flat in London with the luxury of a bedroom, sitting room, kitchen and bathroom entirely to himself.

He was tired. It had been a long day following a fitful night's sleep and an arduous train journey, but he was buoyed by having been given the responsibility of the investigation and he didn't want to let his chief down. There was work to be done.

Crispin was older than Ryga, possibly by a few years, in his early forties. Ryga wondered how long he had been stationed on Portland and acting as an inspector. Scotland Yard investigations, and therefore its officers, took precedent, but he and Crispin were of equal rank and he would be sure to make that point clear in both his approach and manner. He wasn't going to lord it over the man — it wasn't his style anyway. He needed Crispin's cooperation and his and his officers' insights into the island's people, their personalities, their patterns of life and more.

He quickly brought Crispin up to date with the recent developments and what he and Daniels had discussed. Crispin relaxed a little even though his back to the window remained ramrod stiff, but there was a slight shift in the shoulders and the eyes grew less sharp and wary. He didn't interrupt but listened intently.

Ryga asked for officers to search the cove and the pillbox.

'I can only let you have two, which is two more than I can spare,' Crispin said smartly.

'That's fine. Is the weather forecast good for tomorrow?'

'Yes.'

'I'd also like them to search the footpath up to the small parking area by the Rufus Castle Bridge. Can you reach the cove from the south?'

'The Southwell Landslip area. Yes,' Crispin said. He sounded somewhat reluctant, probably, Ryga thought, because he was worried he was going to ask his officers to search that as well. He'd hold back for now. Perhaps he'd take a look himself. He needed to explore the area more thoroughly on foot anyway, and there was as yet no indication of where the dead man had come from. Once they had photographs of the victim the local police officers could ask around the villages, and he'd also request that they talk to the quarry managers. One of them might remember if the victim had once been employed there. Wakefield had said the dead man might have been a manual worker.

There was a tentative knock at the door. Crispin barked, 'Enter.'

It was Braybourne. 'There's no answer from Miss Paisley.' He addressed Ryga with a brief glance at Inspector Crispin that, Ryga thought, held a hint of apology in it. 'Do you want me to keep trying?'

'No. I'll call round tomorrow if you jot down the address for me.'

'Already done it, sir.' He handed over a piece of paper as though it contained the secret of the universe.

'Do you have an Ordnance Survey map of the area?' Ryga had forgotten to ask Daniels to get him one.

'I'll look it out for you now.' Braybourne slid out, quietly closing the door behind him as though afraid of igniting a reprimand from Crispin.

Ryga said, 'As soon as I get a photograph of the victim I'll let Sergeant Braybourne have it for circulating to all your officers and I'll send one to the press. Is there a local newspaper?'

'Yes, it covers Portland and Weymouth. The local reporter, Sandy Mountfort, has already been on the telephone to me, twice. He wants to speak to you.'

Ryga caught the sour note in Crispin's voice. Perhaps Mountfort had been dismissive of Crispin saying he wanted to speak to the Scotland Yard man only and that had put the inspector's nose out of joint. It was inevitable that the press were pushing for news, and from the officer-in-charge of the investigation. Ryga wouldn't speculate, just give the facts and only those he deemed relevant.

Ryga attempted to mollify Crispin. 'It's a shame that we need to spend time talking to the press, but you know as well as I do that in a case like this where we have no identity we need all the assistance we can get. Someone might recognize the dead man from his picture in the paper, or might have seen him in the area, which will save your officers time. I take it that I can tell the public, through Mountfort, that anyone with any information needs to report here or to their local police officer?'

Crispin nodded.

Ryga added, 'I'm grateful for any help you and your men can give me. Do you have any thoughts on the victim? You saw him in situ?'

Crispin stared hard at Ryga as though he was setting him a test or trap. After a moment, he picked up his slim silver fountain pen and said, 'He must have been meeting someone, his killer — could be a woman. It wouldn't need much strength to stick a knife into a man's neck, especially if he was sitting or crouching down.'

'Motive?'

'Blackmail. Or perhaps she just got tired of him and wanted him out of the way.'

'Anyone you know fit the bill?'

'No.'

But Ryga got the impression he'd like to suggest someone, perhaps the woman who had reported the discovery. Maybe Crispin was right. Perhaps he had already suggested this to the Chief Constable, who had ignored his theories and brought in Scotland Yard and Sergeant Daniels from Weymouth CID. Crispin might resent both the fact that he had been brought in and that a young sergeant from Weymouth CID had been assigned to the investigation — a slur on his capabilities.

'That desk and phone are at your disposal, Inspector.' Crispin indicated the furniture in the far corner to the left of the door. 'Sergeant Daniels can use the desk behind Sergeant Braybourne.'

'Thank you. I need to report to my chief.'

Crispin rose.

'There's no need for you to go.'

'I have matters to attend to.'

'Of course.'

Crispin picked up his cap. Ryga sighed with relief as the door closed. He rose and crossed to the window behind Crispin's desk. All he could see were a few pinpricks of light from the cottages, unlike from his London office, where lights from houses, offices and shops twinkled brightly at night and were reflected on the Thames. Unless, of course, the fog blotted out everything. Then you couldn't even see so much as a hand in front of you.

He reported to his chief. Street said he would update the Dorset chief constable. That saved Ryga a telephone call, for which he was grateful. He collected the Ordnance Survey map from Braybourne, who apologetically said that Inspector Crispin had left the premises but that there was a bus to Easton. Ryga said he'd walk. It was a clear, dry night and he always enjoyed walking. It helped him to think. Braybourne told him the quickest route, which Ryga discovered was the only one unless he wanted to stumble and fall crossing the quarries in the dark.

It was a steep climb up through Fortuneswell, the titular capital of the Underhill area of the small island, where lights shone behind the windows of the small houses rising in terraces to his left and crowding either side of the narrow thoroughfare. The shops were closed but the pubs seemed to be doing a brisk trade. The bend in the road took him higher and away from habitation. To his right the black expanse of the sea stretched out to the west beyond the scarred landscape of quarries. Only a few cars passed him. No bus. Then there were more quarries before he entered Easton, the capital of the island's Tophill area.

Braybourne had told him where he could find The Quarryman's Arms. It was in a street just off the public gardens he'd seen earlier when in the car with Daniels. The mothers with prams and the elderly people had been replaced by a small group of youths, aged about sixteen or seventeen, who were smoking and larking about. Soon their boredom would be channelled in other directions when they set off to do their national service. He felt sorry for them and hoped they wouldn't be called to fight the war in Korea.

The pub, on the corner of a road of terraced houses, was a double-fronted, grey-stoned building, which from the signs in the frosted glass windows boasted a public bar on the left and a snug on the right, whose door was on the side of the building. Beyond that he could see an entrance into the yard and the rear of the place. Ryga plumped for the public bar, where, before even entering, he could hear talking and laughter.

Both immediately ceased as he stepped into the smoke-filled room. He felt like Alan Ladd or Randolph Scott in a Western as he removed his hat and headed towards the bar. Maybe he should swagger a little, he thought, but swagger was definitely not his style. And his fingers couldn't twitch at his side over a gun in his holster because he didn't carry one. Besides, he was carrying his holdall in one hand and the briefcase and his hat in the other.

The bar was crowded with men. A few elderly ones sat in a corner by the coal fire, while standing were a group in their late thirties to mid-forties, who, by their clothes, represented the name of the pub — quarrymen. They watched him in silence as he approached the bar, behind which was a dark-haired, shapely and attractive woman in her early thirties studying him with curious deep brown eyes. Opposite her was a stout, short man in a crumpled raincoat, cigarette poised perilously on the edge of his lip. His eyes narrowed and a wily grin spread across his face as he shifted one of his feet off the rail running along the bottom of the bar counter. He needed no introduction. Ryga had seen his type many times before in London. Unless he was very much mistaken, this was the local reporter in search of news about the body in the cove.

CHAPTER FOUR

'Scotland Yard, I presume,' the little man said in a voice that sounded as though he'd swallowed the gravel from the quarries.

Ryga had hoped to delay the press interview until tomorrow but someone at the station must have told the newspaper man where he was staying. Or perhaps it had just been a good guess. He put down his holdall and briefcase and stretched out his hand, surprising the small man. 'Yes, Inspector Ryga.'

'Sandy Mountfort, local gazette. What can you tell me about this murder?' he launched salaciously, extracting a notebook.

'For heaven's sake, Sandy, can't you leave the poor man alone? He's only just got here.' The dark-haired woman scowled at the reporter before swinging a warm smile on Ryga. Ryga noted the dark smudges under her eyes and the slightly drawn features. 'Sonia Shepherd, landlady.'

'I've got a job to do, same as you and him,' Mountfort replied good-naturedly. 'Pint?'

'Half.' There was no point in antagonizing the local press — he needed their assistance.

Conversation resumed in the bar as Sonia Shepherd drew his beer but it was more subdued, barely above a mumble.

Ryga knew that all ears were straining to catch what he would say. Mountfort offered Ryga a cigarette, which he refused.

'I'll put your bags in your room, Inspector.' Mrs Shepherd lifted the flap and moved round to his side of the bar. Ryga handed over his holdall and briefcase.

'Is that the murder bag?' Sandy Mountfort asked.

Sonia Shepherd eyed it, horrified, and looked set to drop it. Ryga quickly said, 'It only contains some brown paper envelopes, gloves and a magnifying glass.'

'No body parts, eh?' Mountfort winked at Ryga and then beamed at Sonia, who tossed back her head and marched off.

Ryga took a draught of his beer. It was good stuff and he said so.

'It should be. It's brewed locally. So what can you tell me, and don't say "not much" because I can't put that in my newspaper.'

'You've probably got the basics already.' Ryga wondered if Miss Paisley had told the reporter anything.

'Only that a man's body was found in the cove. And he didn't die of natural causes, otherwise you wouldn't be here and Inspector Crispin wouldn't be going around looking as though he's had his lips sealed with glue. Who is the dead man?'

Ryga said that was what they were very keen to find out. He gave the reporter a description of the victim including what he had been wearing — the outer clothes only, which caused Mountfort's thin eyebrows to rise and the cigarette in the corner of his mouth to waggle. He looked up from his shorthand but before he could speak Ryga jumped in and promised he would give him a photograph tomorrow.

'I tried to get one off the woman who found him but she wasn't having it. Said I'd have to ask the police. Bit snotty about it.'

Ryga was glad to hear that. 'Who gave you her details?'

'Can't keep much from me. The local jungle drums work well around these parts.'

'Good, because if anyone has seen that man I want to know about it. I'd also like to hear from any fishermen or sailors who visited the cove or sailed past it on Tuesday night or the early hours of this morning.'

'How was he killed?'

'We won't know for certain until after the post-mortem but it appears he was stabbed in the neck.'

'Nasty. No murder weapon, I take it.'

'Not yet. I'll let you know when the inquest will be held. There's not much more I can tell you at the moment.'

Mountfort withdrew a card from his suit jacket pocket and handed it over. 'What about you? What's your background? What did you do in the war?'

'That's not relevant,' Ryga said.

'Go on with you, readers like a bit of glamour and they don't get much more glamorous than Scotland Yard on the case.'

'There's nothing sensational about our work,' Ryga said. 'I'm just like any other police officer. Seventy per cent or more of our work is routine and requires the cooperation of the local police.'

'Then why send you?'

'Because I can utilize the Yard's facilities.'

'And because you're an outsider, here to make sure no one local is covering up,' Mountfort said in a slightly louder voice to ensure the men in the bar heard.

'I'm here to offer an impartial, fresh view of the case and my expertise as a trained observer. You'll have to make do with that for your newspaper column.' Ryga drained his beer.

Mountfort sniffed, then shrugged his shoulders as if to say 'please yourself', but Ryga got the uncomfortable impression that he'd keep nosing around until he got something on his personal background. He didn't relish that being splashed over the newspapers but Mountfort was sure to get something from the nationals regarding his previous investigations. That was fine by him — they didn't contain any personal information. Perhaps he was being unnecessarily sensitive over it. Most people wanted to forget what had happened in the war and it was five years ago. Only those who had nothing to shout about, who didn't actually suffer, kept banging on about it.

'Anything you can give me, Inspector, would be much appreciated, including that photograph, and I'd like it by eleven a.m. in time to catch the midday edition tomorrow.'

'You can have what I get as long as you keep the national press away from me.' Ryga didn't want them cluttering up his investigation and he knew that Mountfort would be keen to sell his story to them.

'It's a deal.'

Sonia Shepherd returned and offered to show Ryga to his room. It was small, clean and comfortable. The bathroom and toilet were just across the hall.

'I have a son but he shouldn't bother you. He's ten. His name's Steven. His—' She made to say something more, then changed her mind. 'If you're hungry, there's some meat pie I can heat up.'

Ryga said he was but didn't want to put her to any trouble.

'It'll be a pleasure,' she said. 'Be ready in half an hour. You can eat in the parlour. You won't be disturbed there. Steven's in his bedroom. He wanted to stay up to meet you but he's got school tomorrow. He's a great fan of Sherlock Holmes.'

'I hope I don't disappoint him then.'

'I'm sure you won't. But I won't let him pester you. I told him that you'd be far too busy to talk to him.'

'I'm sure I'll be able to spare him some time.'

'Thank you. The parlour is down the stairs, the room at the back.' She hesitated at the door, then someone called her name from the bar below. He wondered what it was she wanted to tell him but was reticent about. Perhaps later she would reveal what it was. Was there a Mr Shepherd? He hadn't been in the bar otherwise he would have come forward.

His eyes swept the room, taking in the small, black iron fireplace and gas fire, the mahogany chest of drawers with swing mirror perched on the top, which was placed in front of the window, and the matching wardrobe to the right of the fireplace. Beside it was a wooden chair with a wicker seat. She had placed his holdall on the seat and the murder bag on the floor beneath it. On the green and purple eiderdown of the double bed was a large towel and either side of the brass bed were bedside cabinets, one with a clock on it. There were no pictures or personal items in the room, but then there wouldn't be if she let it out. He sat on the bed and tested its springs. It creaked a little — like him, he thought — but it seemed comfortable enough.

He approached the window. A large rug covered the polished floorboards. The darkened street was deserted but he caught the sound of men's voices as they left the pub. They paused on the pavement. Hearing mention of the body in the cove, Ryga strained to hear more, wishing he could open the sash window without alerting them, but he was convinced it would squeak.

'Why should it be him?' the taller and broader of the men said.

Ryga couldn't catch the reply. The other man was more quietly spoken, blast him.

'Well, I say good riddance if it is. Nasty piece of work,' the louder chap hailed before saying he'd see his friend in the morning.

Ryga pulled the curtains and, plucking the towel from the bed, crossed to the bathroom, washed his hands and face, and descended to the parlour. It was a comfortable room, if not a little over furnished and in much need of redecorating. There was a large crack in the wall, probably caused by a bombing raid. The island had suffered badly because the naval dockyard had been a target for enemy action. He'd also seen a crack in the wall of his room after depositing his towel on the back of the chair and unpacking his clothes in the chest of drawers, wondering if they would last him out. It depended on how long the investigation took. If there was no result, his chief would call him back to London and he didn't much fancy going back a failure.

He was warming his hands in front of the coal fire when Mrs Shepherd entered.

'Is everything all right with your room?' she enquired.

'Yes, thank you, very comfortable.'

She looked relieved. 'Sit down. I'll fetch your dinner.'

He sat at the table in the centre of the room and a couple of minutes later she returned from a room beyond, which was obviously the kitchen, with a steaming plate of pie and vegetables.

'This is really very good of you, Mrs Shepherd.'

'Think nothing of it. Tuck in. I've got to get back to the bar and call time. Don't want to be arrested.' She smiled.

An attractive woman, he thought, especially when she smiled. It lit up those dark, smudgy eyes, which looked weary and troubled.

As he ate he gazed around the room. There was only one photograph on the mantelshelf of Sonia Shepherd and a child, obviously her son. There were none of a man or any evidence of one, and yet when she had put the plate on the table he had noted her wedding ring. Widowed, he wondered, during the war? Was she managing this place on her own? It couldn't be easy. It would be enough to make anyone look tired and anxious. Perhaps she had help during the day.

The sound of men talking wafted in from the bar. Then all he could hear was the clinking of glasses as Sonia Shepherd no doubt collected and washed them. He finished his meal and sat ruminating over the day's events. He hadn't made much headway, but tomorrow with the photograph and the full post-mortem they'd have more information, and someone might come forward to say they could identify the victim.

The door opened. 'It took longer to get rid of them than usual,' she said, cheerfully and not with resentment. 'They're curious about you, and the murder.'

He was curious too about the latter. He wondered what she thought about him, and what had the men in the bar speculated about?

'Tea, Inspector?'

'No, thank you.' He didn't want to use up her ration.

'You can smoke if you wish.'

'I don't. Gave it up during the war.' He'd had no choice.

'And I took it up. Do you mind?'

He shook his head. It was her home after all. She reached into the pocket of her dress and drew out a packet. She seemed reluctant to sit, as though she was waiting for him to give permission. But he could hardly invite her to take a seat in her own house. He made her nervous. Perhaps he should stand.

'Did any of your customers venture an opinion on who the victim might be?' he asked as lightly as he could, trying not to make his enquiry sound like a police interrogation.

'Several.' She lit her cigarette. After exhaling, she said, 'They ranged from some spiv from London, a nutcase from the mainland, a foreigner come in by boat, but no mention of him being a German spy, not this time. We had plenty of that during the war, none of it true, although someone did say this man could be a Russian spy. No doubt Sandy will print all of these theories in the newspaper tomorrow.'

Finally she sat. Ryga thought she did so out of sheer fatigue.

'And who do you think he is?' he asked.

'Me?' She looked startled for a moment, then drew on her cigarette. 'I have absolutely no idea.' She shifted and added, 'Poor man. Fancy being stabbed to death.'

There was a short pause. Ryga broke it. 'How long have you had the pub, Mrs Shepherd?'

'For ever,' she joked with a sigh. 'It was my father's and then passed to me when he died in 1938. By then I'd met my husband, Sam. He was killed during the evacuation of Dunkirk. Steven was two months old.'

Ryga didn't say he was sorry because, just as he had replied to Daniels that the war hadn't been his fault, he sensed that Sonia Shepherd would give him the same answer. It had happened and being sorry didn't alter the past.

In the silence that followed Ryga thought the clock on the mantelpiece ticked a little louder. He rose. 'I've got a busy day ahead.'

'Of course.' She also stood up. 'I'll give you a key to the back door. You don't want to be waiting for me to let you in and you don't want to come through the public bar and get badgered by my customers.' She felt along the top of the mantelpiece and, retrieving a key, handed it to him. Their fingers touched briefly.

'What time would you like breakfast?'

'I don't want to put you to any trouble.'

'Steven has his at eight o'clock *if* I can rouse him from his bed, but if you want to avoid his questions then come down before or after, when he's gone to school.'

'Eight will suit me fine.' On his past record he'd be awake long before then.

He lay listening to the noises of the house. He heard her clearing away downstairs, drawing a bolt and climbing the stairs. The footsteps paused for a moment outside his door before continuing. The toilet flushed, water gurgled in the pipes. He wondered why there were no pictures of a man who had died at Dunkirk. Maybe it was too painful for her to be reminded of him and his sacrifice. Perhaps having her son, Steven, was enough to remind her of the man she had lost. Not everyone wanted their loss displayed on the sideboard, he thought as he began to fall asleep, and not everyone wanted the world to know about it — certainly not strangers.

He woke with a start. Not, this time, as a result of a nightmare. It took him a few moments before he could fathom what had shaken him from, for a change, a dreamless sleep. It was the sound of a child crying. Then into it came a woman's soft, soothing voice as she tried to calm and reassure. Ryga felt his stomach knot and forced away the memories of his own mother lost to illness two years before his fifteenth birthday.

He lay there listening to the soft rhythm of her voice without being able to hear the exact words spoken, and after a while the cries ceased. He waited for the return of the soft footfall for some time but it didn't come. Closing his eyes, he tried to return to sleep but knew it would be hopeless and his brain, predicting that, obliged him. Just before five a.m. he gave up.

Quietly he crossed the passage, had a cold wash, dressed hastily and, plucking his raincoat and hat from the hook on the back of the bedroom door, hurried downstairs as stealthily as he could, praying he wouldn't disturb Mrs Shepherd. He scribbled a hasty note to her apologizing for skipping breakfast and not seeing Steven, but he said he'd see him later that day, if he could.

At the back door he drew the bolt and let himself out. Under the light of a nearby streetlamp he negotiated the small yard full of barrels and bottles, stepped out onto the pavement and headed for Church Ope Cove. In the lane down to the bay he switched on his small torch and soon was once again climbing down the rough track to the shore. There was a glow on the horizon across the sea that heralded the dawn, a sight that reminded him of his days in the merchant navy. The tide was almost at its lowest point, the waves rolling gently onto the stones. There wasn't a breath of wind in the shelter of the cove.

He recalled what Captain Wakefield had said about the timing of the victim's death. He gazed around. The killer and victim must have come here with torches. Why meet here? For privacy obviously, and if that was the case then the victim hadn't feared his killer or expected to be killed. If the victim had been brought by boat, already dead, then why hadn't his killer dumped the body at sea, where no one was likely to find it? If by chance someone had found it or it had been washed up, it would by then have been difficult to identify once the marine life had eaten into it. Someone had gone to a great deal of trouble to eliminate all the victim's identification, or had he done that himself? Had he left his papers and personal belongings somewhere? A beach hut, perhaps? That didn't mean to say they were still there — the killer could have taken them.

Suddenly his heartbeat quickened at the sound of footsteps behind him. The thought flashed into his mind that history was about to repeat itself and he'd end up dead with a knife in his neck. He spun round to find himself looking into the pale blue eyes of a tall woman in her late twenties or maybe early thirties, wearing navy-blue trousers, flat shoes and a sweater under a well-worn and disreputable dark-navy donkey jacket, which only seemed to enhance her casual elegance rather than detract from it. Around her slender neck was an expensive-looking camera. Her shoulder-length blonde hair framed a slightly tanned, open face sculpted by high cheekbones and endowed with a generous mouth, which was smiling at him while the cool blue eyes assessed him shrewdly and critically.

'I'm sorry, I didn't mean to startle you, Inspector Ryga,' she apologized with a slightly playful air. Her voice was rich and rounded but without any noticeable accent.

'And you are?' This couldn't possibly be the woman who had discovered the body.

She swiftly corrected his thought. 'Eva Paisley.'

What was it Sergeant Daniels had said? That she was a 'nice party, tall, not what you'd call pretty but attractive in a sort of no-nonsense way'. Ryga saw exactly what Daniels had meant. And he thought Eva Paisley very attractive indeed.

CHAPTER FIVE

'May I ask what you are doing here?' Ryga said, keeping his tone light. There was no reason why she shouldn't be on the beach. It wasn't out of bounds to the public.

'The same as you, revisiting the scene of the crime, *if* he was killed here. And no, I didn't kill him.' There was a gleam in her eyes and no defensiveness about her tone.

'What makes you think he wasn't killed here?' he asked, intrigued by her and keen to hear her views.

'Because the lie of his body looked as though someone had placed him like that.'

'Have you seen many bodies?'

'Sadly, yes.'

Ryga raised his eyebrows. 'You're a doctor?'

'No, a photographer.' She indicated the camera. 'And finding a corpse in the cove yesterday did make the morning shoot far more interesting. You find my flippancy distasteful?'

Did he? Had his reaction been so obvious? 'I'm just surprised by it.'

'I surprise myself most of the time. I saw you walk past the cottage. It's on the main Wakeham road, and I didn't fancy shouting, "Hey, Inspector, want to see some photos?" The neighbours already think I'm a little odd.'

He couldn't help smiling.

'I guessed where you were heading. I didn't really need the camera but it's my occupation and a photographer without a camera is like a policeman without a whistle. I take it you do have a whistle?'

He stretched his hand into the inside pocket of his raincoat and withdrew it. 'Want me to blow it?'

'Only if you think I'm dangerous and need arresting.'

She was arresting and maybe her charm was also dangerous, he thought. 'Did you take any pictures of me?' he asked.

'Yes, from the path. The great detective at work.'

'Staring out to sea. Hoping for inspiration. Or, as the newspapers might say, the great Scotland Yard detective looking baffled,' he added, frowning.

'They're only pictures of your back but it's OK, I won't use them or sell them to the newspapers, including that diminutive local reporter, Mountfort. You can have them and I'll burn the negatives in front of you if you're really that worried. But you'd like to see the pictures I took of the corpse, so let's take a look.' She struck out and it was all he could do to keep up with her long-legged stride. 'Maybe I can tell you a thing or two about him when we examine the photographs,' she tossed over her shoulder, not the least out of breath.

'What do you mean by that?' Did she know the victim? If so, why hadn't she told Inspector Crispin?

'I see things through my photographer's eye, which might give you a different slant on what you and your colleagues see. Or perhaps add to it,' she replied.

But would it be relevant? he wondered. Still, he needed all the information he could get and he wasn't going to refuse to examine any ideas, no matter how wacky they sounded.

He looked back over his shoulder. 'Did you take this path down to the cove yesterday morning?'

'Yes.'

'Then you must have seen the body from here.'

'Of course.'

'You didn't tell Inspector Crispin or Sergeant Daniels that.'

'They didn't ask me.'

They came out at the top of the path.

'But why did you go down? Why not go straight to the police station?'

'Don't be obtuse, Ryga, you know why.' She indicated her camera. 'Besides, I didn't know the poor man was dead, although I thought it extremely likely,' she continued, striding up the lane towards Wakeham. 'I could tell by the way he was lying, although there was a chance he was unconscious. As I got nearer, though, I ruled that out because then I could see by his colour that he was dead and had been for some hours, but I tested for a pulse anyway.'

No screaming and running off for this woman, thought Ryga. 'You've seen bodies in that state before then?'

'And worse. I'm a war photographer.'

He took a breath. 'I see.'

'Do you?' she said, slightly hostile, but the anger vanished from her eyes as she stared at him. 'Yes, you do,' she said quietly before looking away.

They walked on in silence.

Ryga was grateful she didn't ask about his war. His admiration for her increased. As a war photographer she would have witnessed some dreadful carnage. Now he understood why a single body on the beach had not been a traumatic event for her.

Turning into the main street, she led the way across the road to a small Portland-stone cottage with navy-blue garage doors on the right that must once have held horses, and a window above them. A narrow alleyway on the left looked as though it led into the backyard or garden. A handful of men heading for work on foot passed them on the opposite side of the road. By their apparel they were making for one of the nearby quarries. Ryga noted their inquisitive glances and a couple of the older men touched their caps, not to him but to Eva Paisley, who waved a greeting back. A bus thundered past as she slipped a key into the lock and pushed open the door.

They stepped directly into a sitting room. It was comfortably furnished with an array of mismatched armchairs, a table pressed up against the far right-hand wall, two thick Persian rugs on the flagstoned floor, a large inglenook fireplace on the left and behind it stairs that led up to the first floor. There were also some paintings on the thick-stoned, whitewashed walls — urban landscapes showing workers making for the factory gates, men toiling in the quarries, who by their clothes were convicts from the nearby prison, seascapes featuring fishermen. But these weren't the usual cosy type of picture — these showed the workers' raw features and heavy labour.

Seeing him looking, she said, 'My late aunt's.'

'They're . . .' He searched for the right word, feeling a little self-conscious that Eva Paisley would be scornful if he said 'good'. It was the wrong word anyway because it didn't do them enough justice. 'Striking and thought-provoking,' he said after a moment, admiring the way that hope, fear, struggle and hardship had been captured in the eyes and mouths.

'They are.' She threw him an assessing glance. 'Come through to the kitchen. I inherited this place and all of Pru's paintings. I'm not sure what to do with either yet, although several galleries have approached me wanting to know if I'd sell her paintings.'

He'd love to own one but considered they would be way out of reach of a police officer's pay.

'I thought I might sell the cottage but now I'm not so sure,' she said. 'It might be nice to have somewhere to stay near the sea now and again.'

But not for long, he thought. 'Where do you usually live?'

'Wherever the job takes me.' She put the camera down on the kitchen table and shrugged off her donkey jacket, which she placed on a hook on the back of the kitchen door. 'But I do have an apartment in London.'

'Now there's no war, what do you photograph?'

'There's always a war, Ryga. I might go off to Korea. Don't look so horrified. You're thinking what's a nice girl like me doing tearing around war zones taking snaps?'

'Not quite.'

'But along those lines. The answer is I don't know. It's just something I feel I have to and want to do, a bit like you wanting to solve crimes and put people in prison or get them hanged.'

'Only those who are guilty.'

'Ah, but it's not always the guilty.'

'I don't sentence them, and I like to think that I have enough evidence to prove they are guilty.'

'But you're *compelled* to keep the public safe from murderers, thieves, cutthroats and rapists?'

'Compelled? I'm not sure. It's just something I do.'

'Life shouldn't be just something one does, Ryga.'

'But it often is.'

'Maybe. But you can always change that.'

'Some people can't.'

'No,' she said thoughtfully. Then, crisply, 'Coffee?' She lifted a contraption made of double-glass jars and must have seen his surprise. 'It was Pru's. She developed a healthy love for coffee, having lived on a plantation as a child for many years. As soon as these came on the market she bought one. It makes great coffee. But if you're a mug of tea man—'

'Coffee is fine, thank you.'

'Did the locals in The Quarryman's Arms tell you about me, the mad woman in old Pru's cottage?'

'No. I didn't talk to them. Sandy Mountfort was intent on grabbing all my attention and your name didn't come up, although he has asked me for a photograph of the victim.'

'Which you shall have shortly. It's a wonder they didn't gossip about me.'

'Is there something to gossip about?' He watched her spoon the coffee into the glass machine and switch it on.

'There's always something and someone to gossip about in a place like this.'

'Such as?'

'How I, a stranger, and a rather queer one at that, managed to find a dead man in the cove. And no, I don't know who he is, and I have never seen him before.'

'Why do you say a "rather queer one"?'

'I wouldn't have thought you needed to ask that.' She pushed her blonde hair back off her forehead and looked at him impishly. 'It's what Inspector Crispin thinks. I don't exactly conform to his image of a woman, and he's not the only one. I had hoped the war would have changed views of what women can do but it's amazing how quickly people forget.'

Ryga's mind flicked to Sonia Shepherd managing the pub on her own. He wanted to ask Eva Paisley about her but wasn't sure why. He wondered what she had thought when she had found his message propped up against the teapot on the table. Did she think he was avoiding her and her son? That was foolish. Why should he? But he recognized that he didn't want her to think badly of him. Impatiently, he brushed away the thought. He had no time for such wasted emotions or entanglements. His job saw to that.

'Breakfast?' Eva said. 'It'll have to be scrambled eggs only, no bacon,' she continued without waiting for him to reply.

'I couldn't possibly—'

'Oh, don't be so stuffy, and for heaven's sake take off that ridiculous-looking mackintosh, it makes you look sixty-four.'

'I feel it sometimes,' he replied with a smile.

'Sling it anywhere.'

'I don't want to take up your ration,' he said.

'You're not, but then I probably shouldn't tell you that, you being a policeman. A very nice local man lets me have one or two eggs, or, that is, he let my aunt have them during the war and the tradition has continued.'

Ryga reentered the sitting room, placed his coat over the back of an armchair and his hat on top of it, noting this time the photographs on the sideboard of a woman in her mid-fifties with strong features, short grey hair and a wide mouth looking reflectively into the camera, and another of a slender, tall woman in a swimsuit on what he thought was Church Ope Cove. It was Eva. Who had taken that picture? Perhaps she had taken it herself on a timer.

'There's plenty of bread,' she said as he returned to the kitchen. 'So hack yourself off a couple of thick slices and a couple for me while you're at it. I'll stick them under the grill.' The grill popped and hissed into life.

She began whisking the eggs. 'There's no butter or margarine. I've got some left on ration but I was preoccupied yesterday with more important matters than to queue for it. While we eat and drink I'll tell you what happened. Sergeant Daniels has probably already brought you up to date but there's no harm in repeating it to fresh ears and an open mind — at least, I hope you have an open mind, Ryga. You look as though you might. Which is more than I can say for Inspector Crispin and Superintendent Meredith. If Meredith hadn't been so anxious to get rid of me he might not have slipped and broken his ankle. Sit down.'

He did.

'Egg on or off your toast?'

'On.'

'Good decision.'

She placed the plate in front of him and poured them coffee. Both tasted good. He was amazed that he was eating breakfast with a witness. It was unprecedented in his short police career, but then the person discovering a body didn't usually take photographs of it that could assist in their investigations. Somehow both the breakfast and the fact she had photographed the corpse seemed perfectly natural.

'So here's my statement—'

It was as Daniels had told him: there was nothing new or different. By the time she had finished so was their breakfast.

'Right, let's look at the photographs.' She made for the door leading off the kitchen. 'This used to be the scullery but Aunt Pru had it converted into an artist's studio and the inner sitting room became the kitchen. I turned this into a temporary darkroom when I arrived here two weeks ago.'

She flicked on the light and he saw several photographs laid out on a table against the wall. They were of excellent quality, and he felt guilty as his comments to Daniels yesterday flooded back about them probably being fuzzy and of no use. Daniels certainly didn't need to take his camera to the mortuary today.

The first picture he studied was taken from the path that led down into the cove with the body laid out as Daniels had told him and as Eva Paisley had confirmed. The victim was lying on his back with his legs slightly apart and his arms angled away from his body but straight.

'I see what you mean about knowing he was dead,' he said. 'He doesn't look as though he's just fallen asleep, and why would he be on the beach wearing a suit? If he had fallen from the cliff or been thrown over it, or had had some kind of seizure, his body would have been crumpled up, lying on its side or on its face.' And now that Ryga could actually see a picture of the body, he agreed that it did look as though the victim might have been placed there. Could he have been standing or sitting when he was stabbed in the neck and his body repositioned? But why bother to do so?

'His clothes are interesting,' she said, echoing Wakefield's comments. 'I've done some fashion shoots — needs must when there's a lull in hostilities around the world,' she said, slightly tongue-in-cheek. 'And that suit is very Cary Grant, Clark Gable or Winston Churchill, although the corpse's build lends itself more to the former two. Those kinds of suits were very popular in America in the twenties and thirties.'

'You think he could be American?'

'Why not? There were a lot of them over here during the war. He might have stayed here or returned from America, perhaps because he left someone behind.'

It was an idea well worth considering. Had he fathered a child while being stationed close by and had returned to his lover only to discover an irate husband had also returned from the war? Was jealousy and revenge the motive? Crispin had already mentioned that. Perhaps Church Ope Cove had been the lovers' meeting place and therefore chosen by the killer as the death place. The dead man could have arranged a meeting with his lover in the cove and her husband, overhearing it, had caught them and killed the man.

He brought his attention back to Eva as she continued, 'Those suits were also the uniform of gangsters during Prohibition — flashy, a bit spiv-like, until the two aforesaid actors made them more respectable. This is much more like Cary Grant's pinstriped suit. Wide lapels, double-breasted, padded shoulders, slightly fuller and shorter sleeves allowing something of the shirt cuff to show. The corpse's jacket was unbuttoned, the buttons intact and with matching thread. The trousers are fuller too on the waist and hips, with button flies not zipped. I'd say this suit was made sometime in the mid-thirties, possibly later, but then it would have had a zip fly unless it was made especially for him and he preferred buttons. The fly buttons were all in place and not sewn on with different coloured thread.'

'You examined them?' he asked.

'Don't sound so shocked, Ryga. It's my job to notice things.' She gave him a slightly teasing glance. 'I see what other people take for granted. I look for the unusual, the emotive, the . . . Well, let's just say I look for more and he didn't look right — his features and hands were at odds with that suit.'

'In what way?' He was fascinated to hear what she had to add to what he had seen on the mortuary slab. It was seldom he had such a knowledgeable and observant witness. In fact, he had never had one like Eva Paisley.

'He was wearing an expensive, good-quality suit, and yet has a hard-featured face, not that you can see what his background or experience in life was from it, because death has wiped that clear. I took some close-up shots though.'

It wasn't a pretty sight, but then as she said, she had seen worse. So too had he. Into his mind flashed the image of her standing over the dead body while the seagulls and crows squealed and squawked around her. Why hadn't they pecked at the dead man's face and eyes? Because birds don't fly at night, at least that type didn't, and she had discovered the body fairly early in the morning, thank goodness, otherwise these pictures would have been a darn sight worse.

She said, 'Note his broad face, the shallow but prominent brow over the eyebrows, which are dark and heavy. The wide mouth. What were his teeth like?'

'Dentures.'

'Thought as much. So probably not a healthy diet. And possibly he came from a background where it is normal to have all your teeth extracted at twenty-one and replaced with dentures. It's much more a working-class habit than a middle or upper-class one, wouldn't you say?'

He would have agreed except for the fact that many returning from prisoner of war camps overseas had lost their teeth because of starvation and appalling or non-existent medical care. He'd been lucky — his were intact. Had this poor man been in such a camp? He looked bulky now but he'd have had five years to build himself back up.

'It would be interesting to know when the dentures were fitted, or, to be more precise, if they are new or old ones,' Eva added.

'I'll get a dentist to tell us that.'

She rearranged the photographs. 'Then there are his hands.' She indicated a few prints showing the victim's hands and wrists. 'Strong labourer's hands, I'd say.'

Ryga would, as Wakefield had also highlighted, and he'd be very interested to know if the pathologist could find anything of use on the skin, under the fingernails, or when examining the organs that might give them some indication of where the victim had come from and what his line of work had been. The same with the lab's analysis of the clothes.

'And have you noticed that the suit doesn't fit right? Of course you have,' she said.

It had been one of those anomalies that he had silently considered after leaving the mortuary yesterday.

'Perhaps it was made for him when he was slimmer,' she continued, 'although the trousers are a little too short in the leg and I wouldn't have said he'd have grown much since having them fitted.'

'They could have shrunk on cleaning.'

'Not a suit of that quality. Any labels in it?'

'No. And nothing in the shoes either, but they look to have been handmade.'

'How worn is the suit?'

'A little but not much. Our analyst will take a closer look.'

'He was obviously prudent as he's kept this suit since say about 1935, possibly earlier. That's over fifteen years.'

'That's not unusual, especially as there was—'

'Don't say it.' She held up her slender hands in mock horror. 'I know we were at war but even you've bought yourself a new suit since then, Ryga — wider jacket, double-breasted, longer in the trouser leg. Fits nicely.'

'He could have stored it away and after the war returned to where he lived and dug it out again.' Ryga ignored her compliment. He'd had no option but to buy new clothes on his return from Germany. His clothes and personal effects, not that he'd had many, had been destroyed in the bombing, along with the owners of the house where he had left them, an elderly couple who had been friends of his father. Besides, nothing would have fitted him. He'd lost weight in the camp. He'd put some of it back on since but not all.

It crossed Ryga's mind that the victim could have been in a British prison for some years for a crime he'd committed and the suit he was found dead in had been the one he'd been wearing when he'd been sent down. 'It could have been his favourite suit, or he'd fallen on hard times since returning from the war. He couldn't afford a new suit or many new clothes.' But Ryga recalled that the victim's vest was silk as were his socks and had looked pretty new. He mentioned this to Eva.

'Interesting,' she remarked. 'His tie is also silk and modern.' She pointed at it in the photograph. 'I didn't touch it but I could tell just by looking at it. Its geometric pattern is not dissimilar to yours. Where did you buy it? Austin Reed,

Regent Street, I'd say.' She laughed at his amazed expression. 'I told you, I notice things and I've done fashion shoots. Do you know the maker of the victim's tie?'

'Van Heusen.'

'American company and very discerning. They're renowned for their quality clothes, in particular their shirts. Was the victim's shirt from Van Heusen?'

'There was no label in it.'

'Probably wouldn't have been. Van Heusen shirts and ties are worn by movie stars — Bob Hope and James Stewart, for example.'

'Expensive then.'

She nodded.

More anomalies. And now for the one that had puzzled him the most. 'And the cufflinks?' He watched her expression carefully.

'I didn't see them. I didn't want to lift his arms and change the position of the body in any way.'

'Then take a look.' He retrieved the envelope from his inside jacket pocket and tipped them out onto her open palm, noting there were no rings or ring marks on her fingers and that her nails were cut and not painted. He didn't know why he was showing them to her except that within the brief time he had known her he had developed trust in her and valued her eye, her judgement and the additional information she had already furnished him with.

'Handmade,' she said, turning them over, 'and if I'm not mistaken, that is a real diamond in the centre.'

His thoughts exactly, especially after what she had said about the shirt and the tie.

'Unusual colour too, pink,' she added. 'Not the natural choice for a man. So it seems as though your victim was not hard up, or rather he was wealthy at some stage.'

'They could have been a present from a woman or he stole them.'

'Wouldn't the Yard know if something like these had been stolen?'

'It might not have been reported to the Yard. It could have been reported to the local constabulary, who didn't think them valuable or important enough to pass on to us.'

But she had thrown up several possibilities, including some he hadn't considered. He was grateful for that.

She continued, 'There isn't a maker's mark on the cufflinks, unless it is so tiny you need a magnifying glass. Have you looked?'

Ryga had to admit he hadn't. She reached into a drawer, pulled one out and studied each of them in turn through the lens. 'Here, have a look. I can't see any mark but there are some tiny scratches on them.'

'I can see them.'

She leaned against the bench, frowning. 'No maker's mark or signature could suggest that the artist either didn't want his or her identity known, or it was a personal gift and therefore didn't need a signature.'

'Could you take some very close-up photographs of them for me?'

'With pleasure, and I'll keep a set of prints and ask around my fashion and artist friends.'

Ryga didn't even bother to say that it wasn't her job to do so. She could speak to people it would probably take him or Daniels days to unearth and to talk to.

'I've printed off several copies of the victim photographs for you,' she said, shuffling them up and reaching for a large brown envelope. 'Because they're black-and-white prints you don't see the hideous colour of his face, due to the lividity, so the press will be able to use them and they might be suitable for your posters.'

'And they might help us to identify him if he's in our rogue's gallery,' Ryga added, taking the envelope from her.

She reached for her camera. 'I'll take the photographs of the cufflinks now.'

He watched her as she clicked away taking pictures from all angles. Within seconds she'd finished. 'I'll let you have them later today and those I took of you in the cove. Where will I find you?'

'At the police station at Fortuneswell. If I'm not there leave them with the desk sergeant, or I can send Sergeant Daniels over to collect them, but only the pictures of the cufflinks.' He didn't want the ones of him being bandied about. Daniels or someone at the station might not be able to resist peeking in the envelope.

'Fine.'

He thanked her for her help and for the breakfast, thinking he sounded ridiculously like a policeman but then that was what he was. He saw her amused expression and left feeling slightly irked by it. He didn't like being laughed at, but perhaps he was being oversensitive. He wasn't one of those men threatened by clever, self-assured women, although he knew some of his colleagues in the police were. Inspector Crispin was possibly one of them. And perhaps one of a band of men who still believed the police force was no place for women. He was aware that some constabularies across the country still had no women police officers which, given the roles women had undertaken during the war, was amazing and extremely short-sighted, as Eva Paisley had intimated. He'd learned that everyone had a part to play in society, and he had returned home from the war hoping that a new, enlightened era would ensue. In some ways it had. In others not.

He wondered what kind of war photographs Eva Paisley had taken and where she had taken them. She'd been extremely helpful and her insight had been invaluable but he still needed the experts' opinion on the clothes, shoes and those cufflinks. And with regard to the latter it meant sending them up to the Yard and asking if a Hatton Garden diamond expert could confirm whether they were in fact real diamonds. Once he had photographs of them he would do so.

He consulted his watch. It was time he was heading back to The Quarryman's Arms where Daniels was to collect him, but he paused. There were two people, aside from the local police officer, who knew what went on in any village — the milkman and the postman — and Ryga had spotted a uniform. He crossed the road and made for the postman.

CHAPTER SIX

After introducing himself Ryga asked the postman if he had seen any strangers dressed in a pinstriped suit.

'Several,' was the surprising and unexpected answer. The postman gave a semi-toothless grin and pushed back his cap. 'I'm exaggerating but I've seen two gents up at the hotel wearing them, one of them about the age of the man you say is dead, though I can't say it was him.'

And Ryga didn't think it was, because surely by now the hotel would have reported one of their guests missing. 'Where is this hotel?' he asked.

'Just along the road there.' The postman pointed to his left in the opposite direction of Easton and Eva Paisley's cottage. 'See that stone archway? Well, that's the entrance to it. The Pennsylvania Castle Hotel. Big place, overlooks Church Ope Cove.'

Does it indeed!

'It's only just become a hotel,' the postman elaborated, in no hurry to get on with his round. 'It's been a private house until now — a bloomin' great ugly thing if you ask me. Built in the late 1700s for John Penn, the Governor of Portland and the grandson of William Penn. You'd know about him, of course.'

Ryga said he didn't.

'He founded Pennsylvania in America,' the postman answered, somewhat amazed that a Scotland Yard detective didn't know such an important fact. 'His sons, Thomas and Richard, also owned the Pennsylvania state. Makes you think, doesn't it?'

Ryga said it did, though he wasn't quite sure what it was supposed to make him think about.

'There was a quarry named after the castle south of it,' the postman continued, 'but it went out of use sometime in the 1920s. Winston Churchill, Eisenhower and de Gaulle met there to finalize plans for D-Day — the castle, that is, not the quarry.' He laughed throatily. He seemed about to embark on a tale about the war so Ryga hastily thanked him and set off towards the hotel. It was only a few minutes' walk.

He entered the impressive archway and walked briskly up the equally impressive tree-lined driveway with its sweeping lawns on either side. To the north the grounds gave on to a wood, while to the south more landscape gardens spread out. To the east there was a silver glow in the sky heralding the bright morning with a pale blue sky, a good omen for the officers who would be searching the cove. He couldn't see that from here because of a wooded area beyond the lawns. Was there a footpath through it? he wondered.

Ahead was the grand white Portland-stoned sprawl of a building, which didn't look at all ugly to Ryga. In fact, he thought it majestic with its square castellated towers and arched mullion windows. Staying here wouldn't come cheap and the fact that the place had only just become a hotel indicated more affluent times were ahead, for some at least. Not so Scotland Yard detective inspectors. This was leagues away from The Quarryman's Arms. Not that he would have preferred being billeted here — on the contrary, the pub suited him fine. It was where he'd stand more chance of picking up information that could help progress the investigation.

His thoughts flicked to the overheard conversation last night of the two men leaving the pub. *Why should it be him . . .*

good riddance if it is . . . nasty piece of work. Who was? Ryga wondered. Had they been discussing the victim?

He noted the two cars parked in front of the hotel. One was a green Rover 12 salon, another a Daimler salon, both registered about 1939, he thought, certainly pre-war. Stepping inside the spacious plum-coloured hall, he made for the wide mahogany reception desk, his tread silenced by the deep-pile carpet. No expense spared, he thought as he showed his warrant card to the thin, middle-aged woman behind the desk, whose smile of greeting vanished in an instant to be replaced by a worried, censorious frown, as though the smell of paint, wallpaper and new carpet had suddenly turned to one of bad drains and sewers.

She peered disapprovingly at him over the top of her rimless spectacles before gliding off to fetch the manager on Ryga's request. On the wall behind where she had stood was a sign declaring the house had once belonged to the founder of Pennsylvania as the postman had told him.

He turned. Across the hall, through the open door, he could see the lounge giving on to a conservatory, where a couple in their early sixties were reading newspapers over their coffee. The other guests must be in the dining room having breakfast, he thought.

A quiet throat-clearing made him turn back. A man, as lean as the receptionist but about twenty years younger, had appeared as though out of nowhere. His narrow face was puckered with anxiety and his light brown eyes were fearful. 'Is this about the man found in the cove?' he asked in a whisper.

Ryga said it was.

'Then we'd better speak in my office.' He stretched out an elongated arm and glanced around nervously as though someone might see them. When Ryga didn't move the manager's arm flapped impatiently as though he wanted to push him into the room to the right of the reception.

Ryga obliged by stepping into it. The door closed silently behind him and the manager slid his way around his massive and untidy desk to a worn leather armchair. The cramped office smelled of stale tobacco and a sickly scented aftershave that Ryga had caught a hint of from the manager as he'd brushed past him. Ryga didn't think there had been any scent on the victim's clothes but then the mortuary smell didn't exactly help to identify if there had been. He'd leave that for the analysts to determine. He was no expert on either women's perfumes or men's aftershave. Eva Paisley hadn't been wearing any perfume but Sonia Shepherd had — a very soft, slightly musky smell, the memory of which stirred his loins. Hastily he pushed such sensations aside.

'Please be seated.'

Did anyone speak like that anymore? wondered Ryga as he eyed the nervous specimen in front of him. This cadaverous, obsequious man was like something out of a novel by Charles Dickens. Uriah Heap, thought Ryga. He'd read and reread the scant supply of Dickens many times in the prison camp. Or perhaps the manager felt obliged to act out the part of an eighteenth-century man as befitting the founder of Pennsylvania in 1787, according to the notice he'd just read.

'Cedric Dington,' the manager introduced himself, perching on the edge of his chair, as though he didn't intend staying long. His ancient desk was covered with papers. 'I really don't know how I can help you, Inspector Ryga — the dead man has nothing to do with this hotel.' He spoke the words distastefully, his nostrils twitching with disgust at the very idea that someone should choose to die so violently and so close to his hotel.

'How do you know that?' Ryga asked politely.

Dington gave Ryga a superior and condescending look. 'This is a high-class establishment, Inspector, and I can assure you that all our guests are present and would not—'

'End up being murdered,' Ryga interjected, again with the same polite manner, wondering about Dington's background. What had this slimy little man done during the war? Probably dodged it on some trumped-up grounds. But Ryga swiftly and silently reprimanded himself. What had he just been telling himself? That prejudice had no place in his job, and here he was jumping to conclusions.

Dington made a moue of distaste as though the word 'murdered' offended his senses.

Ryga said, 'But you do have some gentlemen guests who wear pinstriped suits.'

'Well, of course, that's not unusual.'

'Has a man wearing a pinstriped suit, about five feet eleven, broad-shouldered with square, rugged features and strong hands, aged between mid and late forties visited the hotel in the last few days?'

'No.'

'But you don't see everyone.'

'Well, no, I—'

'Then I'd like to talk to your receptionist.'

'Is that really necessary?'

'Do you have a night porter?'

'Of course.'

'I'll also return and question him. What time does he come on duty?'

'Seven o'clock. I can assure you that neither will be able to help you.'

Ryga ignored the remark. 'How many guest rooms do you have?'

'Eight at present. We hope to—'

'Are they all occupied?'

'Not at the moment. We've only just opened. It takes a while to build good custom,' he said.

'How many are occupied?'

'There were three but only two at present. We have, of course, other couples booking in tomorrow for the weekend.'

Ryga wasn't interested in them. 'I'd like to know who was booked into the hotel on Tuesday.'

'Well, I—'

'Shall we check the register, Mr Dington?' Ryga rose, indicating it wasn't a question.

'I'll ask Miss Maudley to bring it in.' Dington quickly scrambled up.

But Ryga had other ideas. 'I'll examine it at the desk and talk to her at the same time.'

Dington clicked his tongue but acquiesced. He had no choice really and saw that humouring the Scotland Yard detective would get him off the premises far quicker than protesting. Ryga caught the anxious glance between Miss Maudley and Dington before Dington's nervous narrow eyes shifted around the hall. There was no one present, but another couple in their sixties had joined the one in the conservatory at a different table.

Ryga asked to see the register. A Mr and Mrs Waverley of Bristol had signed in on Friday. They were the owners of the Rover. Then there was a Mr and Mrs Farringdon of Hartlepool, who had booked in on Thursday and were the owners of the Daimler. A Mr James Legg had booked in on Sunday and had checked out on Wednesday morning. There was no time entered in the book for when he had left the hotel. Mr Legg was the owner of a Jaguar XK120 sports car, which, Ryga knew, had only come on to the market two years ago and was very expensive. Mr Legg was obviously immune to austerity. Why? How? A war profiteer, perhaps, or someone who had inherited wealth or made money legitimately. Did it matter? Not really. But the time frame was interesting. The address Legg had given was Croydon.

'Was Mr Legg here on business or pleasure?'

Miss Maudley answered, 'I don't know. It's not my job to pry.'

'But it is your job to make the guests feel welcome.'

'Of course, but that doesn't include interrogating them. Mr Legg was a gentleman who made it clear he didn't want questions asked.'

'How?'

She looked taken aback at the question. 'One just knows when one has been in this business for years.'

'He wasn't curt or rude?'

'Not at all. On the contrary, he was a very pleasant man.'

'So what did you talk about?'

'I really can't remember — the usual,' she added with an exasperated air. 'The weather, his journey down here, if his room was comfortable.'

'His occupation? It's not entered here.' Ryga stabbed at the register, where there was a column for it. The other male residents were listed as 'retired'.

'It's not obligatory to complete that column. He didn't mention what he did for a living and it was not my place to enquire.'

Ryga addressed Dington. 'Did you meet him?'

'Yes. I asked him if everything was to his satisfaction and he said it was. Why are you so interested in Mr Legg? He left on Wednesday morning.'

That's why I'm interested. 'What time did he check out?'

Dington looked to Miss Maudley to answer.

'I don't know, he'd already left when I came on duty at eight o'clock.'

'How did he pay for the room?'

'By cash, when he arrived on Sunday,' she answered.

Ryga removed his notebook from the pocket of his coat and jotted down Legg's address. Croydon came under the jurisdiction of the Metropolitan Police, so he would get Sergeant Jacobs to make enquiries. It was the home of London's aerodrome, although the new Heathrow airport had been designated London's primary airport a few years ago and flights were getting fewer at Croydon, but Mr Legg could have returned home. Or perhaps he'd flown out of the country having completed his task, that of stabbing the victim. Or was Legg the victim? If so, his killer must have driven away his car.

He was getting ahead of himself. He noted the vehicle registration number. Jacobs would contact Croydon town council to see if the car was registered there. 'Describe him to me, please.'

After a nod from her boss, Miss Maudley said, 'Mid-forties, well dressed, quiet, light brown hair, very polite.'

'Any accent?' Could Legg be American, as he and Miss Paisley had discussed? He'd returned to be with his English lover only to discover her married. He'd stabbed the husband in order to be with her. Or was Legg the jealous husband? Probably neither. Nevertheless, Legg needed looking at more closely, especially as he had checked out on the morning of the murder.

'No accent,' Miss Maudley answered. 'He spoke nicely.'

'Did he wear a pinstriped suit?'

'Well, yes, he did.'

Dington interjected in his usual *sotto voce*, 'I concur with Miss Maudley's description. Mr Legg also wore a very smart light-grey lounge suit. Now if that's all—'

'I'd like to speak to some of your other staff who would have spoken to him — the waitress in your dining room and the chambermaid who cleaned Mr Legg's room.'

'Is that really necessary?' Dington looked annoyed.

Ryga answered firmly that it was.

With a sniff and a tut Dington showed Ryga into the oak-panelled, starched and shining dining room, where a dark-haired, plump waitress of about twenty dressed in crisp black and white was clearing a table among others already set for lunch. Dington gave a brief introduction. Only when Ryga said he wouldn't keep Miss Kernerk long and that he'd return to the reception desk when he had finished did Dington get the hint to leave.

The waitress confirmed the description of James Legg but had nothing new to add. He'd had breakfast on Monday and Tuesday morning and dinner both Monday and Tuesday night. He had chosen an expensive wine and asked for a whisky after his dinner. He'd read his newspaper at breakfast — no, she didn't know which one, but had read the local newspaper both evenings. She had no idea why he was staying. He was pleasant, talked about the weather but had mostly had his head stuck in his newspapers, which indicated to Ryga that he'd wanted to avoid conversation. That was no crime, but he was growing more curious about James Legg and his purpose here.

When Ryga returned to the reception area, Miss Maudley said that Mr Dington had the chambermaid waiting for him in his office. This time Dington, stiff and upright with a cold, determined gleam in his little brown eyes, clearly had no intention of leaving. Mrs Irene Wilmington was in her early fifties, a small, wiry woman with a lined, sorrowful face, quick, slightly arthritic hands and a sharp eye. She had only seen Mr Legg once, on Tuesday morning when she'd gone in to clean his room and make up his bed. He'd said he'd leave her to it and abruptly left the room. No, she didn't see any pinstriped suit lying around, and it wasn't her job to look in drawers and wardrobes. He'd had a very nice pair of paisley-patterned pyjamas and a matching silk dressing gown, was very neat and tidy, and the room had hardly needed doing, which was more than she could say for some. His bed had been slept in on all the nights he'd stayed, his pillow dented.

Ryga told Dington that he wanted to explore the grounds of the hotel alone. Dington turned pale and shifted agitatedly as though he had hot coals in his pointed shoes.

Probably scared I'm going to find another body, thought Ryga. Thankfully Dington's telephone rang and he had no choice but to answer it.

Ryga entered the conservatory, nodded a greeting to the two couples inside and stepped out onto the terrace and across the lawn in the direction of the cove. Soon he was in the wood. There didn't seem to be any set path through it but there was one track that looked more trodden than the others and he took it, weaving his way through the ferns and bushes under the canopy of oaks, hawthorns and elms. The leaves were beginning to change colour and some had even fallen. He was heading downwards and although the undergrowth was growing thicker there was still a narrow path through it. Branches either side had been broken off and some had been beaten down. Recently? he wondered. It looked that way to him but he couldn't say how recently. The ground was dry and he couldn't make out any footprints. As he progressed the terrain became more rock-strewn and the undergrowth less dense.

Suddenly he came upon a set of wooden steps. They were a little slimy and rickety but passable. As he descended, he studied them, looking for evidence that others had passed this way but couldn't see anything. The steps didn't lead down to the cove but ended abruptly at a deep square hole about nine feet deep hewn out of the stone. It was surrounded by ruined walls. Stone slabs had fallen into the hole, which was scattered with earth, weeds and grass. Ivy trailed around the twisted trunks of fallen branches and he caught the sound of scurrying animals and birdsong. There were the remains of a small stone doorway and steps leading down to the hole. It looked like some kind of old tomb or vault minus its coffin. To the right were the remains of a small graveyard.

Ryga nimbly eased his way into the hole and eagerly scoured it, wishing he'd had the foresight to bring along his magnifying glass. He found the remains of three cigarettes — one tipped, two untipped — which he put inside a small brown envelope retrieved from his inside coat pocket. The cigarette ends looked to be recent. They weren't wet or damp and there were no traces of lipstick on them. He made a mental note to ask when it had last rained here. The hole was fairly well sheltered by the trees so the fact that the cigarette ends didn't look as though they'd been doused by rainwater didn't necessarily mean they had been here only recently. And if they belonged to the murderer, would he have been foolish enough to have smoked here and then discarded his cigarettes?

Ryga shrugged. Possibly. Maybe he had used this location to lie in wait for the victim and had believed nobody would ever find it or be able to link the smoked cigarettes with a killer.

He squinted through the canopy of trees. The sun was rising. It was growing warm, and he removed his hat. The smell of the earth mingled with that of the sea. He stood for a moment, listening to the birdsong and the cry of the seagulls out to sea. Then, replacing his hat, he climbed out of the hole, studying the ground around the ruin. There was no evidence of fresh footprints but then the ground was dry and rocky. As he continued towards the sea he noted that the bushes had been broken back and the undergrowth trampled down. It was a perilous climb down to the cove but someone had done it. And maybe not long ago.

He came out in a clearing on the cliff edge where the rocky ground and evidence of the quarries that had once graced this area spread out all around him. He had a good view out to sea and, beyond it, the Dorset coastal hills and sweeping green countryside. On the other side of the cove was more evidence of quarries and below him two uniformed officers were combing the ground where the body had been found. He'd proved that it was possible to climb into the cove from the hotel but not feasible to drag or carry a body there. Someone, though, could have left the hotel and met the victim on the shore. Equally, as he'd already previously considered, the victim's body could have been brought ashore by boat. Did any of the hotel bedroom windows give out to sea? Had any of the guests or staff seen the lights of a boat on Tuesday night or early Wednesday morning? He'd have to ask them and Dington wouldn't like that one bit. He'd postpone that for now as Daniels would be waiting for him at The Quarryman's Arms. He needed to return to the hotel later to talk to the night porter anyway, unless by then Mr Legg had been located and eliminated from the inquiries.

He found Daniels outside The Quarryman's Arms waiting in the car. 'I hope I haven't kept you.'

'Only been here a few minutes, skipper.'

That was better. Daniels had reverted to the form of address Ryga liked.

'Mrs Shepherd said you'd left a note to say that you'd be back and that I should wait for you. Where do you want to go?'

'The police station.'

Daniels started up and pointed the car in the direction of Fortuneswell. 'I spoke to Doctor Tremaine this morning and asked if he could do the post-mortem, but he said the new National Health Service had considerably increased his patient workload and he was up to his armpits with sick people and paperwork. I asked if he minded if Captain Surgeon Wakefield conducted it and he said he'd be delighted. I called the hospital but couldn't speak to Wakefield, so I left a message for him to call the station to let us know when he could conduct it.'

Ryga hoped it would be that day. 'When did it last rain here?'

Daniels thought for a moment. 'Monday night. It didn't amount to much, though.'

'Know anything about a ruin in the grounds of The Pennsylvania Castle Hotel in a wooded area that leads to the cove?' he asked.

'John Penn's Bath.'

'Eh?'

'It's a bath, built by John Penn,' Daniels reiterated, smiling.

'The grandson of the founder of Pennsylvania?'

'That's the man.'

'It didn't look much like a bath to me, more like a tomb. What a strange place to build a bath.'

'It was intended for bathing in sea water. John Penn didn't fancy going all the way down to the beach to take a dip so in 1805 he built himself a bath. It's not actually in the grounds of the hotel — it was built on common land so he had to pay to use it. He did so a couple of times then didn't bother anymore.'

'How did he get water to it?' Ryga asked.

'The servants had to carry sea water up from the cove in buckets.'

'They must have been mightily relieved when he abandoned it,' Ryga said with feeling. He relayed what he had learned that morning about a hotel guest called James Legg and what Eva Paisley had told him. As he finished Daniels pulled up outside the police station and indicated a battered Ford.

'That's Sandy Mountfort's old wreck,' Daniels said. 'No doubt waiting for one of those photographs.'

'Then let's not disappoint him.'

CHAPTER SEVEN

Judging by his agitated state, Sandy Mountfort had been waiting for some time and was itching to get more news.

Ryga asked him to wait a moment longer. 'I've got a deadline to meet,' Mountfort called after him as Ryga crossed to the desk sergeant. 'And about ten minutes to make it. They're holding the front page for me.'

The desk sergeant gave Ryga an apologetic look. Mountfort was a hard man to get rid of. Still, Ryga thought, the newspaper man had a job to do and could prove helpful. He asked the sergeant if any messages had come for him.

'One,' Sergeant Braybourne said in a low voice, as if to avoid being overheard by Mountfort, but Ryga thought there was no chance of that — the man probably had ears like a bat and could lipread. He was also sure to be an expert at reading upside down, as was Ryga. 'Captain Surgeon Wakefield returned Daniels' call to say he would start the post-mortem at midday.'

That was good news. Ryga gave Mountfort one of the photographs Eva Paisley had taken of the face of the victim. He felt the full profile one with the corpse laid out would be too gruesome for many readers, although Mountfort might not agree. He looked as though he'd just been given a Christmas present.

'There's little more I can give you at the moment,' Ryga said. 'I might have something for you tomorrow.'

'This will do for now,' Mountfort said, elated. And with that, he was gone.

Ryga turned to Sergeant Braybourne. 'Is Inspector Crispin in?'

'No. He, er, should be in later.'

Ryga wondered why Braybourne looked so awkward. Dismissing it as none of his business, he gave Braybourne some photographs of the victim and asked him to see that a set was circulated to all his officers. 'Ask them to make enquiries at the hotels and boarding houses on the island with the exception of The Pennsylvania Castle Hotel. I'm dealing with that. And make sure they show the picture to the cove beach hut and boat owners. You have their names and addresses.'

'Yes, sir. Most of them live in Easton and the Grove, that's a village close by and where the borstal is.'

'Could you also detail your officers to ask the local quarry managers if they recognize the victim?'

'Of course, sir.'

Ryga then handed a set of photographs to Daniels.

'Miss Paisley's done a good job,' Daniels said.

'She should, it's her profession.'

'Taking pictures of dead bodies?'

'Yes. She's a war photographer.'

Daniels gave a low whistle. 'Blimey, that takes some guts.'

'Telephone the hospital and if you can't speak to Wakefield, leave a message for him. Ask if he can tell if the victim was deaf, and also if he knows anything about the victim's dentures, the age of them, how good or bad they are, and where they might have been made. If Wakefield doesn't know that sort of thing then perhaps he'll have a dentist colleague who can examine them.'

Ryga made for Inspector Crispin's office after asking Braybourne to get the coroner on the telephone. As he waited for the call to come through he stared out to sea. There were a few clouds building up and the wind had risen but it was still a fair day and very warm.

The phone rang and Ryga quickly relayed the progress of the investigation. The coroner said he would hold the inquest on Tuesday morning in the courtroom adjoining the police station and he wouldn't call a jury. In all probability the inquest would be opened and adjourned, which would allow them more time to gather information, unless by some miracle Ryga had by then the answers to the four key questions the coroner would ask — the place, time and manner of death, and the identity of the victim.

After the call, Ryga considered those questions in order as the sounds of the station filtered through the open office door — a ringing phone, low men's voices and a motorbike starting up outside. Yes, the body had been found in Church Ope Cove but there was nothing to say that was where the victim had been killed. As to the time of death, Ryga hoped that might be more precise after the post-mortem. The manner seemed clear — the victim had been stabbed through the neck — but as to answering the fourth critical question, that of the identity of the victim, Ryga didn't know if by Tuesday he would have the answer. He might never have it, and if that was the case they might never apprehend the killer. Still, it was early days yet.

He lifted the receiver and asked to be put through to Scotland Yard. He wondered where Inspector Crispin was and again why Braybourne had been hesitant in telling him. Perhaps the inspector was busy out on an investigation and had left specific instructions that Ryga shouldn't be told about it. Ryga hoped that Crispin hadn't taken it into his head to follow up a lead of his own on their Church Ope Cove murder.

When Sergeant Jacobs came on the line a few moments later, Ryga quickly briefed him about James Legg. 'Get down to Croydon and check out Legg's address. He might have returned. If not, ask around, get anything you can on him and find out if his car is licensed with the County Borough of Croydon. I'm sending up some mugshots of the victim — ask records if they have anyone who matches them and get them circulated to all officers and constabularies in England and Wales. I'll also be sending up some cigarette ends found in a possible rendezvous point. There might be some vestige of a print left on them.'

Jacobs said he'd get onto it right away. Ryga rose and went to find Daniels, who was with Braybourne.

'Wakefield said he'd be able to look for any signs of deafness in the victim and he's got a colleague who can examine the dentures,' Daniels reported.

'Know any good jewellers?'

'Depends what you mean by good,' Daniels answered. 'There's the honest, decent sort, who sell new and very selective second-hand jewellery, or there's the possibly not-so-honest type who only sell second-hand stuff and act as a pawnbroker, like Sebastian Conrad. He knows everyone and everything.'

'Does he know much about diamonds?'

'Why? Have we got some?'

'Possibly. I want someone to take a look at the stones in the dead man's cufflinks.'

'Then he's your man. He has a poky little shop off the seafront in Weymouth.'

Before calling on Conrad, Ryga instructed Daniels to call at Weymouth police station and leave the pictures of the victim to be circulated. Sandy Mountfort's article in the newspaper might prompt someone who lived and worked in the seaside town to report in. He also wanted to get the latest cigarette ends despatched to the Yard.

He had anticipated a quick visit, but word had got around that he was on the premises and he found himself being summoned to report to Chief Constable Ambrose. He was shown into an office where a shortish, stoutish man with grey hair and a squashed-up, lined face sat behind a desk that looked too big for him. Ryga gave his briefing succinctly. He held back about his forthcoming visit to Sebastian Conrad, and that Eva Paisley had taken pictures of the cufflinks — in fact, he didn't mention them at all and wondered why. Perhaps because he was laying a hunch they were significant and he wanted to see where they led first.

His update didn't seem to please the man. He showed Ambrose the pictures of the body, the one full on and the close-up of the face. Ambrose's fleshy jowls puckered up even more as he peered at them through his spectacles.

'Strange thing for a woman to do, take pictures. Most would have run a mile or had hysterics.'

'Not necessarily, sir,' Ryga said somewhat icily. 'Many women saw horrific atrocities during the war and did incredibly brave things.'

Ambrose grunted. 'Well, I wouldn't want my wife seeing such things, then staying around and taking pictures of it. Doesn't sound natural to me or to a lot of people. If she is this hard—' he stabbed a squat finger at a picture — 'then she could be involved in the murder.'

Ryga said he was sure she wasn't.

'You'd be best to keep an open mind about her, Inspector,' came the sharp reprimand.

Ryga said he would and left feeling disappointed that memories were so short.

As Daniels drove along the seafront, Ryga took in the late summer scene. Elderly people squatted in stripy deckchairs, splay legged, soaking up the warm early afternoon September sun, and a few children played with buckets and spades on the sandy beach. Just looking at them made Ryga feel hotter than he already was. After a short distance, Daniels indicated off the main road and threaded the car through a couple of narrow streets until he pulled up outside three tiny, seedy shops — one that boasted it sold sweets and sticks of rock, which would be in short supply because of the rationing, and another that sold postcards and all kinds of knick-knacks heralding they were 'from Weymouth'. Between these two was a dingy window displaying some dusty relics that had once masqueraded as jewellery.

Their arrival had drawn the attention of three small boys playing with marbles in the gutter opposite and two women on their doorsteps farther down the road towards the corner. A woman pushing a pram paused to browse the window of the shop selling knick-knacks but Ryga knew she was nosy to see who they were and where they went. The car didn't carry any police insignia or a blue light, but Ryga got the impression all their observers knew they were police just as they seemed to know in Wapping or Rotherhithe in London when he showed up.

The property fronted directly on to a small pavement. The bell clanged loudly as Ryga pushed open the door. He found himself in a tiny room crammed with grubby glass-fronted display cases. Behind the grimy glass were watches, brooches and diamond rings that didn't look as though they'd been moved for years. There were no price labels attached to them. The linoleum was dusty and cracked and the place smelled as though it hadn't been aired in decades. Stale food, tobacco and coal smoke pervaded the air. Ahead was a small counter behind which was a door, and through this emerged a diminutive man in his early sixties with a large nose, dark, darting eyes and a shaven, overlarge head perched directly on hunched shoulders. He was dressed in a collarless blue-and-white-striped cotton shirt with the sleeves pushed up his hairy forearms and held in place with navy-blue armbands. Dark blue braces supported a baggy, dirty pair of trousers. His lined, sallow face broke into a broad grin as his gaze rested on Daniels.

'To what do I owe this pleasure, Sergeant?' His small, dark eyes flicked to Ryga.

Ryga wondered what his assessment was. Daniels introduced him.

'From Scotland Yard. I know. About that body found in Church Ope Cove.'

'How do you know about that?' Ryga asked.

'I know a lot of things.' Conrad winked. 'It's in the newspaper.' He stretched down and retrieved the said item from somewhere beneath the counter — a shelf most probably — and put it on the counter.

Mountfort had got his front page. Ryga found himself staring at a picture of the dead man. He didn't think it would offend too many readers' sensibilities. It looked fudged, maybe deliberately so. The eyes were closed and the face mask-like, but there was no mistaking the strong square jawline, prominent brow and wide mouth. Beside the picture was one of Church Ope Cove and the caption *Who is the mystery man found dead in the cove?*

Quickly skimming the article, Ryga saw that Mountfort had mentioned the pinstriped suit and that the post-mortem was being conducted by the naval doctor Captain Surgeon Kit Wakefield, which confirmed that Mountfort had indeed been earwigging his conversation at the station or had glimpsed Braybourne's note. Mountfort had also mentioned Scotland Yard and Ryga by name, but there was, thankfully, no personal background. Good. Mountfort had enough copy on the dead man for now to fill his column. There was also no mention of Eva Paisley having found the body. It just said 'a woman', but Ryga had a feeling that Mountfort would use more on that story in a future edition, especially if there wasn't much else breaking.

Daniels said, 'We need your expert opinion, Conrad, on something that was found on the dead man.'

'Then you'd better come through.' He nipped to the front door, locked it and turned the sign round to *Closed*.

They followed him into the room from which he had emerged. In the centre, taking up most of the limited floor space, was a large round table covered with a grubby, tea-stained red velvet cloth. On it was a small navy-blue velvet pad and an Anglepoise lamp with a flex that led up to the ceiling light. Four chairs were arranged around the table. In front of the small, unlit fire was a battered armchair with wooden arms and a sunken cushion, and in the opposite corner a wireless on top of a sideboard. There were no pictures on the distempered walls and no signs of any jewellery. Beyond, Ryga caught a glimpse of a room that he guessed was the scullery.

Conrad waved his arms for them to be seated and took up position opposite them in front of the lamp and velvet pad. There was a loupe beside it and Ryga wondered what Conrad had been studying through the magnifier before they'd entered and where the items now were. He placed his hat on the table, removed the brown paper envelope from his pocket and shook out the cufflinks.

Conrad's skinny fingers reached for them and gently, almost lovingly, placed them on the cloth. He switched on the Anglepoise and fixed the loupe to his eye. Positioning the light, he examined the first cufflink, making no comment, only the occasional sniff and grunt. In the silence Ryga could hear the ticking of several clocks coming from the shop and a dog barking somewhere out in the street. It was stiflingly hot and he wanted to remove his coat but wouldn't, and by the thin line of perspiration on Daniels' forehead he was suffering too.

After what seemed an age, Conrad put down the cufflink and went through the same ritual with the second one. Daniels tossed Ryga a glance and raised his eyebrows. Someone tried the shop door then went away. The dog stopped barking and a child started crying. The clocks chimed the half hour.

Finally Conrad removed the eyepiece and put the second cufflink beside the first one. He peered at them with lively excitement dancing in his dark eyes. 'Diamonds,' he announced. 'The real thing, and very rare ones.'

Ryga's pulse quickened. All thoughts of discomfort because of the heat vanished. 'Are you sure?'

'Of course I am,' Conrad said, gleefully without taking offence.

'How can you tell?'

Conrad rolled his eyes and looked sorrowfully at Daniels.

'He doesn't know your pedigree like I do,' Daniels said with a smile. 'Conrad served ten years in Portland Prison for his part in a diamond raid in Hatton Garden in 1910, where he was apprenticed to a diamond cutter.'

'I was young and impressionable.'

'Not that young,' quipped Daniels.

'Twenty-three, Inspector Ryga. I got in with the wrong crowd. I wanted money and a good time and I wanted it quick. All I had to do was tell this geezer when we had a new valuable consignment of diamonds in, where they were and how to get into the safe.'

'Not much then,' Ryga said.

'No,' Conrad answered, taking the comment as an earnest one. 'And it got me ten years hard labour over there digging rocks before the prison became the borstal. I was released in 1920.'

'And you settled down here directly after that?'

'No. Although I'd done hard labour, I'd escaped the Great War. Might not be alive now if I'd gone to France up to me neck in mud and shit, scared witless. When I came out of prison my old master, the diamond cutter I was apprenticed to before I went to gaol, gave me a reference to take with me to Amsterdam.'

'A very forgiving man.'

'Yes,' Conrad said thoughtfully and sorrowfully. 'Pity there aren't more of them. I didn't care what I did in Amsterdam, I was just glad to get away and make a fresh start. I worked for this elderly Jew, a diamond cutter called Isaac Abramowski. Oh, I could never cut diamonds like him and I didn't even try, but I knew what to look for and, when it came my way, how to bargain for it and get the best price. We did well until . . . Well, you know what happened next.'

Ryga did. Hitler.

'Isaac told me to get out but I wouldn't go without him and I didn't. I managed to wangle us both a passage to dear old Blighty, but the poor soul died on the crossing from acute seasickness. He left me some money and some diamonds, which

I sold, and I bought this little house and set up shop here. Not that there was much trade during the war and, before you ask, no, I didn't do black market stuff.' Conrad took a grubby handkerchief from his pocket and blew his nose loudly. 'I did my bit with the Home Guard and prayed the house wouldn't get bombed. It didn't. Business got brisker towards the end of the war and has been even better since. Lots of folk are hard up and need to sell things — comes as a bit of a shock for some of 'em who've never had to count their pennies before.' His twisted smile filled Ryga with distaste but he wouldn't let it show. 'Then there are others making money who want to buy good jewellery at knock-down prices which will make them more money in the future. That's where I come in. All of the stuff in the shop is second hand. It might not look much but that's deliberate. Don't want anyone knocking it off. It's good stuff and word gets around.'

'Why did you come back here? It can't have had very pleasant memories for you,' Ryga asked.

'I know it seems strange, but I didn't fancy London and that was before the bombing. Besides, I didn't really know where else to go. When I looked across at that rocky island I didn't see that godawful prison, instead I saw liberty and old Isaac. My days of wanting money and a good life have long gone, Inspector.' He stuffed his handkerchief back in his pocket. 'I don't even need this shop but it keeps me amused. I do valuations not only for the nobs but also for you lot, young Sergeant Daniels here and his super. Heard he's laid up with a broken ankle.'

'He is,' Daniels said.

'That'll teach him to play football at his age.' He winked. 'Now, to these diamonds. You say they were found on the dead man?'

'Yes, and keep that to yourself,' Ryga answered, 'or we might have to take a closer look at your business transactions.'

'I'm not one to go running to the newspapers.'

'I'm glad to hear it. Do you recognize the victim?'

'Not from the picture in the paper.'

'Then take a closer look at these.' Ryga put the picture of the body and the close-up of the face in front of the little man. He watched Conrad carefully, who scrutinized them in silence, but there was only the slight narrowing of his dark eyes before he shook his head.

'Can't say I do recognize him. No.'

Ryga took them back. 'About these diamonds?'

'What do you want to know?'

'Everything,' Ryga said. 'You said they are rare — how do you know that?'

'Do I know the Pope is Catholic?'

Ryga smiled.

Conrad continued. 'The value of a diamond is determined by colour, cut, clarity and carat weight. These are pink diamonds, and that makes them one of rarest stones in the world.'

So how did the dead man come to have two?

'Natural pink diamonds can be found in Brazil, Russia, Siberia, South Africa, Tanzania and Canada, but most of 'em come from the Argyle Mine in Western Australia.'

Ryga threw Daniels a look. He knew the sergeant was thinking the same as him. The strong-featured face of the dead man, the rough hands. Had he been an Australian miner? 'Go on,' Ryga said.

'Lighter pinks are less valuable than deeper hues, but you're still talking big money.'

'How much?'

'Many thousands of pounds. Admittedly these pink diamonds are small but they'd still fetch thousands.'

Then why hadn't the dead man sold them? Wondered Ryga. Was it because he had stolen them and couldn't risk them being traced? Or perhaps they had been given to him and he couldn't bear parting with them. One thing was obvious, though — robbery hadn't been the motive for his murder. But perhaps the killer had been completely unaware of the diamond cufflinks, or that they were in fact real and rare diamonds. He mustn't have been a confederate of the dead man's if he had been involved in a diamond or jewellery theft.

Conrad continued, 'The other thing that makes these diamonds more valuable is the cut, and that also tells us roughly how old they are. The cut is rectangular with rounded corners and the diamonds have a bigger and wider culet, not pointed. You can see it through the stone's top.'

'What's a culet?' asked Daniels. Ryga had been about to ask the same.

'It's the diamond's bottom facet and it's the quickest way to tell if the diamond is antique instead of modern. These diamonds are also fiery and warm rather than brilliant like modern diamonds are today. They've got a kind of inner light,' he said wistfully, staring down at them. 'They're very precious,' he added. 'These diamonds are old mine cut.'

'And that means?' prompted Ryga.

'As I said, rare, beautiful and very valuable. But I know what you're after. Their age.' He sniffed and took a deep breath as though composing his thoughts. Or was that his emotions? thought Ryga.

'There are three cuts,' Conrad continued. 'European, modern and old mine. Modern came into being around about 1920. Before that it was European and before that old mine, which has been used since the end of the seventeenth century, got more popular with the Victorians, and stayed around right up until thirty years ago, but most of them date back to the 1800s. They're usually set in expensive mountings, not cheap pewter like this.' He pointed a bony finger at the diamonds still bathed in light from the lamp.

'Can you tell who cut them?'

Conrad shook his head. 'Wouldn't make much difference if I could. It would be nigh on impossible to trace them by that means. Not unless you can find the cutter's records. Could have been cut abroad. Old mine cut diamonds are very scarce, though.' He shrugged. 'If someone has one they tend to hold on to it, especially if it's pink. Most of these types of diamonds have been kept within the family as heirlooms, passed from one generation to the next.'

'Maybe the family were forced to sell them. As you said, times are hard for a lot of people — death duties, et cetera,' said Ryga. 'And to do so they'd have sold them how?'

'At auction more than likely. You could try the big auction houses who handle this sort of thing. You're thinking if they had two old, pink, mine cut diamonds they might have more?'

'Something like that, and perhaps these diamonds started out as something different — a brooch, necklace or ring. And whoever bought them had them made into cufflinks.'

Conrad eyed Ryga pitifully. 'And destroyed some of their beauty and value? No, not if he bought them.'

'But he or someone else could have stolen them and then disguised them in this way so they wouldn't be traced.'

'Maybe,' Conrad acquiesced.

'Ever seen anything like this before?'

'Only once with Isaac in Amsterdam just before the war, about 1938. It was a ring with three pink stones. Beautiful.'

'Know who it belonged to?'

'No.'

'What was Isaac doing with it?'

'What do you think in 1938? Valuing it for some poor Jew who needed money to get away from that bastard Hitler.'

'But Isaac couldn't have bought it?'

'No, but he could say how much it was genuinely worth and the poor soul who owned it probably sold it for an eighth of its value.'

In the silence that followed Ryga wondered if the owner had managed to escape with his or her life.

'Is it possible these are diamonds from that ring?' Ryga asked.

Conrad looked at the stones as he considered this. Daniels dashed a glance at Ryga, who through his own gaze urged silence.

'It's possible, I suppose. But there are others like this in the world.'

But not others that had ended up as cufflinks on the body of a man in a pinstriped suit in Church Ope Cove.

CHAPTER EIGHT

'Do you think those stones are part of that ring?' Daniels climbed into the car.

'I'm not sure, and I'm not sure about Sebastian Conrad either. How do we know he's telling the truth about Isaac Abramowski? Have you ever checked that Abramowski and Conrad sailed together to England? Have you confirmed Abramowski died on the crossing? Did the shipping company notify it? Is his death registered? Was there a post-mortem?'

Daniels looked troubled.

'No, I thought not. There was no need for you to do so. Conrad is very convincing and he *is* an ex-crook. He could have stolen diamonds from Abramowski in Amsterdam, bought himself passage on a boat to England and used the rest to buy that shop and support himself.'

'But if he had stolen the diamonds from that ring, surely he wouldn't have mentioned it to us?'

'He could have done so to throw us off the scent. To make us believe that the diamond ring ended up with someone else, when in fact he stole the ring, or bought it for a knock-down price from the Jewish seller and split the diamonds.'

'That doesn't explain how the victim ended up with two of them in cufflinks,' Daniels protested.

'It does if the victim was involved with Conrad in stealing them from Abramowski, or the Jewish seller, and had two of them made into cufflinks to disguise them while Conrad kept the third one.'

Daniels looked impressed.

Ryga added, 'But I can't see Conrad tracking our victim to Church Ope Cove and then killing him, and if he had, he'd have taken the cufflinks off the body. No, I don't think Conrad is our killer, and he's probably not involved with the death in any other way, but we need another opinion on these pink diamonds. For all we know, they could be phoney and Conrad could be spinning us a yarn just to watch us run round in circles. An expert at Hatton Garden can tell us more.'

Ryga was tempted to take the cufflinks up to the Yard himself by train that day but he couldn't really spare the time. He gave Daniels instructions to make for Weymouth police station and once there told him to take a late lunch. Ryga was hungry himself but before making for the canteen he arranged for the diamonds to be transported up to London by a police motorcyclist. If they were as valuable as Conrad had said, then Ryga sincerely hoped they'd get there safely. He stressed the importance of them to the police motorcyclist and gave him strict instructions that they were to be personally hand delivered to Detective Chief Superintendent Street and no one else.

Then, in Superintendent Meredith's redundant office, Ryga put a call through to Street and updated him. Street said he would get the diamonds examined by an expert once they arrived. All that would take time, but at least the enquiries both in London and Portland were progressing, not to mention in Croydon, where Sergeant Jacobs was following up James Legg. Tonight Ryga would return to The Pennsylvania Castle Hotel and question the night porter.

It was almost three o'clock when he tucked into cottage pie, peas and carrots. As he ate he mulled over the recent interview with Sebastian Conrad. There was something not right about him, he could swear to that. He couldn't say what it was aside from the feeling that he didn't trust the little man. Perhaps it was the smugness about him. Maybe that was his natural manner, but Ryga had got the feeling that Conrad was laughing at them. He washed his dinner down with a cup of tea and went in search of Daniels.

'I want you to return to Conrad,' Ryga instructed. 'Get the full details of the ship he and Abramowski sailed on to London in 1938, the date it docked, and the doctor who attended Abramowski's death. Find out if there was an inquest and a post-mortem and where he was buried. If Conrad seems to be suffering from amnesia, come down hard on him. I'll take the train back to Portland.'

Before he left the station, he put in another call to his chief. 'Sebastian Conrad claims to have worked at Hatton Garden before serving time for his part in a diamond raid there in 1910. I'd like that checked and any other information we can get on him.'

Street said he'd get in touch with the Prison Commission. Fortified with food, and with his thoughts on Conrad and the victim, Ryga made for the railway station and the train to Portland. From there he walked the short distance to the police station, where he found Inspector Crispin in his office looking a little less crisp than he had the previous day. Ryga updated him on their investigations. When he told him about their visit to Conrad and what he had said, Crispin's brow puckered with distaste.

'I wouldn't stand much store by what Sebastian Conrad says,' Crispin snapped. 'He's a born liar and a crook.'

'He's managed to stay out of trouble with the law since he came out of prison in 1920.'

'He's just not been caught.'

'You have evidence of crooked dealings?'

'No, he's too wily.'

'What do you suspect him of?'

'Handling stolen goods, selling looted jewellery during the war—'

'That's a very serious charge.'

'The Weymouth CID have turned a blind eye to it. Conrad's taken them in, along with a lot of other people.'

'Well, we'll know soon enough if Conrad is telling the truth about those diamonds. A Hatton Garden expert will be examining them.'

Crispin had echoed some of Ryga's thoughts about Conrad, but there was a bitter note to his tone that was almost personal. Had Conrad swindled Crispin or a relative? He knew nothing of the inspector's personal circumstances or if indeed he was married. There was no need for him to know, but he was curious. 'Were you policing here during the war?' he asked pleasantly.

'Yes,' came the short reply.

He'd been wrong then about Crispin being in the army. A master sergeant or warrant officer had been his guess. He wasn't such a good detective after all, he thought wryly, and maybe he was wrong about Sebastian Conrad. He wondered why Crispin hadn't been called up. Perhaps he had been too valuable an officer to lose from here during the war. This had been a vulnerable location targeted by German bombers and a possible base for an invasion and the landing of spies, which Sonia Shepherd had already mentioned to him, in jest perhaps, but the fear and threat had been real enough back then.

'Have you always lived on Portland?' Ryga continued.

Crispin looked as though he wanted to refuse to answer, but Ryga was a Scotland Yard detective and maybe he thought on balance he shouldn't.

'My family are from London. My father was a senior police officer.'

'With the Metropolitan Police?'

'No, with the Royal Dockyards, mainly the Woolwich Dockyard.'

Ah, thought Ryga, and he had wanted his son to follow in his footsteps, perhaps even attain a higher rank, although Ryga had no idea what rank Crispin senior had reached. 'And you didn't fancy London?'

'It didn't suit.' Crispin picked up the telephone, clearly indicating the personal probing was over.

Ryga mentally shrugged. If Crispin didn't want to talk about his background, that was fair enough — Ryga didn't wish to talk about his. He turned his attention to the reports that had come in. The search of the cove had finished with nothing to show for it except a few more cigarettes ends, an empty packet of cigarettes, which the officers had brought back with them, two empty bottles of beer, and that was it aside from stones, sand and seaweed. The enquiries with the beach hut and boat owners were ongoing, as were the ones with the hotels, boarding houses and quarry managers. No member of the public had reported seeing the victim or recognizing him but Ryga wasn't too disheartened about that. Once people returned from work, relaxed later this evening and read the newspaper, the victim's face might ring a bell with one or more of them.

Crispin continued with his paperwork. Once or twice he coughed and took a few deep breaths as though he was about to speak but didn't. Then he rose and left the room. Several times Ryga looked at the clock, thinking the time seemed to be passing very slowly. He wondered how Wakefield was getting on with the post-mortem and when he could expect more information.

He turned his thoughts to the victim's strong hands and again, as he had at Conrad's little shop, considered they could be miner's hands rather than those of a former quarryman. The victim could have come across those diamonds legitimately while working in Western Australia, Brazil, South Africa, Tanzania or Canada. Ryga thought it unlikely he would have worked in communist Russia or Siberia. Perhaps he had stolen them. Then again, maybe Conrad was spinning them a yarn, although Eva Paisley had thought the diamonds genuine. But then she wasn't an expert.

Was the Chief Constable right to be suspicious of her? No, of course not. Ryga dismissed the idea as ludicrous and yet even then the silent voice inside his head urged him to keep an open mind as he'd been cautioned. Then there was Sonia Shepherd, another woman whom he found . . . what? Interesting? No, it was more than that. Disturbing? In what way? Yes, she was attractive, there was that, and in a different way from Eva Paisley's tall, slim figure and confident, strident manner. There was a vulnerability about Sonia Shepherd beneath that businesslike and jovial exterior, the latter a requirement of being a publican. But it was an act. He could see it in her eyes and hear it in her voice.

He recalled the soft sound of the child crying and her gentle, melancholy voice trying to soothe it. It had held a note of real anxiety and love, which had made him feel sad. Thoughts of both women disturbed him in different ways. Maybe he was recovering from the long years of war and was craving to get back into some kind of normal relationship but there had been no normal for him with months away at sea, and certainly not many women.

He typed up the reports of his interviews with the postman, Miss Maudley, Cedric Dington, the chambermaid and the waitress. Daniels would do the report on the interview with Sebastian Conrad. Ryga wondered how the sergeant was getting on. Impatiently he glanced at the clock on Crispin's wall. It was just after six p.m. Why hadn't Wakefield called to say he'd completed the post-mortem? He must have finished it by now. And where were the photographs of the cufflinks Eva Paisley had promised him? Maybe he should call on her and collect them. Her cottage was close to The Pennsylvania Castle Hotel, where the night porter would be on duty from seven o'clock.

The shrill bell of the telephone sliced through the air and he snatched it up. It was Wakefield. At last.

'It's as I said, Inspector. The cause of death was a stab wound to the neck, resulting in very rapid death due to internal haemorrhage. The knife severed not only a major blood vessel but also the trachea, resulting in a massive haemorrhage into the pulmonary tree. I doubt if the victim was capable of any physical activity after being stabbed, and there is no evidence on his hands, wrists or forearms to indicate he tried to defend himself. He probably didn't see his attacker coming, or rather didn't see the attack coming. He could have known this person was there but was looking away at the time of the fatal blow.'

'How tall was the victim?'

'Five feet eleven inches.'

So Ryga's assessment and the information given to Mountfort had been correct.

'I know what you're thinking, Inspector — that whoever stuck a knife into his neck has to be as tall, or taller, than the victim.'

'Not unless he was kneeling down at the time or sitting and the killer came up behind him.'

'Possibly. But it would have taken a very fleet-footed killer to have approached on the stones, because I could find no damage to the ear organs.'

'Had the body been moved?'

'No. There was no lividity on the buttocks, shoulders or the back of the head, which shows that he had been lying in that position since being killed.'

That didn't mean, though, that he hadn't arrived by boat, just that he had been alive at the time. But it did mean that the victim had been laid out in that position, as Eva Paisley had suggested, because after being stabbed he was much more likely to have fallen on his side or face down. The killer had made sure to place him on his back and straighten his legs and arms.

'Can you be more precise on the time of death?'

'Only that you're looking at sometime between midnight and six a.m.'

'Any idea what kind of knife, aside from being a sharp one?'

Wakefield gave a small laugh. Then said, more seriously, 'I couldn't find any trace of it embedded in the neck, so it didn't break on penetration. A knife that was kept sharp, or perhaps a new knife, no longer than seven inches, single-bladed and smooth, not serrated. There must be hundreds like it.'

And none found in the cove. Looking for the murder weapon was impossible. The killer could have disposed of it at sea.

'The victim was in poor shape healthwise,' Wakefield continued as Ryga caught the sound of voices outside. They moved on past his door. 'He was suffering from mesothelioma, a rare and very aggressive form of cancer. He had it in the lining of his lungs. Mesothelioma symptoms can take anything from twenty to fifty years to appear after the first exposure to asbestos. It typically develops in one of three specific areas. The most common type, pleural mesothelioma, which is what your man had, is caused by the inhalation of asbestos fibres. If he had lived it would have spread to his abdomen or his heart. Looking at how far it had already progressed, I'd have said he would have been dead within three years.'

Why kill a man who was dying? 'Would there have been any symptoms?'

'He might have had trouble breathing or experienced chest pain. He might have been vomiting, and there could have been some weight loss, although our victim doesn't look to have lost weight. The clothes he was found in weren't hanging off him.'

Except, thought Ryga, recalling Eva's words, *'the trousers are a little too short in the leg and I wouldn't have said he'd have grown much since having them fitted.'* She'd dismissed the idea they could have shrunk on cleaning because it was an expensive suit, and you didn't lose height with mesothelioma.

'There is no known cure,' Wakefield said.

'Could he have contracted it from working in a diamond mine?'

'Most certainly,' Wakefield said. 'Diamond deposits can be found close to asbestos or there can be airborne asbestos fibres in different diamond mines.'

'And as a quarryman?'

'It's possible, but he would be far more likely to have had silicosis, which he could also have contracted from working in a diamond mine but didn't.'

So the victim hadn't been a quarryman. Or if he had then not for very long. But what Wakefield had discovered tied in with what Conrad had told him, and the possibility of those diamonds being real was now far greater.

Wakefield said, 'Aside from that there is evidence that your man broke his right leg some years ago. That leg is slightly shorter than his left, as we previously discussed. The scar beneath his right rib looks to have been inflicted by a knife or weapon of some kind, but it is too old for me to be precise on that. I haven't any information on his dentures yet but I'll telephone you when I do. Have you got anything further on him? I've seen the newspaper article.'

'Not yet but it's early days. I'm sorry your name was mentioned. I didn't give it to the press but the reporter somehow got hold of it.'

'Don't worry about it. No one from the press has pestered me so far and if they do I'll refer them to you.'

Ryga thanked him and replaced the receiver, deep in thought. There didn't seem much point in officers asking around the quarries now but they'd continue with it nonetheless.

His telephone rang again. This time it was Sergeant Jacobs.

'That address of James Legg you asked me to check up on — there's no such place now, the house got bombed.'

Which wasn't surprising, except from the point of view that Legg had said he lived there. Croydon had suffered badly during the war. It had an aerodrome that had become an RAF station and was also close to RAF Kenley and Biggin Hill. The town had seen five years of bombing attacks and dogfights in the skies.

Jacobs was saying, 'The whole street and a small factory at the end of the road took a hit from a V1 flying bomb, and no one called Legg lived there then or before, and neither was anyone of that name killed or injured.'

Now this was interesting news. Ryga's pulse beat a little faster. Had Legg known that the house and the street had been destroyed, which was why he had used it to give a false address? Why, though? Had Legg lived in Croydon, or perhaps he had just read about the bomb damage and remembered it years later when he needed to give a false address? Or perhaps a relative or friend had been killed there. Into Ryga's head came his conversation with Eva about the victim's pinstriped suit bought or acquired in the mid to late 1930s and Ryga's memory that his clothes and personal effects had been destroyed in a bombing raid along with the house and its elderly owners. James Legg wasn't their victim but perhaps the victim had lived at that address in Croydon, and that was where Legg had come to know him.

'And the Jaguar?'

'It's not registered with Croydon County Borough.'

Ryga sighed silently. That meant a longer job finding it. He asked Jacobs to send a circular to all police forces in England and Wales asking if they had reports of the vehicle having been stolen, and if not, to check with the local authorities in their constabularies to see if the vehicle was registered.

Replacing the receiver, he sat back and considered what this latest piece of news concerning Legg meant. Maybe nothing other than that Legg was a crook. But perhaps he was a man who had wanted to hide his real identity for another reason. Why would a man do that? Because he was a famous actor and wanted to travel incognito without being pestered for autographs? Neither Miss Maudley nor Cedric Dington had recognized him but Ryga set no store by that. He doubted if they knew any present-day film stars. That pair seemed to be firmly stuck in the last century. But neither the chambermaid nor the waitress had recognized Legg. Maybe that was because he looked very different in the flesh from his appearance on film or on stage. Or could Legg be on the run from a wife or mistress? Whatever and whoever he was, Ryga wanted to know why he had been staying at The

Pennsylvania Castle Hotel, as he didn't think it was for the sea air, good though it was.

A glance at the clock told him that the night porter would be on duty. Ryga retrieved his hat and raincoat from the stand. Now he had another unknown man to make enquiries about, but this time one who was alive.

CHAPTER NINE

Before he could leave the station, Ryga was hailed by Sergeant Braybourne. 'These just came for you, sir. Miss Paisley dropped them in. She said she couldn't stay as she was on her way to London.'

Ryga stifled his pang of disappointment and took the brown envelope from Braybourne. Inside were a few prints of the cufflinks. No pictures of him, thankfully, as he had instructed. Ryga slipped the envelope into the large inside pocket of his raincoat and set off for the hotel. He'd have liked to tell Miss Paisley what Conrad had said. If she was on her way to London then she must have a car, but even so he couldn't have entrusted the diamonds to her.

It was a crisp, blustery night and as he briskly walked he considered this latest news regarding James Legg. Could he be an accomplice of Conrad's and have killed the victim under Conrad's instructions? But if that were the case, he would have taken the diamond cufflinks. Perhaps he didn't know about them, or perhaps there had been other diamonds on the body — a tiepin, for example. Why wasn't the victim wearing a watch? Had he owned one? Had that also been stolen from the body? Was it in one of those dusty glass cases in that seedy, run-down shop, or had Legg taken that and a diamond tiepin, if there had been one, to sell? And why hadn't the victim been wearing a belt or braces? Surely he'd have one or the other to help keep his trousers up. Why would someone steal a belt? Had that also contained something valuable? He thought of the pewter-like cufflinks. Perhaps the buckle contained a diamond or there had been diamond studs on the leather.

Could the victim have been bringing those diamonds to Conrad — diamonds he'd stolen from the Argyle Mine in Australia or from a mine in another country? But why have them made into cufflinks? Perhaps they were phoney and the real diamonds had been in the victim's pockets. Legg's instructions had been to rendezvous with the victim, to kill him and retrieve those diamonds. Or perhaps Legg was totally unconnected with the victim and with Sebastian Conrad. And there was nothing to say that Conrad had anything to do with the murder either.

Ryga's musings had taken him to the hotel, where he found a burly man in his late fifties, resplendent in a maroon uniform with shining brass buttons, installed behind the reception desk. He had an upright bearing and looked more like a concierge at one of the more elite London apartments, or a doorman at one of the posh hotels, except his face was more weathered. He introduced himself as Reginald Crawley and greeted Ryga pleasantly. He clearly needed no introduction but Ryga showed his credentials just the same.

'Mr Dington said you would be returning, Inspector, to ask me some questions about the body found in the cove.' Crawley smoothed down his thin, straight white hair over his large head and then repositioned the blotter on the counter in front of him.

Ryga showed him the photograph of the victim and asked if he recognized the man.

'I saw the picture in the newspaper.' His accent was very strong West Country. He put on his spectacles, studied the photograph, and looked back up at Ryga with shrewd, assessing grey eyes. 'I've never set eyes on him and I've a good memory for faces. Need it in this job — the guests like it if you remember them and even better if you can recall their names. Some, though, you never forget, especially the ones that are constantly carping and complaining.'

'You've been in this business a long time?' Ryga replaced the photograph in his coat pocket.

'No. Only just started at this game when the hotel opened, but it doesn't take long to recognize the professional complainers. I worked on Terryman's Farm but the land's been sold for housing and I thought a change was as good as a rest.'

The outdoor life accounted for his ruddy complexion and weathered face.

'Working nights and indoors out of the cold suits me and my rheumatics just fine. I'm a widower — have been for some years now. Lost my wife just before the war. She'd have hated the bombing. We all did but some suffered more from it than others. Nerves,' he added, lowering his voice as though it was a sinister word. 'Me? I was in the Home Guard, spent my nights freezing my knackers off on this windswept coastline trying to shoot down enemy planes with a Lee Enfield rifle. Couldn't hit a fly but it made us feel good for trying.'

'Do you live on the premises?'

'No. Got a small cottage up on the Grove. I keep a few hens and some geese for Christmas, like.'

Ryga nodded. 'Tell me what you know about Mr James Legg. He checked out on Wednesday.'

'Mr Legg? What's he got to do with this?'

Ryga ignored the question. 'Was he one to complain?'

'No, the opposite — very polite and a good tipper. Not a talker, though. Kept himself to himself. Couldn't get anything out of him. I asked him a few polite questions, trying to be friendly — "Where are you from? Have you got relatives in this part of the country? Are you down for a rest and the sea air?" type of thing. But he sort of sneered and fobbed me off, not rudely, just muttered something noncommittal. I soon got the message he didn't want to talk. But he wasn't stuck up. And neither was he a toff.'

'Bit of a mystery man then?'

Crawley nodded. 'Ah, you'm right there, sir. He were that 'n all. But then not everyone likes to tell the world their business. Each to his own is what I say, just as long as they are polite, and even if they aren't you learn to grin and bear it in this game and tell yourself you'll soon be shot of them. Although they can make your life a misery while they're staying at the hotel. I remember one—'

'Did Mr Legg go out at night?' Ryga interjected.

'Yes, he did. After dinner. Every night he was here. Three nights, that is.'

'By car?'

Crawley considered this for a moment. 'The first night, Sunday, he went for a walk. On Monday he took the car and the same on Tuesday night. No, hold on, I tell a lie. He went out on foot Tuesday night. I was doing my rounds. I was in the conservatory, checking the doors, and I thought "Hello, what's going on out there?" Then I could see it were Mr Legg. He was walking across the grounds towards the woods in the direction of the cove.'

'In the dark? How did you see him?'

'The moon was out.'

'But you still couldn't have seen his face. How do you know it was him?'

'He had a very distinctive walk.'

Ryga's ears pricked up at this. 'You mean he had a limp?'

'No. He walked slightly lopsidedly on account of his shoulders — they weren't straight. Oh, it wasn't so that you'd notice much but his right shoulder was down just a touch like this—' Crawley dropped his right shoulder slightly to demonstrate.

This was news to Ryga. He couldn't see how it would help him, though. Mentally he noted it nonetheless, and thought of that worn right heel on the victim's shoe and that Wakefield had said the right leg was slightly shorter than the left. But then the victim wasn't Legg. He'd walked out of the hotel alive and well on Wednesday morning.

Crawley continued, 'I notice these kind of things. It didn't affect his clothes. They fitted him well. He was a snazzy dresser. Good suits, 'specially made for him. None of your off-the-peg-stuff, and his shoes were handmade.'

Ryga didn't ask how he knew about the shoes because Crawley would have cleaned them as part of his duty. 'Who were the shoemakers?'

'Lobbs of London. Black lace-up brogues. They'd been resoled and he'd had steel caps fitted on the heels.'

Ryga jotted this down. 'Did you see him wearing a pin-striped suit?'

'Once. Good fit it was too.' Crawley eyed Ryga curiously. 'You don't think he was involved in the murder of that man in the cove?'

'What time did he go out?'

'Just before eleven o'clock.'

'Did you see him return?'

'Yes. He had to ring the bell to be let in. I had locked the conservatory doors. The front door stays open until eleven thirty. The guests don't have a key because I'm always here on duty.'

'Every night, seven days a week?'

'I have one night off a week, Wednesdays, when Mr Dington does the duty. He says he's going to take on some-one to help me, but with the hotel only just opening it's early days yet and he wants to see how the custom goes first. He says the hotel is advertised in the newspapers up north.'

Ryga wasn't sure whether Crawley meant up country or just the other side of Weymouth. And it didn't matter anyway. But he was extremely curious about Legg's nocturnal walk on Tuesday.

'What time did Mr Legg return?'

'Just before midnight — that clock struck as he walked upstairs to bed.' He pointed to the ornate grandfather clock in the far corner.

'Did he say where he had been?'

'No, and I didn't ask on account of what I've told you — he didn't like questions. He just said thank you and goodnight.'

'Did you notice anything about him? His manner or clothing?'

'His shoes were a bit muddy when he came in, but when I collected them from outside his bedroom door later he'd cleaned them up. There was still some mud underneath on the soles though. And there was some stone dust clinging to the mud, which isn't unusual around these parts with quarries everywhere you look.' He again smoothed down his hair with slightly podgy fingers. 'Why are you so interested in Mr Legg?'

'Did anyone else go out on Tuesday night?' Ryga asked pleasantly, again ignoring the porter's question. And again, he seemed not to notice, or at least didn't take offence.

'Mr and Mrs Waverley went out in their car. They came back just before ten o'clock. Said they'd been for a drive down to Chesil Bank after dinner.'

Ryga didn't think they had anything to do with the case. He began to tuck away his notebook and pen when Crawley said, 'Then there was Miss Paisley.'

Ryga froze. 'Miss Eva Paisley?'

'Yes. I saw her in the grounds.'

'On Tuesday night?'

Crawley nodded. 'It were just before eleven thirty.'

Ryga's mind was racing. Why hadn't she told him this? 'Are you sure?'

'Yes. It were about half an hour after Mr Legg went out. I wondered if they were, you know.' He winked. 'Maybe I shouldn't have said, but she isn't married. I don't know about Mr Legg, though.'

And neither did Ryga. Did it matter if she had gone to meet Legg? Did it matter that she hadn't mentioned this to him? Did he care if she was having an affair with Legg? The answer to all three questions had to be yes, because Legg had given a false address and the next morning Eva Paisley had reported the discovery of a murdered man.

CHAPTER TEN

Ryga walked past Eva Paisley's darkened cottage, wondering if she had gone to London to warn Legg, then dismissed the idea. She couldn't know that he was a person of interest in the inquiry. The news had only just come through from Sergeant Jacobs about the false address. He couldn't believe she was involved in murder, and there was nothing to say that Legg was involved either. Perhaps she was in London enquiring about the cufflinks — she had said she was going to ask some fashion friends and artists about them.

At The Quarryman's Arms he made to enter by the back door then changed his mind. Many of the drinkers would have seen the local newspaper. One of them might have recognized the victim. And even if they hadn't, he might pick up a snippet of information about the man in the pinstriped suit in an unguarded moment.

Thankfully there was no sign of Sandy Mountfort's car parked in the road, which surprised him because he had been certain the reporter would return for an update on the investigation to run another article tomorrow. Maybe he already had what he needed. Wakefield had said he hadn't spoken to the reporter but perhaps the staff at The Pennsylvania Castle Hotel had contacted the local newspaper after his enquiries there that morning, although he thought that Cedric Dington and Miss Maudley were unlikely to do so for fear of bringing the hotel into disrepute, and Dington had probably threatened the waitress and chambermaid with dismissal if they so much as breathed a word to the press about his visit.

The bar fell silent as he entered, just as it had done on his arrival yesterday. Sonia Shepherd looked across the smoky room with eyes that were even more tired than the previous day. The shadows under them seemed to draw her skin tightly across her face. She managed a smile but it had a hint of nervousness about it. 'Half a bitter, Mr Ryga?' Her voice carried a ring of false jollity.

'Please.' He rested his hat on the bar and looked around at his silent audience. In total there were about fifteen men, all but three of them aged between twenty-five and fifty. The other three were the old regulars he'd seen yesterday, well into their eighties and all sitting in the same seats, close to the small coal fire. He waited until he had his beer in front of him and had tasted it before turning to them all. He felt as though he was on stage. Evenly, he said, 'You've all probably seen the picture of the murdered man by now in the newspaper. Do any of you recognize him?'

Silence. A few shook their heads.

'Have you seen him about the area?'

Again, just the shake of a few heads as they looked from one to the other.

'He could at some stage have worked in the quarries,' Ryga said.

One of the men broke their silence. He was well-built, tall and broad-shouldered, late forties, wearing work clothes, and Ryga was sure it was the same man he'd overheard talking last night from his bedroom window.

'PC Hill came round today asking if we knew him, but the dead man's never worked in Perryfield Quarry — not while I've been there — and that's twenty years except for three during the war.'

‘He’s not worked in our quarry either,’ another smaller and slimmer man chipped in. ‘Broadcroft.’

Sonia spoke. ‘What makes you think he’s a quarryman?’

‘His hands and his build. And the fact that he was suffering from an industrial disease linked to the quarries.’ Ryga wasn’t going to mention that it was far more likely the disease linked him to being a diamond mineworker.

‘Silicosis,’ said one of the older men knowingly. ‘I’ve known a few taken off with that.’ There was a general murmur of agreement.

The first man spoke again. ‘So you’ve no idea who he is or where he came from?’

‘Not at the moment.’

Did he detect a general sense of relief in the room? He drank his beer. He had the feeling that they knew who the victim was and why he had been killed but no one was going to say, not yet at least. The quarrymen’s conversation he’d overheard returned to him. *Why should it be him? . . . Well, I say good riddance if it is . . . Nasty piece of work.* Who was nasty and how?

Talk resumed and this time it was more subdued. They were watchful, suspicious, and there was something else, but he couldn’t quite put his finger on it. He wouldn’t get anything from them. Instead of quickly finishing his beer though, he took his time over it and then ordered the other half of the pint, taking it to a seat in the corner where he could watch the men but appear as though he wasn’t interested in them. He was curious to see what they would do. Would someone strike up a conversation with him?

No one did. They fell back to talking in general about work, the rationing, the new National Health Service, someone’s allotment, anything other than the dead man in the cove. From time to time Sonia Shepherd dashed an anxious glance his way and threw him a couple of what he thought were meant to be reassuring smiles but they didn’t quite come off. In between serving she spent her time cleaning the counter, collecting and washing glasses, and disappeared once to see to the pumps and bring in more bottles of beer. His presence created an uncomfortable atmosphere. He made the punters reserved and nervous, and they began to drift away. There was work tomorrow.

Soon only the elderly men were left and one by one even they took their leave, wishing Sonia good night. It was closing time anyway.

Ryga rose. 'I seem to have driven away your customers. I'm sorry.'

'Don't be. Quickest I've ever got them out of the bar.' She draped the beer cloths over the pumps. 'Would you like something to eat?'

'A sandwich if it's not too much trouble.' He followed her through to the parlour after she had locked and bolted the door to the public bar and the one to the adjoining snug. She had some fish paste, which on the label said it was pilchards but Ryga thought it might just as well have been snake for all its taste, and it certainly bore no resemblance to the pilchards he'd eaten in the past. She left him to eat and returned to the bar to clear up. He ate slowly, looking around the warm parlour. There was only the photograph he'd noted before, of mother and son.

Sonia disappeared into the kitchen to wash his plate and to tidy up. He'd have liked to talk to her. He wanted to know what was troubling her, but he sensed that she, like the men in the bar, wouldn't tell him. Perhaps she was worried about her son.

He excused himself and went upstairs, where he washed and retired to his room. He heard her come up and go into the bathroom. Then after a while she went into her bedroom. Was she lying awake, worried? Was her son ill or perhaps an invalid? She'd made no mention that he was. Perhaps that was what she was trying to tell him but didn't know how.

He sighed, tried to shut down his thoughts and concentrate on getting to sleep, but this time Eva Paisley interjected. Had she really been intent on a photographic shoot yesterday morning when she had discovered the body, or had she gone to the cove so that she would be able to report it, knowing it was already there, and throw suspicion off herself? But why take the photographs and be so helpful?

He turned over and thumped the pillow. It felt as though it was full of coals and the mattress lumpy but there was nothing wrong with the bed or its linen. The trouble was him, and the thoughts of two women.

He strained his ears for the sound of Sonia Shepherd's soft, regular breathing that would tell him she was asleep, but with his door and hers shut he doubted he'd hear it anyway. Then there was the fact he was on tenterhooks waiting for the child to cry and for his mother to go to him. But Steven Shepherd slept soundly. Lucky him.

Eventually Ryga drifted into a fretful, half-waking sleep that felt, when he woke for the umpteenth time at 6.35 a.m., as though he'd never been asleep at all. He hoped a cold wash would invigorate him. It did to some extent — that and the stern talk he gave himself that he was determined to resolve this case.

It was just after seven when he descended the stairs and found Steven Shepherd eagerly awaiting him. Obviously the boy had heard him rise and while he'd been in the bathroom had slipped downstairs, not wanting to miss out on seeing him a second morning.

There didn't seem to be anything amiss with the child. He looked a perfectly healthy specimen of a boy, albeit a little on the thin and small side, and his young face was more hollowed that it should have been in a child. He was a dark-haired, thoughtful and intelligent ten-year-old who Ryga immediately took to. The boy's very deep-set, chocolate-brown eyes lit up with delight at his arrival.

'You must be Steven.'

He nodded fervently and launched into his questions. He showed a lively interest in detective work and a child's healthy appetite for the gruesome, wanting to know the gory details. Ryga insisted there weren't any but Steven, tucking into his porridge, refused to believe that the victim hadn't had his throat cut. Sonia scolded him and apologized to Ryga, which he brushed aside. The circles under her dark eyes were deeper than ever. She clearly had experienced a sleepless night like him. She looked worn out, and he found himself feeling sorry for her. There was something about her that brought out a protective instinct in him. His emotions on this case seemed to be getting the better of him. Perhaps it was the sea air, he thought with a rueful grin, glad the morning was bright with a chilly edge in the September wind.

He was also glad to see that Inspector Crispin wasn't in his office. He found his presence depressing and inhibiting. He telephoned the lab and asked if they had any information on the victim's clothes and shoes. The clothes were proving difficult. There were hairs on them, but they could be the victim's. The tie didn't yield much except it had been fixed with a tiepin at some stage, which again made Ryga wonder if such a tiepin had contained a diamond. The shoes they'd had more luck with. Close examination had given them part of the shoemaker's name, 'LO', and looking up London-based shoemakers they suggested it could be James Lobb, Jermyn Street, London. Ryga felt a quick thrill of excitement. It was the same shoemaker that Crawley had told him had made James Legg's shoes.

Ryga put a call through to Sergeant Jacobs and asked him to get the victim's shoes from the lab and take them around to Lobbs. He apologized that he seemed to be making Jacobs do all the footwork, 'No pun intended,' he added. He relayed what Crawley had told him, including the bit about Legg's right shoulder being lower than his left. 'Find out if Legg had his shoes made there and when, and what address he gave. Ask around the London tailors to see if any of them made the victim's suit and sold him the tie. It's by Van Heusen so is very select. And if no one stocks that tie, send a telegram to Van Heusen in Pennsylvania and ask them if they can tell us who they supplied in the UK.' He didn't hold out much hope of it leading anywhere but it was worth a try. He again pondered over the Pennsylvania connection. Maybe it was just coincidence.

He was also keen to hear what the Hatton Garden expert said about the diamonds and perhaps someone would come forward today with new information about the victim, although after his experience in The Quarryman's Arms last night he didn't think it would be anyone local.

He reported to his chief in London. Street said the diamond cufflinks had arrived safely. There was no information yet on Sebastian Conrad from the Prison Commission. When Ryga came off the phone he was informed by Sergeant Braybourne that Sandy Mountfort was waiting to speak to him in reception.

Ryga obliged even though there was little he could tell him. He made no mention of James Legg, although it was possible Mountfort could have helped them by publicizing the fact that they were anxious to talk to him, but he didn't want to give everything away just yet. It was very much a case of enquiries progressing and too early to say yet, which was the truth.

Inspector Crispin arrived an hour later and Ryga updated him without mentioning the tension and reserve in The Quarryman's Arms. He'd have liked to ask him about Sonia Shepherd but that would have made the inspector curious and Ryga didn't want to do that yet. Some ideas were forming in the back of his mind but he wanted more information before he aired them with anyone, not because he thought he might make a fool of himself if he got them wrong but because he didn't want to cause any unnecessary stress. Then there was Eva Paisley. Ryga knew what Crispin thought about her, so he wouldn't get an unbiased opinion there. Perhaps she would be back from London today and he could question her about her nocturnal visit to the hotel.

He spent the next couple of hours waiting for reports to come in and going through those that did, looking for something that might take them forward. In the early stages of an investigation it was often like this, putting out enquiries, following up leads that often filtered away to nothing, gathering information, analysing it and waiting, and yet he felt restless, wishing there was something he could do to cause a breakthrough.

He decided it was time to stretch his legs and get a late lunch. He walked into Castletown, past the hospital, and took lunch in The Royal Breakwater Hotel, where he asked the manager and reception staff if they had seen the victim and, as expected, got a negative result. The dead man had got to Portland somehow. If he hadn't come by boat had it been by private car? If the latter then why drive him across the island to Church Ope Cove when he could have killed and left him on Castletown beach just across the causeway? Admittedly Castletown was busy, being close to the naval base, but there was also Chesil Cove nearby.

He called in at the railway station and showed pictures of the victim to the staff, but no one recognized him. The same went for the bus drivers that he managed to ask. He knew Inspector Crispin's officers were out and about doing the same but he couldn't just sit around and do nothing.

It was almost four p.m. when he returned to the police station, wondering if by now Eva Paisley was back from London. He had decided he would telephone her to establish whether she was at home, but as he made to enter the building a car drew up.

It was Daniels. Good. He hoped he had something on Conrad. Ryga climbed in.

'Sorry I've been so long getting any news, skipper,' Daniels said, but Ryga waved that aside and asked him to go ahead with his report.

Daniels silenced the engine. 'Eventually, after some threats and persuasion, I managed to get some information out of Conrad yesterday as you instructed, skipper. The name of the ship he and Abramowski had sailed on was the MS *Poelau Laut*.'

'Part of the Nederland Royal Mail Line.'

'Yes, how do you know that?' Daniels asked.

'I was in the merchant navy and the Thames River Police.' He'd seen her sail into London and read of her exploits during the war when she had carried American troops across the world to Townsville, Cairns and Brisbane, and not just once. She'd packed in a fair few miles during the war, mainly in the Pacific, and was now restored to her original state, which meant the guns had been stripped off her. She was back in service, carrying cargo and a limited number of passengers.

'In the 1930s the Nederland Royal Mail Line carried tin and tobacco from the government-run plantations and industries in the East Indies,' he said. 'They probably do now but to a lesser extent. Their European route carries factory equipment and manufactured goods. They called regularly at Amsterdam, and still do.'

'Conrad said he couldn't remember the exact date they docked in London.'

Ryga scoffed.

Daniels grinned. 'When I pressed him he said he thought it was late August. I telephoned the General Register Office at Somerset House and they got back to me earlier today to say they had the register of death of an Isaac Abramowski on 30 August 1938. The cause of death was severe dehydration caused by sea sickness, certified by Doctor P Grossly in Albion Street, Rotherhithe. I asked the exchange for the number, thinking he's bound to have been bombed out or retired or died, but miraculously he's still in practice there. I was told he was out on patient rounds. I left my number with the woman who answered the phone and asked if the doctor could phone me on his return. He was a bit short with me at first, said he couldn't possibly remember every person he'd certified as dead. And didn't I know we'd been at war when people were dying in their hundreds of thousands.'

'Must have had a couple of difficult patients this morning.'

Daniels smiled. 'I said this one was on board the MS *Poelau Laut* of the Nederland Royal Mail Line from Amsterdam in 1938 and had died of severe sea sickness. That prompted his memory. He said he hadn't had many of them in his career, being a landlubber, but now that I mentioned it, he remembered he was called out to a ship in the Port of London where a man, a passenger, had been taken very ill. By the time he arrived the man was dead. Two crewmen said the man had been violently and continuously sick on the crossing. It was very rough across the Channel and there was nothing they could do until they docked. Once I'd got his memory going Doctor Grossly remembered that the dead man's companion had been a very small man, slightly deformed, his head hunched on his shoulders, but he couldn't remember his name. The body was removed to the mortuary at St Olave's Hospital, Lower Road, Rotherhithe. There was no post-mortem.'

'Very convenient.'

'I returned to Conrad this afternoon and asked him about the funeral. I thought he might have overseen it or at least attended it.'

Ryga shook his head sadly.

'Naive of me, I know. You're right, he didn't. He took off as fast as his short little legs could carry him and let the local council bury the man. Southwark Council are looking at their records but say he was probably buried at Nunhead Cemetery. There's no special plots for Jews.'

They might need that burial location if they had to exhume the body. Could Conrad have poisoned his so-called friend to steal from him? Ryga thought it highly possible. But where did that leave them with the man in the pinstriped suit?

Ryga asked Daniels to drive to Wakeham and Miss Paisley's cottage. As he did, he brought him up to date with his interview with the night porter and the instructions he'd given Sergeant Jacobs at the Yard. He said nothing about Crawley mentioning seeing Eva Paisley. First, he wanted to tackle her about that.

At the cottage, Daniels made to switch off the engine but Ryga forestalled him and told him he could return to Weymouth, and that unless something new came in over the weekend the sergeant could spend it with his girlfriend.

'How did you know I had one?' Daniels asked.

'I'm a detective.' And, he hoped, one who could solve this case and soon. Perhaps Eva Paisley was the key to that.

He waited until the car was out of sight and then knocked on the door but there was no answer. Disappointed, he made his way to The Quarryman's Arms, which by now would be open. It was just after six thirty. He entered the parlour but froze as he heard voices from the bar. Two women were talking and he recognized them instantly. One was Sonia Shepherd. The other was Eva Paisley.

CHAPTER ELEVEN

'Miss Paisley, I'm surprised to find you here,' Ryga said, entering the bar and noting Sonia Shepherd's startled look.

'Why? I get thirsty like you,' Eva answered with a smile.

'I wouldn't have thought this was your usual haunt.'

'Why not? And what do you know about my usual haunts?' she said good-naturedly.

Nothing, he thought. He stepped around to the public side of the bar as the door opened and the three elderly regulars entered. At the same time there came a rapping on the counter of the adjoining snug and with a parting glance of concern Sonia slipped away to answer the summons. Taking the opportunity afforded by her absence, Ryga said, 'I'd have thought The Pennsylvania Castle Hotel was more to your taste.'

'Then you don't know my tastes at all, Ryga.' She swallowed some beer.

He'd given her a lead to see if she would volunteer the fact that she had been in the grounds on Tuesday night but she didn't. Neither did she look concerned.

She said, 'From a photographic point of view this is much more up my street.' She gestured around the pub. 'There are some great studies here. Look at those lined faces and gnarled hands.' She pointed to the elderly men who had taken up their usual position and were obviously waiting for Sonia to return and deliver their beer. 'Their life story is etched in every pore, every crease and every bone. It's in their eyes and their smiles. Did you get anything on those dentures, by the way?'

'Still waiting,' he said. She was right. Here was life in the raw.

'If you look deeply, really look, you can find all kinds of emotions in even the blandest of faces, including those of policemen, who I've been told practise not giving away their feelings and thoughts by standing in front of a mirror. Is that true?'

Now she was teasing him.

She added, 'But you can never quite hide it from the depths of your eyes.'

He wondered if she was alluding to him and what she saw in his eyes.

'Let me buy you a drink, Ryga.' She reached into the pocket of a leather jacket that had replaced the more disreputable donkey jacket she'd been wearing on the beach yesterday. She was still wearing trousers, tailored navy-blue ones this time, flat shoes and a brightly coloured silk scarf at the neck of a close-fitting jumper.

'No. I couldn't,' he said.

'On duty, are you?'

He was in a way, because he wanted to interview her, but that wasn't what he had meant. He had never let a woman buy him a drink and he wasn't going to start now, but she misread his intentions.

'Don't be so stuffy. Sonia, a pint of bitter for the inspector.'

'Make it a half.'

Sonia served it up. She seemed reluctant to leave them. Ryga got the impression she wanted to talk to him but she had to draw the old men's pints and when she returned from serving them at their table another two men had entered.

Eva said, 'I know you can't possibly tell me what's been happening with the investigation today, particularly not in here if you were inclined to do so, but can I confirm you got the photographs?'

'I did. Thank you.'

'I hope they help. You can have the negatives of those I took of you any time you want them, just call in.'

'There are some questions I need to ask you, Miss Paisley.' He watched the curiosity and amusement flicker across her eyes. She must think him dull and boring. 'I'd prefer it not be in here.'

'Fine.' She drained her glass and called out to Sonia, 'I'm just leaving with Inspector Ryga.'

Ryga swallowed a mouthful of his beer and left the rest.

'Make sure he don't put the cuffs on you, love,' one of the old men joked.

One of his companions replied, 'If he does I'll come down to the station with a pair of pliers.'

There was a cackle of laughter. She smiled and waved her hand at them before they stepped out into the cool evening and silence. They set off in the direction of her cottage. He left the silence undisturbed, wondering where it would lead.

It was some time before Eva broke it. 'Sonia is a lovely lady. She may look as though she can cope with that business and life, and she has no choice, but she's very fragile.'

It was not what he had expected. Was she trying to distract him from questioning her about her movements on Tuesday night? 'Why should I be interested in Sonia Shepherd?'

'Because I think she's fallen in love with you.'

Ryga dashed her an incredulous glance.

'Not that she has said anything or even mentioned you. But I saw the way she looked at you when you came in.'

Ryga felt angry. She was teasing him and trying to divert him. Sharply he said, 'Why did you go to The Pennsylvania Castle Hotel on Tuesday night?' If he had expected her to be disconcerted by his question and the sudden change of subject, he was sorely disappointed.

'Why shouldn't I?' she said, giving him a quizzical glance.

'Because by your own admission a few moments ago it is not your type of place. Was it to meet someone?'

A car noisily changed gear as it crunched past them.

'Who did you meet there?' he pressed.

'No one. I went to take some photographs of John Penn's Bath.'

'In the dark!'

'No, in the moonlight and with a strong torch, the latter to guide me.'

'I didn't think topography was your usual subject matter,' he said slightly cynically.

'Sometimes you just need a break.'

'But John Penn's Bath is a ruin.'

'You've been there?'

'Yes.'

'Then you must have seen how mystical it is.'

He'd just seen stone, brambles and a big hole.

She continued, 'It was a crazy idea building a bath there to begin with, which tells you something about the man — eccentric and with reclusive tendencies, not wanting to bathe with other people in the cove. Or perhaps he thought that would have been too demeaning. Instead he thought nothing of his poor servants trudging up the cliffs with buckets of water. The fact that he built the bath on common land also showed a total disregard for others — a man who thought he was above the law. Bet you've met a few of those in your time, Ryga.'

'I have.' And one I'd very much like to apprehend, a killer, he added silently as she continued.

'It resembles a tomb. I wanted to see if I could capture its rawness and magical quality in the moonlight through the dead trees around it, but the moon taunted me by deciding to disappear behind a fast-moving bank of cloud.'

'What time did you go there?'

'You probably know that already if Crawley, the night porter, saw me. It was him who told you?'

'You know him?'

'My aunt mentioned him to me. And I've met him once or twice.'

Ryga got the impression she didn't think much of Crawley, or perhaps her late aunt hadn't.

She said, 'It was about eleven thirty.'

Crawley hadn't seen her again. He said he had let Legg back into the hotel just before midnight. 'Did you see anyone?'

'No.'

Ryga remained silent for a moment. He wanted to believe her but according to Crawley's evidence she must have seen Legg. Then his spirits lifted. Just because Legg set out in that direction it didn't mean he was at John Penn's Bath. He could have taken the path down into the cove to wait by the beach huts or boats for his victim.

'Do you know a man called James Legg?'

'No.'

'He stayed at the hotel from Sunday and checked out early Wednesday morning. Tall, well dressed, one shoulder slightly lower than the other, drives a Jaguar XK120 sports car.'

'I saw the car parked outside the hotel but I don't know any James Legg.'

'According to Crawley he also set out in the direction of John Penn's Bath just after eleven p.m. on Tuesday night.'

'What does this James Legg say?' She eyed Ryga closely. 'You can't find him.'

Was he really that transparent? he thought. Maybe he should practise more in the mirror!

'And you think he could be your killer?' she mused. 'I guess it's possible, which means he could have met the victim in the cove that night, killed him then returned to the hotel. But his motive wasn't robbery unless the dead man had valuables on him other than those cufflinks. Are they real diamonds?'

'It seems so. Pink diamonds and very valuable, but we're having that checked.'

'So why didn't the killer take them?' She answered her own question with the same thoughts that Ryga had come up with. 'Because he didn't know they were diamonds. But the dead man might have had others on him, which Legg, or whoever the killer is, stole. Where are the cufflinks now?'

'At the Yard. An expert will be examining them tomorrow.'

'Another one, you mean, because you've obviously already consulted one.'

'A man called Sebastian Conrad. Runs a seedy little second-hand jewellery shop in Weymouth, has a background in diamond cutting and a prison record to go with it. Served time here on Portland as a matter of fact. Released in 1920.'

'I know of him,' she said. 'But have never had cause to meet him. I drove up to town last night. I've been calling on a couple of my fashion friends. I showed them the photograph of the cufflinks but nobody recognized them. I believe pink diamonds are mined in Australia, South Africa and Canada.'

'And Brazil, Russia, Siberia and Tanzania.'

'Could your corpse have come from one of those countries? Pity you didn't have his passport, but then that would have been too easy and too foolish of the killer to leave it on the body. Did the post-mortem tell you more or aren't you allowed to say?'

Maybe he shouldn't but he didn't see what harm it would do. She had held out on him about her visit to the hotel grounds but then why should she have mentioned it to him when she didn't know that it or rather Legg and John's Penn Bath might be connected to the murder? Also giving her more information, and seeing what, if anything, she did with it, might help him in the investigation. Or trip her up, said the silent, disturbing voice inside him. He relayed what Wakefield had told him.

'So it looks as though your victim worked in a diamond mine,' she said. 'It would account for his strong, gnarled hands and the mesothelioma.'

They drew up outside her cottage. She unlocked the door and invited him in. 'For the photographs and negatives I took of you,' she added when he hesitated. He removed his hat but not his coat, and stood just inside the door while he watched her cross to the table, where she picked up an envelope.

'They're all in there.' She eyed him keenly. He made sure to return her gaze while wondering what she was thinking. He felt slightly uneasy. Her close scrutiny and photographer's eye made him wonder how much of his inner thoughts and feelings she saw. She made to speak when her telephone rang. Excusing herself to answer it, it was clear from her greeting that it was a friend. Ryga was glad to take his leave.

In his room later that night he opened the envelope and spread out the photographs on his bed. There were several of him on the shore, mainly of his back as he looked out to sea, but there was one where he had turned southwards. It was a profile shot. He had removed his hat and lifted his head, probably to look up at the coastal path, but as Ryga peered at the picture he thought it looked awfully like he was gazing out to sea reflectively and with longing, for what, though, he didn't know. Inspiration most probably, and he needed some now on this case. Well, if the sea could give it to him, tomorrow he would follow its path by the land. He'd take that coastal path above the bay and make his way to the lighthouse. One of the keepers might have seen some boat movements on Tuesday night or in the early hours of Wednesday morning.

CHAPTER TWELVE

Saturday

Ryga surprised himself by sleeping well that night. He had been convinced he wouldn't. In contrast, Sonia Shepherd, at breakfast, looked as though her eyes had hardly closed. He considered what Eva had said about Sonia falling in love with him. He'd seen no sign of it on his return last night and Sonia Shepherd showed none of it now. She was still uneasy about something, Ryga could see that, but he was convinced it had nothing to do with any burgeoning emotions for him.

He asked if she would mind making him up some sandwiches, explaining that he wanted to explore the rugged, hilly coastline. She did so without questions. Unlike her son, who had more than enough demands to make up for his mother until she tetchily ordered him to go out and play. With reluctance and a sly glance at Ryga, he did, probably in the hope he'd be able to nab him as he left. Fortunately, by the time he did, the child had found some friends to play with and had vanished. Ryga was able to make his escape. Once again, he set off through Wakeham and towards Church Ope Cove, only briefly glancing at Eva's cottage before turning on the road down.

Carrying his greaseproof-paper-wrapped sandwiches in one coat pocket and a small flask of tea in the other, which Sonia had insisted he take, he decided he'd start from where the victim had ended up dead. He'd already consulted his Ordnance Survey map, also nestled in his pocket, and from the cove would head south towards Portland Bill and the lighthouse. It was only a little over two and a half miles, possibly three allowing for detours.

Of course, if the victim or his killer or both had come by boat, it didn't mean the vessel would have sailed around the Bill. It could have approached the cove from the opposite direction of Weymouth or via the English Channel without negotiating Portland Bill's treacherous rips. Maybe this need to visit the lighthouse was just an excuse for him to stretch his legs and think.

He would have preferred stouter walking shoes and to have discarded the suit and raincoat but he'd only packed four shirts, underwear and socks in his holdall, not hiking gear. Besides, he didn't have any. There was no need for it in London, although he liked to walk as much as he could, but smog and smoke made that impossible on quite a few occasions.

He also wanted to see if the victim could have approached the cove on foot from this direction. Instead of descending to the cove, though, he continued along the clifftop path, pausing where it branched off to a rough, overgrown track, which from the map led to John Penn's Bath. He walked along it for a few yards, studying the undergrowth and the hard, stony ground for signs of recent passage. The track had been used, that much was certain, and he'd say fairly recently looking at the shrubs and branches, but it wasn't possible to say when or by whom.

He turned back, wondering if Eva Paisley had left John Penn's Bath, walked down to the cove to meet the victim and stabbed him? Had she become hardened by her experiences in the war? So hardened that death meant nothing to her?

No, he simply couldn't believe it. And what would have been her motive? He considered this as he climbed onward.

Revenge? For what? Had the victim robbed her or a member of her family? Or robbed a friend? Did she know or believe that the victim had killed someone she loved? He knew only what she had told him of her background. He needed to know more. The very thought of her being guilty of such a heinous crime and as a result her neck in a hangman's noose made him feel physically sick. Could he really bring that about? But if he couldn't then he'd better pack in the job and go back to sea.

He came out on the clifftop. The blue-green water stretched out before him, its waves short and choppy in the brisk, south-westerly wind. There wasn't a boat in sight. So different to the crowded Thames with its barges, tugs and river boats trammelling up and down it and the never-ending rows of tramp steamers and liners in the docks jostling for space.

He leaned into the wind as it whipped around him and raced across the barren, rocky landscape. Taking deep breaths of the fresh, salt-laden air, he continued his speculation. Had Eva come across the body the night of her nocturnal trip to John Penn's Bath and failed to report it, returning instead the next morning claiming to have discovered it then and taking those pictures? The only reason she would do that was because she had an accomplice and was protecting him. James Legg. It had given him time to get away. It made sense but it didn't feel right. Was he really that blind when it came to her? Had she completely bewitched him? Had she done the same with Legg and got him to kill the victim? But if she had, why had she allowed herself to be seen by Crawley?

The landscape spread out before him, great grey boulders of rock, rusting iron machinery, discarded quarry derricks. It must have been physically challenging labour here hewing the stone against the elements. There was little protection from the weather, save where a few cave-like shelters had formed along the way. Below him the sea washed onto the rocks and the shallow shores. It was low tide.

He looked for any paths or ways inland that the victim could have taken but soon gave up that idea, because it occurred to him, looking down at his own shoes, that the victim's would have been covered with grit and the telltale white-grey dust. The same dust that Crawley said Legg's shoes had been covered in on his return to the hotel that night. But when he had examined the victim's shoes in the mortuary the soles and upper leather had been clean. He wondered how Sergeant Jacobs was getting on at Lobbs. Ryga hadn't heard from him yesterday. Maybe Jacobs would report in today, and maybe the analysts would pick up traces of stone dust.

It was good to be here with the wild, rugged landscape and the endless space of the sea. He always felt that the rhythm of walking stimulated mental action. Pity it didn't produce the answers, although given time it might. He barely saw anyone, just an occasional walker and a man with binoculars strapped around his neck. Each time Ryga showed his identification and asked if they had been on the path on Tuesday afternoon or early evening. They hadn't. And unless the victim or his killer had used a very powerful torch neither would have been able to see their way along here in the dark. More than likely they would have ended up over the cliff edge.

He headed inland towards Southwell, noting the construction work of the new Admiralty Gunnery Establishment where the Heavy Anti-Aircraft Battery had been during the war. Did it never end? War, that was. Evidently not. The thought of Eva going to Korea appalled him. He felt sick at the idea of something happening to her. He knew he wouldn't be able to dissuade her. Besides, he had no right to. He turned onto the quiet road for Portland Bill. The small fields lay around him. The day had clouded over a little and the wind was getting stronger.

It wasn't long before the red-and-white lighthouse loomed in front of him. Judging by the number of cars in the car park it was popular with the tourists and to the left of it was a café and beach huts. He hadn't thought that he'd be competing with tourists for the attention of the lighthouse keeper, but on enquiring he discovered there were three of them, and after declaring who he was he was soon directed to the head lighthouse keeper, a grey-haired man in his early fifties with a weathered face and lean body, who introduced himself as Ivor Palmer.

'If you're fit, how about climbing to the top?' Palmer said, with a gleam of challenge in his hazel eyes. 'It's only 153 steps.'

Ryga enthusiastically agreed. The view alone would be worth the exercise. He received a running commentary on the way up the spiral staircase.

'The lighthouse is built of stone quarried from the island,' Palmer said over his shoulder. 'It's 136 feet high, with the tower measuring 115 feet and the lantern section twenty-one feet.'

Ryga wondered how many times he had said this to tourists.

'We've got a cast-iron balcony running around the lantern room, as you'll see. The first level houses the sector light room, the second contains the diaphone and its sounding receivers. The next level, directly below the lantern room, contains the clockwork mechanism used to rotate the lantern. From there it's a steep climb to the lantern room.'

It was, Ryga agreed, trying not to show he was out of breath. He'd taken as much time as he could to get fit and stay so after the war and he was in good condition, but the lighthouse keeper, for all his years, was in a better one.

Once in the lantern room, Ryga's breath was taken away by something other than the steep climb. The view. He remained silent and was grateful to Palmer for respecting that, for letting him soak in the vast expanse of grey sea stretching out to the horizon and to the west and east, while inland Portland and the rolling Dorset countryside lay before him.

Palmer broke the silence. 'Lord of all you survey, eh?'

Ryga nodded.

'You could get drunk on it,' Palmer continued. 'And it's better than any liquor I've ever tasted.'

Ryga agreed. It was a clear morning so he had the best of views, but even on duller days it would still look spectacular and at night the lights of Weymouth and the small Dorset towns would flicker and glimmer in the distance. Not so during the six years of war, though, and Palmer and his colleagues must have been thrilled to see them light up again after victory. Ryga thought back to Tuesday night and the early hours of Wednesday morning. It would have been dark, not so easy to spot a boat out at sea, but one making around the treacherous piece of coast would have used lights onboard in order to do so.

Before Ryga could ask about any ship movements, Palmer said proudly, 'Last year Trinity House chose us and St Catherine's lighthouse on the Isle of Wight for the experimental use of a new navigational aid known as Ramark beacons.'

'You have radar to track vessel movements?' Ryga asked, excited.

Palmer shook his grey head. 'No, it's a non-directional, continuously transmitting radar beacon from here, designed to give an indication of bearing only to the vessels, helping them to identify aids to navigation — buoys, lighthouses, landfall or positions on inconspicuous coastlines.'

No use to him then. He looked across to the Shambles Lightship about three miles out to sea, placed there by Trinity House to warn coastal traffic of the Shambles Sandbank, wondering if the crew onboard had seen anything.

'I need to know if any boats were seen in this area between, say, nine p.m. Tuesday and seven a.m. Wednesday.'

'Heading or returning from Church Ope Cove, no doubt.'

'Yes. You've heard about the murder.'

'Read about it in the newspaper. We've been discussing it. I asked the crew on the Shambles Lightship if they'd seen anyone. It's a new one,' Palmer again said proudly. 'Put there three years ago. Know much about the sea?'

'A fair bit,' Ryga admitted. 'I'm ex-merchant navy.'

Palmer nodded appreciatively. 'You lads did a sterling job in the war — damn dangerous one too.'

Ryga only hoped he wouldn't ask him about his experiences. Like many, he didn't want to talk about it. Maybe

Palmer picked up on this because he simply continued talking about his pet subject, which Ryga had no problem with on this occasion. 'Then you'll know about lightships, easily seen by the naked eye in the daytime and marked at night by a revolving light, visible for ten miles. The lightship also gives out a fog signal. There's a crew of eleven on her, but only seven on active duty at a time, a master and six ratings. I've spoken to the master. Unless a vessel radioed them they wouldn't know who was passing. A crew member was on watch, though, and saw the lights of two vessels passing. But they were way out to sea and I doubt if they would have put in to Church Ope Cove.'

'Do you or any of the crew or the other keepers recognize the dead man?'

'No. Sorry we can't help you, but you might have more luck with the fishermen at Chesil Cove. One of them might have been out that night.'

Ryga said he would talk to them and asked Palmer to let him know via the police station if any information came his way. They chatted about the lighthouse and the sea a bit longer, then made their way down to ground level. Palmer suggested that Ryga also try the naval base. 'They'll have radar and if someone got to the cove by sea, they could very well have come round the island from that direction.'

Ryga said it had been his intention to speak to the commander there.

Before setting off again he found a quiet spot away from the tourists, sat on one of the giant rocks and ate his sandwiches. He postponed all thoughts of the case and of both Eva Paisley and Sonia Shepherd and instead savoured the view, the air and the peace. After drinking his tea, he made for Chesil Cove, the most southerly part of an eighteen-mile stretch of pebble beach that began in West Bay, Dorset. Chesil Beach, or Chesil Bank, as it was called, was famous for its length and its high bank of stones as well as for its shipwrecks. His walk took him past more abandoned quarries, along the coast and inland until he saw ahead the long pebble bank and the small town of Fortuneswell below him. From there he could return to the station and review what had come in.

He considered the idea that the victim didn't have any connection with Portland and that his body had been dumped here by boat en route to and from elsewhere as a matter of convenience, but that didn't add up. If that was the case then why not ditch him in the sea? No, he was certain this rocky, windswept island figured in the murder somehow.

His thoughts had brought him down the steep roads, past the terraced houses, the school and above the cove. There were a handful of fishing boats on the shore and some men mending their nets, but it wasn't them who made him start with surprise, but the person who was talking to one of them. Eva Paisley.

CHAPTER THIRTEEN

Ryga hurried down to the shore, wondering what she was doing here before telling himself that there was no reason for her not to be. She had a right to go anywhere she liked. Her appearance wasn't sinister at all, and judging by the camera around her neck her purpose was obvious, a fact she confirmed when he asked her what had brought her there. Her next words, though, surprised him.

'I've also been asking Harold and the others a few questions about our dead man. Harold, tell the inspector from Scotland Yard what you've just told me about the man in the pinstriped suit.'

'He wasn't wearing it when I saw him.'

'What?' Ryga said, shocked.

'He was wearing a pair of those dark blue cowboy work trousers.'

'Denim jeans,' Eva translated.

'And a navy-blue pullover under a black donkey jacket, bit like Eva's here but older. Oh, and a Breton cap like mine.' With the stem of his pipe he pointed to the dark blue, well-worn fisherman's cap. 'He was dressed a bit like Frank, the coalman, except there was no dirt or grime engrained on his face or his hands. Could have worked on the buildings or in the quarries but not round these parts 'cause me and the others have never seen him before. He weren't no fisherman. He was carrying a sailor's duffel bag. If you asks us, we think he come off a ship.'

Ryga's eyes narrowed as he peered at the ruddy, weather-beaten, lined face. How much of this was fantasy? 'What did he have on his feet?'

'Stout boots,' came the instant reply. 'Clean ones too. But old.'

'How do you know it was him?'

'Because Eva showed me a picture.'

Ryga flashed Eva a startled look. He'd deal with that later. 'Where did you see him?'

'In the pub, over there.' Harold pointed to the lone building fronting the beach some several yards away. 'He were the only stranger in the pub. If you don't believe me, ask Billy or Oswald. They was with me.' He jerked his head to two younger men by the fishing boat. 'It was Tuesday night about seven thirty. He had a beer and then left.'

'Alone?' Ryga asked, still doubtful about this new evidence.

'Yes. No one talked to him and he didn't talk to no one, except Bert, the landlord, and that was only to order his beer. Bert will tell you. The stranger didn't seem uncomfortable or nervous. Just drank quietly then left.'

'Are you sure it was him? Sometimes it's difficult to compare a picture of a dead man with one living.'

'It were him all right because I remember thinking when I saw him alive that here's a man who can take care of himself. And that's what struck me when Eva showed me the picture. Don't matter that he's dead — you can still see it in his face.'

Fanciful. But maybe instinct had a part to play in this, Ryga thought. And there was no harm in going along with it because he needed all the information he could get. Even if Harold was mistaken and the stranger was not the dead man, he was still a stranger and should be followed up. Was it possible Harold and the others had seen the killer rather than the victim?

'What makes you say he was a man who could take care of himself?' Ryga asked.

Harold took his time lighting his pipe. Ryga flashed Eva a glance. She raised her eyebrows slightly. When Harold was satisfied that his pipe was functioning as it should, he continued.

'It was his hands. Strong hands — wouldn't fancy them round me throat,' he cackled, before his expression became serious and thoughtful. 'Then I noticed his eyes. I thought, "hello, they've seen a lot of life and not always good things." But then we've all seen things these last years that we never thought humanly possible.' His expression fell and he eyed Eva sadly. Ryga saw a flicker of sorrow cross her face that hadn't been there when she had talked about her war photography. Yet the atrocities she must have witnessed were surely worse than anything else. Perhaps she'd been masking her feelings for his sake. Or perhaps, he thought, the things that Harold was alluding to were more personal to her.

Harold removed the stem of his pipe from his mouth and looked at Ryga. 'He had a strong face too, not sad or angry but . . . I don't rightly know how to put it.' His face screwed up as he sought the words to express his thoughts. 'He didn't look uneasy. It was as though—' he paused and drew on his pipe — 'as though he belonged here. As though he was at home.'

Ryga wasn't sure he could believe these sentiments. Harold could be spinning him an old fisherman's tale, not because he deliberately wanted to deceive him or that he craved the limelight — perhaps he genuinely wanted to help.

'I've racked my brains trying to remember if I knew him from somewhere, but I can't say I do. And Bert said he'd never seen him before, but then Bert's only had The Cove Inn these last five years since the war ended. Came from London but we don't hold that against him.' He winked and grinned, showing the gaps in his teeth.

Ryga said, 'Didn't you think of striking up a conversation with him?'

'No. He made it clear he didn't want anyone talking to him. Oh, not by anything he said because he didn't speak, but you could tell by the way he looked and stood. We watched him go.' He directed his glance to Eva. 'He marched to the door, and before leaving turned and looked around, not at us but at the place. There was nothing in his expression but it was as if he was thinking that was the last time he'd see it.'

And now Ryga thought Harold had moved into the realms of fantasy. It was time to thank the man for his information, say that a police officer would be along to take his statement and those of his colleagues and make his farewells. Eva told Harold she'd see him later with some of the pictures she'd taken of him and his crew. 'And don't forget, you said I could come out with you sometime.' Harold said he wouldn't, touched his cap and turned back to his crew.

'Are you really going out fishing with them?' Ryga asked as she fell into step with him, heading back up to the promenade.

'Of course. I should be able to get some great shots, especially if it's a bit rough. Well? What do you think of Harold's evidence?'

'What do you?' he tossed back at her.

She thought for a moment. 'A little bit of poetic licence interspersed with reality. Yes, the stranger was there. Yes, I believe it was the victim, but perhaps not that he was as silent as Harold says and certainly not that final, lingering look.'

Ryga smiled.

Eva continued, 'Harold has got imagination but he's solid and trustworthy. And the landlord will back up his story, along with the other drinkers, which is why we're heading to The Cove Inn.'

He noted she had included herself. He didn't mind. He saw no need to be frosty and exclude her. He pushed away any inkling of the idea she might be involved in the murder. As far as he was concerned that was preposterous.

'What made you ask Harold about the dead man and show him the picture?'

'Like you, I wondered if the victim had arrived at the cove by boat and his body had been placed there, and I thought if anyone had seen another boat in the area, or anything suspicious, it would be Harold. He didn't see any boat Tuesday night or Wednesday.'

Ryga realized he had forgotten to ask that, which was slipshod of him. Had Eva's presence and the startling new information distracted him? If so, he was slipping up on the job.

'But I was surprised when he said he saw a stranger in The Cove Inn. I showed him the photograph. I kept a set — well, you do need the public's help,' she said before he could comment, and she was right. 'And without any hesitation he identified our man in the pinstriped suit as the stranger. It was interesting what he said about his features and hands. It was exactly as we discussed.'

They stepped onto the short promenade, where a few elderly people sat taking in what was left of the sun before a lowering bank of cloud from the west would soon blot it out. They seemed oblivious of the brisk wind. Ryga wondered what had happened to the stranger's duffel bag. The killer could have buried it in the undergrowth or taken it away with him.

'Why are you so interested?' he asked casually. Despite his best efforts to ignore it, Chief Constable Ambrose's words rang in his ears. Could she and Harold have fabricated this story to throw him off the scent? But if so then the landlord and the other drinkers in the pub would be involved in it.

That wasn't impossible. He was an outsider. Did they all know exactly who the victim was and were keeping quiet over it? But you couldn't silence an entire island, even a small one. Someone would have come forward to say who he was.

She said, 'I'm a very curious person. It's an occupational hazard of being a photographer, or rather it's a prerequisite of the job, particularly as for me it involves people and not landscapes. And I don't mean portraits. Aside from my war photography I like to photograph working people at leisure or people at their occupations, caught unknowingly when their faces tell a story.'

As she had done with him on the shore. 'And the fashion photography?'

'Despise it.'

'Which is why you're going back to war.'

She made no comment.

Ryga continued, 'Isn't there enough in Britain for you to chronicle? Hardship, poverty, suffering, all the effects of six years of conflict. Can't you bring that to the public's attention?'

She studied him and there was something new in her eyes he hadn't seen before, a kind of quick admiration or understanding perhaps. Before he could analyse it and his reaction to it, though, they had reached The Cove Inn. They entered the small, gloomy bar. Only two old men sat around a table in the window overlooking the sea, playing dominoes.

Eva reached into the pocket of her jacket. 'Beer, a half pint, I remember.'

But Ryga reached for his wallet. 'I can't—'

'Don't be an idiot.' She gave the order to the landlord and handed across the money.

Ryga felt uncomfortable. She had now bought him two drinks and by his code that was two too many, but he saw that he had no choice. He withdrew the photograph of the victim and his warrant card and asked the wiry, dark-haired man in his mid-fifties if he recalled serving him on Tuesday night.

'I do. He had a pint of mild then left. Why, what's he done?'

'Don't you read the newspaper?' Ryga asked.

'Only the sports pages. The rest is rubbish.'

'Describe him to me.'

Bert did and the description matched that of the one Harold had given them.

Eva sipped her half pint of bitter. 'Did you notice anything about his hands?'

'Big ones, strong. No rings or tattoos.'

'What about his nails?' she persisted.

Ryga let her continue with her questions, watching the landlord's expression carefully to see if he might betray the fact that he might have been rehearsed in his responses.

'Clean, short.'

'Not bitten?'

'Could have been, don't know.'

Ryga interjected. 'Did he speak with any accent?'

The landlord considered this for a moment, which made Ryga think that there had to be one but perhaps he couldn't place it.

'Not so you'd notice. He only said pint of mild, put the money on the counter, drank his beer and left. Didn't say thank you, nice day, nothing.'

'Did you attempt to make conversation with him?'

'You know when a man wants to be left alone.'

Which was what Harold had said. Ryga left a short pause, hoping that Eva wouldn't butt into it and she didn't. After a moment, he said, 'Have you seen any other strangers in here over the last week?'

'No.'

'Has anyone else asked about this man?' Ryga pointed at the photograph lying on the counter.

Bert shook his head. The clock struck three. 'I've got to close up — don't want to fall foul of the licensing laws. Not with a copper on the premises.' He winked at Eva.

Ryga drained his beer. 'Did you see where the stranger went after leaving here?'

'Too busy serving to notice.'

'Did anyone leave immediately after or before him?'

'No.'

Maybe someone would come forward to say they'd seen him climb the streets of Fortuneswell. Ryga asked if the two elderly men were in the bar that night, but the landlord said they were lunchtime drinkers not evening ones. Nevertheless, Ryga showed them the photograph of the victim and asked if they had seen him around. The answer was no. Returning to Bert, Ryga said he would send an officer around to take down details of all the men who had been in the pub on Tuesday night and to get a statement from him. Perhaps one of his other customers had noticed something that might help them.

Outside, Ryga looked up the beach towards the fishing boats where Harold and the others were still working, then to his right down towards Chesil Bank, and finally out to sea, where in the far distance he could see a motorboat. Eva, watching him, interpreted his thoughts. 'He could have met someone who came into this bay on a boat.'

'But why get on a boat?'

'Because someone was taking him somewhere and I don't mean to Church Ope Cove to kill him. Perhaps he was being taken abroad, or thought he was.'

'On the run, you mean. If he was he wouldn't have gone into the pub, a public place.'

'Why not if he thought he'd be safely away within the hour? And perhaps he wanted one last pint of beer before leaving England. He was given a new set of clothes to start a new life.'

'When all the time his murder had been planned,' Ryga said. He thought of that silk vest and socks — would he have been given them to change into? And what of the high-quality white cotton shirt and silk tie? If he hadn't been given them then underneath that dark blue jumper and donkey jacket he had been wearing some expensive clothing and that didn't fit with a working-class man. It might, though, with someone on the run.

He turned away, heading for the narrow alleyway that led into the street. Eva caught up with him. Ryga continued, 'He donned the clothes and new identity papers, the latter of which the killer removed from the body after killing him. But why leave the diamond cufflinks?' If they were real diamonds, he added to himself, which had yet to be confirmed by the Hatton Garden expert.

'Perhaps the killer didn't know the true value of the cufflinks. Yes, I know it seems unlikely but perhaps they belonged to the dead man and he told his killer they were just worthless trinkets of sentimental value and the one thing he wanted to keep.'

'You mean they were given to him by a lover?'

'Or that's what he told his killer and he fell for it.'

'Possible,' Ryga acquiesced. They crossed the road. There wasn't much traffic about, it being Saturday afternoon and half-day closing.

'He could have had the clothes stashed away somewhere and changed into them on the shore.'

Ryga considered this. 'So he left the pub and went somewhere close by. Where?'

'A beach hut or in one of the boats, where he'd earlier put the clothes or where someone had left them for him. He changed and then waited for his rendezvous, a boat arranged to take him out of the country, only the skipper had been told to kill and dump him.'

But there was another possibility, thought Ryga. Could the dead man have made his way to John Penn's Bath to fetch the hidden clothes left there by James Legg — or, dare he think it, Eva — changed into them, gone down to the cove as instructed at the allotted time, only to have the person meeting him from the boat kill him?

Or James Legg had murdered him and there was no boat. If so, Legg hadn't known the value of the diamonds. The suit and the handmade shoes could have been Legg's. And that fitted far more as a theory because if there had been a boat, why let the victim change his clothes? Why kill and dump him in the cove? Because, as he had considered previously, it would have been much easier to take him out to sea and ditch his body there.

They were heading towards a small pale blue-green, two-seater sports car. 'This is mine.' Eva stopped by it. 'I'll give you a lift?'

Ryga was very tempted. He'd love to ride in the MG TC sports car, which was only a few years old, maybe less, and likely one of the last models to have been produced by the company a year ago, but it was only a short walk to the police station. And if he intended calling in at the naval base, that too was no distance away. But on a Saturday afternoon he'd be hard pressed to find anyone in authority at the base to answer his questions, so he would need to postpone that until Monday at the earliest.

He politely declined and walked to the station wondering what Mountfort would make of this new information. And what of Harold's impression that the victim had been a sailor? The duffel bag seemed to also confirm that view. Not an enlisted man in the Royal Navy, but had he come off one of the cargo vessels or the ferry service from Weymouth to the Channel Islands? They'd certainly need to circulate the new description and make enquiries with the Weymouth harbour master to ascertain which vessels had sailed into Weymouth on Tuesday.

At the station Sergeant Braybourne greeted him with the news that the Yard had telephoned for him — a Sergeant Jacobs. Eagerly Ryga made for Crispin's office, glad to find the inspector was not on duty, and returned the call.

CHAPTER FOURTEEN

'Your James Legg is quite a character,' Jacobs said. 'He's been giving me a right run around.'

'How?' Ryga asked.

'All in good time, sir,' Jacobs teased. 'You wouldn't want to miss my full report.'

'God forbid. Go on, Sergeant.'

'The shoemakers, after some huffing, puffing, tutting and running off to get authority high up, finally declared that they had made shoes for a customer fitting the description I gave them, he of the lopsided shoulder. They'd made two pairs — one tan-and-brown lace-up, and one black lace-up. The first was in September 1945 and the second two years ago in February 1948.'

'They're quite certain it is the same man?'

'Yes. No doubt about it. There were several appointments and at the first of these the master last maker takes detailed measurements of the customer's foot. I wouldn't want to bore you with all the details, sir, so, skipping the nitty gritty, a trial shoe is created so that the customer can see and feel what it looks like and can make any alterations to the design. It's a very intimate business.'

'And during these several appointments they'd get talking to the customer.'

'The master last maker and his assistant would, yes. While wearing the trial shoe, final measurements are taken, a pattern is made according to the specified style of the client and the artisan cuts out the shapes from the selected leather that will form the upper. The customer also gets special shoe trees to fit the shoe. All the customer's details are kept on their records for when "sir" wants to request a new pair of shoes — only "sir" in this case was not a Mr James Legg but a Mr Joel Laycock. Naturally I asked for the address.'

'And?' Ryga asked, not missing his cue.

'The Savoy Hotel, London, on both occasions.'

'Which you checked.'

'Yes.'

'And?'

'Nothing doing. Wherever Mr Laycock was staying it wasn't there.'

'Just like the false address he gave at The Pennsylvania Castle Hotel, with the exception that the Savoy is not a bombsite.'

'He paid for the shoes by cash.'

'Didn't they think that strange?'

'It wasn't their business to ask, the manager told me. I don't think they worried where the money came from or how they were paid. Business is business. I managed to speak to the master last maker without his superior breathing down my neck as fortunately he got called away. The master last maker said that Laycock, although pleasant enough, wasn't their usual type of customer. Not top drawer.'

'New money?'

'Yes. He hinted at it possibly being made out of the war but he didn't know that for certain. Could have been prejudice talking. He said that many of their wealthy clients were having to tighten their belts.'

'A black market operator,' Ryga said. 'And one with a taste in handmade shoes.'

'We haven't got anything on him at the Yard. Keevil is still looking through the records but he's certain he's never come across him before, or the victim for that matter, and you know Keevil's got a memory like an elephant. If Laycock, or our victim, had been arrested and charged or connected with any of the criminals we're on the lookout for, or had been picked up, he'd know it. Maybe Laycock came into money, inherited it.'

'Or stole it — because why the false names and addresses?'

'Despite not being top drawer and new money he was a smart dresser. He wore good-quality, tailor-made clothes, modern and tasteful. He knew what to buy and how to wear it — that was the master last maker's opinion. I'll try Savile Row on Monday to see if Laycock or Legg had his suits made by any of the gentlemen outfitters there. None of the tailors in Jermyn Street knew him and neither did they recognize the dead man from the photographs I showed them, but they said that judging by the style of the suit it was probably made in the late 1930s.'

Which was what Eva Paisley had said.

'Legg was always alone. Didn't speak of any family or a wife.'

And if Jacobs did get anything from one of the Savile Row tailors, Ryga knew it would be the same as he had obtained from the shoemakers. But they had to try. There might be one new piece of information that could help find him. Was he wasting his time on Legg, though?

'I asked the master last maker about the victim's shoes but he was adamant they hadn't been made by his company, despite there being a faint marking of L and O inside one of them, as our analysts picked up. He didn't know who the shoemaker was. The leather and craftsmanship were good. When pushed he suggested they could have been made in America or Australia, probably about 1937, judging by the design.'

'Any news on the tie?'

'No. The gentlemen's outfitters in Jermyn Street all recognized the make and the design and had stocked that tie but none of them could say who they had sold it to. I'll also ask about the tie around Savile Row on Monday.'

'Did Laycock have an accent?'

'The shoemaker thought there was a slight burr.'

'West Country?'

'Or Irish. He told me that he was good at making shoes, not identifying dialects. His assistant claimed it was West Country but the manager said he didn't hear any accent, but then as far as he's concerned accents are lower class. No one could tell me anything more about Laycock.'

Ryga relayed the news he'd discovered about the dead man and his new apparel.

'Could have come in by boat to London and travelled down by train to Weymouth,' Jacobs suggested. 'I'll check with the shipping companies and send them details but it'll be difficult identifying him that way. You know as well as I do the docks are crowded with ships. If we had an idea of where he had come from we might be able to narrow it down but if he was a passenger on one of the liners or one of the migrant ships returning from Australia I doubt we'll ever be able to find him.'

Ryga agreed. Ships sailed into London from all over the world. He asked if there was news from the diamond expert.

'If there is, Superintendent Street hasn't told me.'

Ryga rang through to Weymouth police station and issued the new description of the victim's clothes, then he asked Sergeant Braybourne at Portland police station to circulate them to his officers and requested that an officer return to The Cove Inn to take the landlord's statement and to take statements from Harold, Oswald and Billy. Next he telephoned the newspaper and asked to speak to Sandy Mountfort.

'You've got something for me?' Mountfort asked.

Ryga told him that new information had come to light and that the victim had been seen drinking in The Cove Inn on Tuesday night. Mountfort tried to prise out of him the bearer of this news but Ryga wasn't having that. He knew, though, that as soon as he put down the phone Mountfort would hotfoot it along to The Cove Inn, where he'd get the information out of Bert and maybe even Harold himself if he was in the bar drinking later that day. Mountfort rang off after cursing the fact that tomorrow was Sunday so there wouldn't be an edition, but on reflection he said it gave him time to pull together a bigger story.

Ryga had still made no mention of Legg, because there was nothing to say save that he was a possible suspect, and he didn't see how releasing that information to the press would help them at the moment. It could possibly help in tracing him, but if Legg was alert to the fact they were after him then he might take off and they might never apprehend him.

Ryga again reviewed the reports then walked back to The Quarryman's Arms. It was a blustery evening with the occasional short, sharp shower. He could see through the window that the pub was already busy so he let himself in the back door with the key Sonia had given him and found Steven in the parlour tucking into a thick slice of bread spread with a layer of jam, some of which had managed to end up round his mouth. The sound of men's voices and laughter came from beyond the door. He wondered if Sonia Shepherd had some help. A busy bar and snug on a Saturday night was a lot to manage for one woman.

Steven quickly swallowed his food. 'Have you got the murderer?'

'Not yet.'

'But you will get him,' he asked excitedly and maybe a little fearfully.

'We will,' Ryga said with more conviction than he felt. He hung up his somewhat wet coat on the peg by the door, placed his hat over it and then, sitting down opposite Steven, put his hand against the teapot. It was warm. He pulled over a cup and saucer and poured himself a cup of tea, indicating that he could refill Steven's if he liked, but the boy shook his head and pushed the rest of the bread into his mouth as a swell of voices reached into them. Ryga noticed that

Steven's clothes were clean but old. The V-neck grey pullover was darned in several places and the shirt beneath it frayed around the neck, but then he'd hardly be dressed in his best clothes to play in the street or yard.

'What's it like being a detective?' Steven managed to ask between swallows.

'Interesting and varied.'

'Exciting?'

'Not really, although when new information comes through, or you get a breakthrough and catch the criminal, it can be.' He sipped his tea. It was a little too strong for his taste, made stronger because it had been stewing for a while. 'But most of the time it's hard work, very methodical, sometimes very boring.'

'Go on, I don't believe that,' Steven said. Then he squirmed and dashed a glance behind him to the door that led into the bar. Ryga could see he was working himself up to say something. The child leaned forward. 'Can I see your murder case?'

Ryga saw no reason why he shouldn't and said so.

'Now?' Another fearful glance behind him.

'If you like.' Ryga rose. 'It's in my room.'

'Then we can sneak up the stairs. You won't tell Mum, will you? Only she said I wasn't to ask you.'

'No, I won't tell her.' Ryga smiled as he followed Steven up the stairs. 'Has your mother got help in the bar tonight?' The sound of people talking and laughing seemed to be increasing by the minute.

'Mr Purdy comes in on Saturday night.'

'And who is Mr Purdy?'

'Lives a few doors down, in Cromswell Street. He's old.'

'Older than me?'

'Bags older. And he smells.'

'Of what?'

'Fish.'

'He's a fisherman?'

Steven shrugged his bony shoulders. 'This is my room.'

'I'll bring the murder case in to you. Then if your mother does find us, I can say it was my fault because I brought it to you.'

Steven's eyes lit up with this. Ryga was gone a couple of minutes. Returning, he found Steven lounging on the maroon-patterned eiderdown of his single bed pressed up against the wall. The room was neat and clean. There were some clothes draped over the back of a wooden chair next to the chest of drawers and a pair of shoes underneath it — Steven's best by the look of them, perhaps ready for Sunday. Some pictures of aeroplanes were stuck on the faded wallpaper and a couple of model planes the child had made himself were perched on the narrow mantelpiece above the small fireplace along with two Dinky cars. He noted that one was a police car, the other a sports model.

Steven discarded the comic he'd been reading and leaped up, his small face flushed. Ryga put the case on the bed and opened it. As he explained each item the child looked on, awestruck. He asked some intelligent questions and they were both so engrossed that Ryga only heard the footsteps on the stairs at the last moment and turned to see Sonia Shepherd in the doorway. The sight of her almost stole Ryga's breath. Her dark hair was styled back, accentuating her deep-set, large brown eyes, her smooth skin was flushed and the dress that clung to her shapely figure did nothing to hide the curves beneath it. Maybe Mr Purdy wasn't that old or smelly after all.

'I'm sorry, Mrs Shepherd,' Ryga said. 'I asked Steven if he'd like to see the case.' He closed it as he spoke. He could see that Sonia Shepherd didn't believe him for one moment. Steven looked anxious and hopeful that his mother would.

'I'll heat your meal up, Inspector. Steven, read your comic, then clean your teeth and go to bed.'

'Yes, Mum.'

Ryga threw Steven a final conspiratorial glance, which he noted lit the child's eyes with real warmth and pleasure. He wasn't sure why, but he felt sorry for the boy and concerned about him. And perhaps, he thought as he followed Sonia onto the narrow landing, it was because he felt worried about his mother. Despite her careful grooming she looked drained. He held her anxious eyes and felt something connect between them. He couldn't say what it was but it made him want to reach out and take her hands, to pull her towards him and hold her. Then silently he scolded himself. What the devil was wrong with him? First an attraction towards Eva and now Sonia. Was he turning into some kind of sex-starved maniac? Were the effects of those long years of imprisonment finally over and now he was overcompensating by finding himself physically and emotionally attracted to every woman he met? Oh, there had been women in London since his release but none he had felt as close to as Eva and Sonia. In fact, the opposite — they had left him feeling cold and empty inside. He'd concentrated on the job and earned himself a quick promotion. But now . . . It must be the sea air, he again thought wryly. He had to pull himself together.

'I'm sorry if I shouldn't have encouraged Steven,' he said, breaking the moment between them, 'but he's a bright boy and it's only natural for him to be curious. That's a good thing.'

Her expression softened. She relaxed a little. 'I just don't want him bothering you.'

'He's not. It's a pleasure to talk to him. You must be proud of him.'

She smiled warmly.

'It can't be easy bringing up a child on your own.'

'Lots of women have to these days.'

'Yes.' He remembered some of the men who had been on the ship with him when it had been raided by the Germans using a heavily disguised merchant ship posing as a friendly vessel. The cargo had been seized and he and the crew taken prisoners. As a result he'd spent four years in MILAG — *Marine Internierten Lager* — a German prisoner of war camp. Some of his fellow crewmen and inmates who hadn't returned had had wives and children.

The sound of voices rose from the bar.

'I expect he asked you about the body,' Sonia said. 'Is there any more news? Sorry, now I'm being nosy.' She flushed and pushed her hands together. 'It's just there's a lot of talk about the dead man in the pub. Is it true that he was drinking over at The Cove Inn on Tuesday night before he was killed and that he wasn't wearing that suit then?'

'It is. How did you know?'

'Bert telephoned me.'

Of course, one landlord to another, or landlady in this case. 'Did you see the dead man?'

'Me? No,' she said, startled. 'I'd better get back to the bar. Charlie Purdy's good but it's busier than usual.'

'On account of me.'

'Yes, and the body. I'll put the gas on. Your dinner should be ready in about twenty minutes. It's on a plate over the saucepan. All you need to do is remove the cover. Would you like me to bring you a beer?'

Ryga said he would like that very much and that he would wash his hands first. He did so, after which he crossed the hallway to the bedroom to the left of Steven's. There he carefully turned the handle and, checking no one was in sight, stepped into a double bedroom — Sonia Shepherd's. He stood just over the threshold, swiftly surveying the room with its faded wallpaper of roses, a sturdy mahogany wardrobe and chest of drawers, on top of which was a mirror and some women's toiletries. There were some clothes draped over a chair, much as there had been in Steven's room. A beige nylon slip lay over a floral dress. The room was clean and tidy, and apart from one picture of a bunch of nondescript flowers on the wall there were no pictures, just a photograph of Steven on the cabinet beside the bed.

Silently he eased the door shut and knocked softly on Steven's door. 'It's all right, you're in the clear,' Ryga said. 'I took the rap,' he added in an American drawl. It was a pleasure to hear the child giggle.

Ryga found his dinner on a saucepan as Sonia had said and was eating it when she entered with a half pint. 'You can have the other half whenever you're ready.' She placed the glass in front of him. 'I've got to get back.' Ryga could hear that. He considered going into the smoky, crowded bar after his meal. He would be the focus of attention and curiosity but perhaps only for a while. He was fairly certain the customers would clam up though when it came to talking about the dead man.

He ate slowly and steadily, mulling over the events of the day and trying not to think about the two very different women who had entered this case and his life and were causing him all sorts of inner turmoil. He had no idea what they thought of him, or perhaps he did. Eva probably thought him stuffy and boring and Sonia was suspicious and slightly afraid of him.

As he finished his meal he considered why Sonia should feel that way. Two things stuck in his mind. The first was the conversation he'd overheard on the day of his arrival between the two men. The other that there wasn't a single photograph of Steven's father and Sonia's husband in the entire house. It hadn't been just to save Steven the embarrassment of being caught looking at the murder case that Ryga had suggested taking it to the boy's bedroom, but because he had been keen to see if Steven had a photograph of his father. If, as Sonia had said, her husband had died at Dunkirk, then why wasn't the child proud of his father? Why didn't he have a picture of him in uniform on his mantelshelf or beside his bed? Why didn't he talk about him? Why didn't Sonia? Three things suggested themselves to Ryga: one, that Sam Shepherd had never been the child's father; two, that he had not died at Dunkirk; and three, that he did not exist.

CHAPTER FIFTEEN

Sunday

Ryga spent a restless, dream-filled night where he was back in the prisoner of war camp, which turned into quarries where he'd been put to hard labour. He woke with a start and perspiration on his brow. It was dark. He lay immobile and focused his thoughts on the case as a means of sending the prison camp memories back to where they belonged. He knew that any further chance of sleep was hopeless and, with that in mind, after a few minutes he rose, shaved and washed in cold water, not wanting the ignition of the gas boiler to wake Sonia or her son. Changing and picking up his hat and coat, he crept stealthily down the stairs in the dark. There was no sound from either Steven's or Sonia's bedroom. Steven's night had been undisturbed. No nightmares for him, and Ryga was glad of that.

It was a little after five o'clock. There was nothing he could constructively do to progress the investigation at this hour, but walking might help him to shake off the dreams and think over the case. The clop of a horse and the clink of milk bottles caught his attention. Previously he'd considered that the two people in the village who would know everyone and everything would be the postman and the milkman. The first he'd already spoken to, the second he could hear just around the corner.

He turned it to find a placid, solid brown-and-white horse towing a milk float and a small, busy-looking man with thinning brown hair and a cigarette smouldering in the corner of his mouth collecting empty milk bottles from a doorstep and replacing them with two full ones.

Ryga made to show his warrant card but the milkman interjected. 'No need, guv, I know who you are.'

'How?'

'Because you've just come from the direction of The Quarryman's Arms where I've been told a good-looking, well-dressed man in his mid-thirties wearing a hat and mackintosh is staying. Word gets around.'

Ryga wasn't sure about the good-looking bit. The milkman was teasing him. And how could the milkman — who said just to call him Ned — know he'd come from The Quarryman's Arms unless he could see around corners? Perhaps milkmen could! Or perhaps Ryga reasoned that only strangers, milkmen and police officers would be awake at this hour of the day, on a Sunday.

Ned placed the empties in a crate on the cart. 'You any closer to catching who did the fellow in?'

'Still working on it. Does your round take you through Wakeham and the area around The Pennsylvania Castle Hotel?'

'It does. Do you mind if I work while we talk, otherwise I'll never get finished.' He didn't need to tell the horse to walk on, it did it automatically as a matter of a long routine.

'What time do you start your round?'

'About four in the morning.'

'Do you deliver to the hotel?' Ryga followed him to a doorstep, where Ned again went through the routine of replacing empty bottles with full ones.

'Yes.'

'Did you notice a Jaguar XK120 sports car there Sunday to Wednesday?'

'No, I go round the back.'

Of course. 'So you have never seen any of the guests?'

'Still fast asleep when I deliver, like the staff. I leave a churn outside the back kitchen door of the hotel. Then I go on through Wakeham.'

'And to the cottages that lead down to Church Ope Cove?'

'Yes.'

'Did you see anything unusual on Wednesday morning?'

'No.'

'Over the last few days, have you seen a man wearing denim trousers, a black donkey jacket and a Breton cap?'

'No, and before you ask, I haven't seen a man wearing a pinstriped suit. Those sort get up long after I've finished my round. The only men I've seen wearing suits like that are in the movies and on some of the spivs you used to get in Weymouth during the war.' He removed his cigarette from the corner of his mouth and spat in the gutter.

Ryga didn't need any explanation as to the meaning of that gesture. He also loathed spivs. He walked with Ned towards a row of three terraced houses. 'Maybe your dead guy was a spiv and finally got his comeuppance.'

They returned to the milk cart and the horse plodded on. Ryga noted that Ned didn't ask why he wanted to know about the cap-wearing man. Word must already have got around.

'I heard that Eva took pictures of the dead man,' Ned continued. 'Still, that doesn't surprise me. That woman's got guts. Nothing stuck up about her, just like her aunt, Pru. Prudence Paisley. Nice party. Shame about the way she died.'

'How did she die?' Ryga asked.

'Heart attack, I guess. Not sure. Found her dead on the landing.'

'You did?'

Ned nodded as he continued with the same bottle-replacing ritual. The streets were still deserted and silent.

'Most folk are in their beds when I do my rounds — not Pru, though. Always an early riser, although sometimes

I don't think she even bothered going to bed. When I didn't see her two days running and her milk was still there I knew something was wrong. I got young Trevor, the paperboy, to fetch the constable. I stayed until he came, and he let himself in with her key. She kept it under a flowerpot to the right of the door.'

'Didn't you think to use it yourself?'

'No. That's the law's job.' Ned paused to light another cigarette from the butt of the one he was just finishing and to wave to a man on a bicycle. 'It was strange to see her dead like that.'

'You went in with the constable?'

'Yes, and while he looked downstairs I called out to Pru and went upstairs. She was lying face down on the landing as though she had been making for the stairs and collapsed.'

'She was fully dressed?'

'Yes.'

'Had she been lying there all night?'

'No idea. Probably. I had to leave it to PC Mitchell and go on my rounds.'

Ryga wondered if there had been an inquest. Or perhaps her doctor had signed the certificate because he knew of a pre-existing heart condition.

'Pru was very spirited,' Ned went on. 'She spoke her mind and folk don't always like that. She was educated, clever and well off, but she'd have none of this "Mrs Paisley" with me. It was always Pru, and if I didn't say it she wouldn't speak to me. Her niece is like that. None of this "Miss Paisley" stuff with her. She said, "Good God, Ned, you'd think the war and what we've seen and been through would have got rid of all that rubbish," but I told her it was out of respect and good manners.' Ned grinned. 'She swore just like Pru used to. Pru did a lot for the people on the island — she spoke out for the ones who couldn't.'

'Such as?' Ryga asked.

'The boys in the borstal. Those who lost their jobs because they went against the bosses when the bosses were wrong. Girls who got themselves into trouble, and bullies, like that husband of Sonia Shepherd's.'

Ryga's ears pricked up at this new information. He tried not to let his interest show. So there was a husband. The idea that there wasn't one he could mentally cross off his list.

'Best thing that ever happened to Sonia was him being called up and getting it at Dunkirk. I know I shouldn't say that, but I'm not the only one. Pru said it too. Sam Shepherd used to knock Sonia about. Nasty bastard.' Ned removed his cigarette and again spat in the gutter.

That explained why there was no picture of the man in Sonia's house and why neither Sonia nor Steven talked of him. It might also explain the conversation he'd overheard of the two quarrymen, or did it? Before he could consider this further, Ned was speaking again.

'Pru was fearless,' Ned continued with admiration in his voice. He put some milk bottles in his carrier and Ryga walked with him to the next few terraced houses. He was glad they didn't have to climb up and down stairs. 'And Eva is just the same — must be to have done the job she did during the war.'

'A war photographer.'

'You seen her stuff?'

'Only the pictures of the body in the cove.'

'That's nothing,' he dismissed. 'You should see her war pictures.' Ned shook his head in wonder and a little sorrow. 'Pru showed me. She cut them out of the newspapers and they're in a book — two books — published and all that. Pru had the books in the cottage. One was quite tame for Eva — *Women Throughout the War Home and Abroad*, but the one on the liberation of the camps in Germany . . .' He let out a long breath and shook his head. 'How that girl could stomach seeing that and take pictures I don't know. Seeing a body in the cove was probably a picnic for her. Then there's her photographs of D-Day.'

'What? How did she get those?'

'How do you think?' Ned replied. 'She went over with the boys from here. Hundreds of thousands of Americans. Official photographer. Didn't you know?'

Ryga said he didn't. He was beginning to feel uncomfortable and embarrassed. He tried to recall what he had said to her. Had he been patronizing? Had she been secretly laughing at him? She must him think him a fool.

He took his leave of the milkman and walked slowly towards Fortuneswell. He didn't want to return to The Quarryman's Arms for breakfast. He savoured the silence of the Sunday morning, thinking over what Ned had told him both about Sonia and Eva. He thought of all the British and American servicemen who had embarked from Portland for D-Day and one woman who had gone with them. Had she been the only female? Perhaps there had been others. But not Sonia Shepherd, who had been abused by her husband.

Sergeant Braybourne had the day off. Ryga asked his replacement about the trains and buses to Weymouth. The former didn't run on Sunday and the latter were sparse, with the first not starting until an hour's time. There was nothing new in. Ryga said that he would make for Weymouth and asked the officer to call the police station there if anyone wanted him.

It was a cloudy morning but dry with a brisk breeze. Weymouth was five miles to the north. He had time on his hands. Not much could be achieved on a Sunday — not unless someone suddenly remembered they had seen the victim and reported it. Soon he was walking across the causeway.

Only a couple of cars passed him heading for Weymouth. He caught the sound of a church bell in the wind and the cry of the seagulls along with the soft rhythm of the sea. Chesil Bank stretched out on his left and Portland Harbour and Weymouth Bay on his right. There were some naval ships in the base and a few yachts anchored in the bay. By the time he reached Weymouth he was hungry. There wouldn't be many places open to eat, it being a Sunday, even though this was a seaside resort. But there was one place he was assured of food — the police station.

After a hearty cooked breakfast and two mugs of tea he set out for Weymouth Quay. The harbour master couldn't recall seeing the dead man or any strangers alighting from any boats, but that didn't mean there weren't any. He said he had seen the pictures in the newspaper but Ryga gave him a photograph and asked if he would pin it up in his office and ask around the mariners when he had the chance. Ryga left with the names of the vessels that had come into the harbour and moored up alongside the quay on Tuesday. Aside from the ferry there was a small freighter, a fishing boat that had suffered engine problems and two leisure craft — the *Beatrice May* and *Dancing Sunlight.* The first had come from Poole to the east and the other from Yarmouth on the Isle of Wight. Ryga noted down the names of the owners.

It was still only eleven and the quayside and promenade were beginning to show a few strollers. The clouds had dispersed leaving a clear blue sky and it was getting hot. There wasn't much more he could do here, but as he walked towards the seafront he thought of those diamond cufflinks and Sebastian Conrad. Had Daniels extracted from the jeweller all the information about that passage to England in 1938 and Abramowski's death? Probably, and it surely had nothing to do with why a man had ended up dead on Portland twelve years later. Nevertheless, while he was here . . .

He turned off the main road into the narrow street, and soon he was standing outside Conrad's tiny shop. As expected, the sign read, *Closed.* He knocked loudly on the door.

There was no answer. He tried again — still nothing. Conrad could be a heavy sleeper. He could be avoiding people, or maybe he was out.

Ryga made to leave but turned back. He reached for the handle and the door opened. The shop bell clanged. He stood just inside waiting for Conrad to emerge from the back room but no one came. He called out. No answering call.

Strange that Conrad would slip out and leave his door unlocked with all this jewellery around. Admittedly some of it might not be valuable — in fact, most of it probably wasn't, just costume stuff — but to a thief it would still be an attractive proposition and fetch a few pounds. Perhaps

Conrad thought no criminals would be about on a Sunday morning.

He gazed around at the dusty cabinets. The smell of neglect and stale food greeted him. There was a stillness in the air that seemed to penetrate right through to his stomach.

Feeling uneasy, he made his way across the shop to the back room where Conrad had examined the diamond cufflinks. He pushed open the scratched and faded door and stepped inside. The fire had long burned out, but it wasn't that which drew his attention and caused the breath to catch in his throat. In front of it, in one of the chairs around the table, was the stone-cold dead figure of Sebastian Conrad.

CHAPTER SIXTEEN

Ryga's first action should have been to head for the police station or the nearest police box and summon officers requesting that one of them bring a camera, but he had a better idea. After finding the key to the shop on the mantelpiece and ensuring the door was locked, he found a public telephone box and asked for the number for Mrs Prudence Paisley, and then to be connected. He waited with bated breath and a racing heart and prayed that Eva would be at home. Miraculously, she was. He inserted the coins and quickly announced himself. 'I need you to do something for me,' he said. 'Can you bring your camera and meet me outside number fifteen Cameron Street, Weymouth? It's just off the seafront.'

'I'll be there in ten minutes.' She hung up.

Ryga breathed a sigh of relief and a silent thank you that she hadn't asked him any questions. But then she was unlike any other woman he had met, and Ned's information had confirmed that. Would he have called her if he hadn't known about her experience during the war? he wondered, hurrying back to the shop. Yes, he thought he might have done, although he knew his action would probably draw censure from Ambrose, who might possibly report him to his chief at the Yard. But Ambrose couldn't know of Eva's background or he wouldn't have uttered that nonsense about her possibly being involved in the murder at the cove.

He let himself into the shop and returned to the body. He wanted to assimilate the scene and, as he looked upon the icy, sad features of Conrad, he wanted to understand what had happened here. Conrad's death had to be connected with the man in the cove — the timing was too coincidental for anything else. And it was clear from his initial study of the body that Conrad had died in the same manner as their pin-stripe-suited man.

Ryga's eyes swept the room. Was anything missing from when he and Sergeant Daniels had sat around this table? He didn't think so, but he couldn't be sure, and he'd very much like Daniels here to assist him. That would be his next request. He caught the sound of a car pulling up and hurried through the shop to see Eva alight from her sports car.

'What have you got?' she asked.

'You'll see.' He locked the door behind her and led her into the back room. He stepped back so that she was facing the dead man. She didn't flinch, and neither did she look horror struck, but then he hadn't expected her to.

'I take it this is Sebastian Conrad.'

'Yes.'

'I'll take photographs.'

He stepped back to watch her work. While she took pictures from all angles he again studied the pathetic figure of Sebastian Conrad. He was wearing the same pair of faded and threadbare black trousers as he had on Thursday. His shirt was collarless and frayed around the cuffs, which were open, and the sleeves were pushed up with elastic armbands, revealing scrawny, hairy forearms. His grey waistcoat displayed evidence of food stains. The top button was undone, the bottom button missing. His hands and eyes were open.

As Eva took close-up pictures of the neck, she said, 'Just like our man in Church Ope Cove — stabbed through the neck and by the same or similar instrument.'

Ryga agreed. There was little blood, only a few spatters around the wound and on the shirt collar.

She continued to talk while taking photographs. 'I'd say Conrad had no idea he was going to be killed. Either he sat here calmly while his killer talked to him and moved around to stand beside him and then stabbed him, or he was drugged first.' She nodded at the chipped mug on the table, which she also began to photograph. Ryga was impressed by the fact that he didn't need to tell her what he wanted. Her words made him think of the man in the cove. Could he also have been drugged? Wakefield hadn't found any signs of that but perhaps he hadn't been looking for any.

On the table alongside the mug was the velvet pad and the loupe. As though reading his thoughts, Eva said, 'He could have been examining a piece of jewellery while the killer came round behind him. Then he sat back to pronounce a verdict or give a price and that was when the killer struck. I'd say by the look of him he's been dead for over eight hours. He's stiff as a board, Ryga. Including his legs and feet. And his colour isn't too good either. It's cold in here, thank goodness, which means the flies haven't yet laid their eggs in the body.'

Ryga studied her curiously. 'I was talking to Ned, the milkman, this morning. He told me about your war work.'

'You want to know how I could do that? How I take pictures of carnage and destruction, of bodies like this and worse and talk dispassionately about it? I can't give you the answer any more than you can tell me how you do it. Unless you count the fact that someone has to, and there is a strong sense of purpose inside you that makes you want to catch whoever took a human life cruelly and callously and needs to be stopped because he or she will do it again. This is war on a much smaller scale.'

She paused to look at him, her expression earnest. 'If we hadn't stopped Hitler and the others, if we hadn't recorded the bravery and sacrifice of individuals and the cruelty of some to show future generations then who can say that callous killers and megalomaniacs who think they are above the law and superior to others won't do it again? I'm not saying I'm a righteous avenging angel. It's a job and I am intrigued by it and I want this—' she touched her camera — 'my third eye, to see what others miss, to make them feel, think, speculate, wonder, discover, question.' Her eyes flashed with passion.

'And what do you see here?' he asked.

'A man who was cunning, mean and selfish. A lonely man who couldn't find what he was looking for and would never be able to find it even if it was right under his nose.'

He eyed her sharply.

'It's what I see,' she reiterated. 'Do you want me to take pictures of the rest of the house?'

He did. He followed her into the scullery, which was little more than a lean-to. It was untidy and dirty, with crockery piled up in the cracked stone sink and fat-caked saucepans on the grimy ancient gas cooker. Beyond the dirty, curtainless window was a brick building in the small yard that Ryga guessed was the toilet.

He said, 'You'd have thought he would have sold some of his jewellery and lived in better surroundings.'

'As I said, he was mean.'

'Or perhaps he was a man who didn't care about his surroundings.'

She fired off a few shots. 'Want to go upstairs?' she added with a slight leer.

Ryga found himself flushing and was annoyed by it. He nodded. The stairs were behind a curtain in the room where Conrad sat dead. He stepped back to let her go first but she said, 'No, after you. You're the boss here.'

He climbed the steep stairs with its carpet so threadbare that there was hardly any fibre left on it. It gave on to a small landing that could only take two people at a push. Either side was a room, one facing the front, the other overlooking the backyard. The front one was Conrad's bedroom. It was in the same state of decay and dirt as the rest of the house and what clothes there were lay scattered over the floor and chair. There was no wardrobe, only a chest of drawers and a single bed.

The house would have to be searched but he'd left his murder case in his room at The Quarryman's Arms. He hadn't counted on finding anything like this. He let Eva take some pictures before crossing into the back room, which was carpetless and contained some broken sticks of furniture, peeling wallpaper and lots of cobwebs and dust that hadn't been disturbed. From the doorway, Eva again took pictures.

They returned to the ground floor. 'I need to report this.'

'I'll see if the beat constable's about, or I can drive to the police station and fetch an officer.'

He walked with her to the door. Unlocking it, he gazed up and down the street. There were a couple of women eyeing them inquisitively opposite and some children playing in the road who seemed more engrossed in Eva's car than their games. Ryga could see curtains twitching across the street. Soon they'd have plenty of observers.

She drove off but had barely been gone a few minutes when the car returned and a uniformed officer climbed out. Ryga showed his identity and reported what had happened, telling the policeman that this death was connected with the one he was investigating in Portland. He left instructions for the officer to lock the door behind him and stand guard outside. He was to let no one in except himself or another police officer. Then he asked Eva to drive him to Weymouth police station.

As she pulled away two more women emerged from the houses opposite and an old man walking along the pavement stopped to talk to them. Their eyes followed the sports car while the children ran after it, yelling and laughing.

'Can you develop that film for me now?'

'Of course.'

She dropped him off at Weymouth police station and headed back to Portland.

In Detective Superintendent Meredith's empty office Ryga telephoned the Chief Constable at his home. Ambrose sucked in his teeth when Ryga told him he had called in Miss Paisley to take the photographs she was currently developing.

'I was with her the whole time,' Ryga said. 'She's an experienced war photographer used to seeing all kinds of terrible carnage and death so it didn't upset her, and she was carefully instructed by me as to the photographs I required. The quality will be far better than anything we could have taken. I'm just about to report in to the Yard, sir,' he added. Ambrose would get his meaning. If anyone was going to reprimand him for his decision it would be his chief. He asked if he could summon Sergeant Daniels from his day off to assist with the investigation. Ambrose gave his permission and added that his police officers were at his disposal but to keep him informed.

Sergeant Daniels was only too eager to leave the comfort of his bachelor flat on a Sunday and head for Cameron Street. His girlfriend was working in one of the tearooms on the seafront, he explained. Ryga sent a car for him and despatched a police motorcyclist to The Quarryman's Arms to fetch his murder case and to bring it to him at Cameron Street. He wondered what Sonia Shepherd would make of that. She and her son would know it meant another murder. The pub would be open by now. It was just after twelve thirty. Word would spread like wildfire. He suspected that, Sunday or not, it would soon reach the ears of Sandy Mountfort.

Ryga put a call through to his boss at his home and quickly briefed him. Street made no comment about using Miss Paisley as police photographer. 'Looks as though you're going to be down there longer than anticipated.' Street's deep voice rang down the line. Ryga could picture him with the inevitable pipe in his mouth and smoke haze around him, unless Mrs Street didn't permit him to smoke at home. 'Any thoughts on the killer?'

'Some, yes.' Ryga expressed the ideas that had been swirling around his head since finding Conrad dead. 'The connection between the two murders is diamonds. The Church Ope Cove victim could possibly have worked in a diamond mine and certainly had diamond cufflinks, if we believe Conrad's expert opinion, and I think we can because he too is dead. Conrad was also involved in a diamond robbery years ago that saw him imprisoned on Portland.'

'Another connection.'

'Yes. He also worked with Isaac Abramowski in Amsterdam before they fled to England in 1938, when Abramowski died of seasickness — if that can be believed. Abramowski could have been killed, possibly poisoned. Conrad could have stolen his diamonds and retired to Weymouth.'

'You think the Church Ope Cove man was Conrad's accomplice?'

'Possibly. But I'm not sure why he would come back to Weymouth and end up on Portland, dead. I don't think Conrad killed him, and if he had connived in his death then why not tell the killer to take the diamond cufflinks?'

'Because he didn't know they existed until you showed up flourishing them. Didn't you say the dead man had been seen wearing working clothes?'

'I did, yes,' Ryga said, encouraged. 'He could have come in by boat to London on Monday and headed for Weymouth by train and visited Conrad. Sergeant Jacobs is going to get an officer to enquire with the shipping companies. After I showed Conrad the cufflinks he must have contacted the killer and told him about them, hence he was silenced.' And was that killer Legg? Was he the other man in this? 'I'll send up the photographs of Conrad as soon as I have them, Chief, and fingerprints. It will be interesting to see if they match any known criminals.'

'We should be so lucky.'

Ryga secretly agreed.

Next he put a call through to the naval hospital on Portland and asked if a message could be sent to Captain Surgeon Wakefield to telephone Weymouth police station as soon as possible.

The car that had been sent to fetch Daniels arrived. Ryga left a message with the desk sergeant to tell Wakefield they had another corpse, a man who had been killed in the same manner as their man at the cove, and that if possible he would like him to examine the body and conduct the post-mortem if his commanding officer gave permission. Ryga said he would speak to the commanding officer himself if it helped.

He gave the driver instructions to head for Conrad's house. On the way he quickly briefed Daniels about what he had found and relayed that Eva Paisley had taken photographs of the victim for them. By the time they drew up outside Conrad's house there were several people in the street and the crowd of children had doubled. Ryga instructed the beat constable to stay on guard outside. They entered the house.

CHAPTER SEVENTEEN

'I didn't expect to see this, skipper,' Daniels said at the sight of Conrad's body. 'It means he knew more about those diamonds than he told us.'

'And more about the man in the pinstriped suit, who is also our man in the black donkey jacket and Breton cap. Do you remember what Conrad said when we came here? He knew I was from Scotland Yard and had come about the body found on Church Ope Cove. I asked him how he knew. He showed me the newspaper. I can't see it under the counter and I haven't seen it in the parlour. See if you can find it.'

'He might have used it for toilet paper.'

'Then you'd better check.'

As Daniels went off to do so, Ryga recalled what Conrad had said: *I know a lot of things*, and he had winked. It seems he did know more than he had let on. Had Conrad contacted the killer to blackmail him in return for his silence? Ryga recalled his discussion with Eva. By the evidence here Conrad didn't look the type to be motivated by money. He didn't spend it on himself or his surroundings.

Daniels returned with a shake of his head. 'It's not in the lavatory.'

'Must have thrown it out. Get on to the exchange and find out what calls Conrad made over the last week.' Ryga had noticed the phone in the shop but Conrad could have used a public telephone box. 'Also if any calls were made from the nearest public telephone.'

Daniels made a note in his notebook. The sound of the police motorcyclist arriving drew their attention and Ryga went into the shop. Outside, a handful of men, having returned from the pub or their allotments, had joined the crowd.

Ryga took his murder case from the officer as the ambulance pulled up. Before he gave instructions for the body to be removed he searched the dead man's pockets. He found only a grubby handkerchief, which he put into an evidence bag. He issued Daniels with a pair of rubber gloves and told him to search the bedrooms and the scullery. 'See if you can find any money Conrad might have stashed away, including under floorboards.'

Ryga took scrapings from the dead man's chair arms and labelled them up. The killer could have worn gloves, but if they were lucky they might still be able to match a print with the glove. There could also be hairs that didn't belong to the dead man but that might match their killer when they apprehended him — Ryga didn't like the word *if*.

He tipped what little liquid was left in the chipped mug into one of the small bottles in his case, labelled it and put the mug into a paper bag. Then he set about taking fingerprints in and around where the body had been and from the Anglepoise lamp on the table. The rest of the room and the shop would be fingerprinted by the officer tomorrow and despatched to Scotland Yard to be checked against their records.

Daniels came in from the scullery to say he hadn't found any money. He climbed the stairs while Ryga continued with his examination of the crime scene. He put the small cloth and the loupe into evidence bags. He'd send those and the other items up to the analysts.

Standing back, Ryga again surveyed the room as he had done with Eva. He recalled his first impressions when he had been here with Conrad and looked for anything that had been moved. Only the chair that had held the body had been moved slightly away from the table, as though Conrad had pushed it back. The large round table was covered with the same red velvet cloth he'd seen on his previous visit. That too would need to be folded, placed in a plain paper bag and sent to the Yard. He didn't have a big enough bag to take it. He'd give Daniels instructions to see to that. In front of the small gas fire was the only armchair in the room. It was battered with wooden arms and a sunken cushion, and, judging by the indentations in the soiled, worn carpet, it hadn't been shifted. In the opposite corner was the wireless on top of a sideboard. Could Conrad have been listening to the wireless and the killer turned it off?

He took some fingerprints from the knobs and the large tuning dial, then turned his attention to the sideboard on which it rested. After taking prints from the handles he opened the drawers to the sound of Daniels searching upstairs. There was the thud of his steps, then the creak of wood as he was testing and probably lifting up floorboards. The sideboard contained only a handful of dusty glasses, a half-full bottle of whisky and a couple of empty chocolate boxes.

A cough from the doorway announced the police constable. 'A message from the station, sir, to say that Captain Surgeon Wakefield will be pleased to examine the body and conduct the post-mortem. Shall he make for the hospital mortuary now?'

'Yes. Tell him I'll meet him there in about thirty minutes.'

The constable saluted and left to deliver the message to the police motorcyclist who had brought it.

Daniels emerged from the stairs. 'No money stashed away.'

'Anything strike you, Sergeant?'

They moved into the shop. Daniels gazed around. 'Nothing broken or disturbed in here or in the parlour. There's no access to the property from the rear, and even if chummy climbed over the yard wall from the house that backs onto this or from those houses either side, he didn't break in.'

'And this shop door wasn't damaged. It was unlocked when I arrived.'

'Conrad let his killer in. He was either a customer or posing as one, or Conrad knew him and could even have been expecting him.'

Ryga opened the door and asked the beat constable to step inside. There was now a large crowd and two more police officers had been deployed by the sergeant at Weymouth police station to keep the onlookers in check, not that they looked as though they were going to storm the place, although one of them might — Sandy Mountfort. Ignoring his cries, Ryga closed the door and addressed the constable.

'This is your beat, I understand.'

'Not always, sir. It varies according to manpower and priorities but mostly it is.'

'What time did you patrol yesterday?'

'The same as today — from six in the morning until two o'clock.'

Ryga looked at his watch. It was 2.34 p.m. 'I'm sorry this has prevented you from going off duty.'

The constable looked taken aback for a moment. 'That's all right, sir. It goes with the job.'

If Conrad had been dead for between eight to ten hours that put the time of death between one a.m. and three a.m., which meant this officer wouldn't have seen anything suspicious, but perhaps Conrad was killed later.

'What time did you patrol this street yesterday?'

'Just after seven, then again at nine and then at eleven, as I was doing today, when the lady asked me to come.'

'Is it usual to do it three times on a shift?'

'No, sometimes I can only do it once. Depends on the day of the week. Saturdays I usually only get to do it twice but yesterday it was quieter than usual. Sundays are usually the quietest, when I do it three times. There's not so many folk about to ask me for help or for directions or to stop and chat to.'

'Did you see or hear anything out of the ordinary either yesterday or earlier this morning?'

'No. It was quiet as the grave. And when PC Robinson handed over to me at six a.m. he didn't have anything to report for last night expect for the usual: a few Saturday-night drunks staggering out of the pub, some youths making a nuisance of themselves, larking around, and a domestic row. But there was nothing down this street.'

'Did he mention any cars parked down here that he hadn't seen before?'

'No, and he would have done because this isn't the kind of street where folk have cars. One parked along here would have stuck out and he'd have taken the licence number. Conrad's customers weren't usually well off enough to own a car.'

'Did you know Mr Conrad?'

'We all knew him, sir, and his record.' The constable threw Daniels a glance. 'But he kept his nose clean. We used to call on him from time to time when we had reports of stolen goods to see if he was receiving them, but we never found anything and he was always cooperative. In fact, he went out of his way to help us if he could on valuations of stolen jewellery.'

'Was he friendly with anyone in particular?'

'Not that I know of.'

'His neighbours, perhaps?'

'I think he acted as a pawnbroker for some of them when they were hard up, or he helped to sell their stuff, but these residents haven't really got much of value to sell. There's an old lady that lives to the left of him, owns the sweet shop, but she's deaf as a doorpost.'

Which would explain why she hadn't come out to see what was going on. 'Must be difficult for her to hear the shop bell clanging when she has a customer.'

'It flashes a light. Besides, she hasn't really got many sweets to sell, not since the rationing and not many customers. It's just force of habit for her to keep the shop open — that and the company. The shop on the other side that sells postcards and knick-knacks is run by a woman in her late fifties who likes to go out dancing on a Friday and Saturday night.'

'Where is she now?' Ryga wondered why she hadn't emerged during all the activity.

'With one of her fancy men, I expect,' came the reply. 'Likes to spend her Sundays with one or other of them.'

Ryga got the point. 'We'll have to question everyone in the street. Perhaps your relief can start that. And you can also make enquiries when you're next on shift. We'll get you some photographs of Conrad, and you've got the ones of the man found in Church Ope Cove plus an amended description of him.'

The constable nodded to indicate he did.

'Is your relief here now?'

'Yes, sir. PC Jenkins.'

'Then ask him to come in and you can go off duty.'

The constable saluted again and left. Ryga went through the same process with the new officer and got the same set of answers. Sergeant Daniels would talk to the night constable when he came on duty.

As Ryga stepped outside Sandy Mountfort called out to him. Ryga nodded at the police constable to let him through and Mountfort scurried over, notebook in hand.

'Is this murder connected with the one on Portland?'

'It looks that way, but we don't know for certain. Did you know Sebastian Conrad?'

'No.'

But Mountfort would have been gathering background on him from the neighbours while waiting and would get more when Ryga had left.

Mountfort said, 'How is the investigation progressing, Inspector? Are you close to making an arrest?'

'There's nothing I can tell you at the moment.'

'The people around here will be getting worried. Two murders in less than a week — does that mean there is some kind of maniac abroad?'

Already Ryga could see the headlines but there wasn't much he could do about it. 'I'm confident that the law-abiding citizens of Weymouth and Portland will be safe. We're doing all we can to apprehend the criminal. Meanwhile, if anyone has any information about the man found in the cove or saw anything suspicious around here over the last two days, we urge them to contact the police or to notify their beat officer.'

Mountfort scribbled this down in his shorthand then looked up expectantly.

'That's it for now.' Ryga opened the car door and climbed in. Daniels followed suit. Ryga gave instructions for the police driver to take them to the hospital mortuary.

CHAPTER EIGHTEEN

'There's not a lot I can tell you right now,' Wakefield said as they stood around the fully clothed body of the late Sebastian Conrad. 'From my initial examination the method of murder matches that of the man in the cove. A single stab wound to the neck, causing an instant massive internal haemorrhage,' he added. 'No blood on his clothes save for a few spots and small splashes on his shirt collar. Nothing on his cuffs, sleeves, arms and hands.' He picked one hand up and turned it over, looking at it with a frown on his keen-featured face before laying it down again. 'It doesn't look as though this man put up a struggle. His forearms show no signs that he raised them to try and ward off the killer or defend himself. How was he found?'

Ryga told him and ventured the view that he could have been drugged given that there was a mug on the table containing some dregs.

'I'll certainly look for evidence of that.'

'When can you conduct the post-mortem?' Ryga asked.

'If you're happy to have the body transported to the naval hospital at Portland I can do it today. I'm not needed in surgery until tomorrow morning.'

Ryga thanked him and asked if he needed a lift back to the island but Wakefield said he had a navy driver on standby. Before leaving the hospital Ryga made arrangements for the body to be taken by ambulance to Portland. Now they would have two inquests to hold. Tomorrow Ryga would need to inform the coroner.

He gave instructions for Daniels to return to Weymouth police station, where their first point of call was the canteen. Ryga hadn't eaten since breakfast and he was so hungry that neither the smell of the mortuary nor the sight of Conrad's body could put him off his roast dinner, which was served throughout the day on Sundays. Daniels also ate hungrily.

After satisfying the inner man, Ryga made sure that the fingerprints, hair samples and the remains of dregs in the mug on Conrad's table, along with the mug itself, were biked up to the Yard. Daniels reported that the duty sergeant had officers out making enquiries around Cameron Road.

Ryga got Daniels to drive him to Eva Paisley's house. There he alighted, telling Daniels to return to Portland police station to review the statements of the landlord of The Cove Inn, those of the customers there on the night the stranger had had a drink, and of Harold, Billy and Oswald to see if anything new had cropped up.

Eva answered the door promptly. 'Good timing. I've just finished. Come through.'

Ryga removed his hat but instead of following her through to her darkroom he paused to study the paintings on the walls, this time with the milkman's words about Prudence Paisley running through his mind. The first time he'd seen these pictures he recalled saying they were striking and thought-provoking, and now he looked more closely at them he also thought them slightly disturbing, especially the ones of the convicts.

Eva stood beside him. 'My aunt was a great advocate for prison reform, or at least trying to reform the ways of Portland Prison before it became a borstal in 1921 when conditions improved. She was a young woman in her twenties when it was a prison and the convicts were put to hard labour in the quarries, as you can see. She hated the way they were treated and even more that they were a tourist attraction.'

'And yet she painted them.'

'Not for material gain or to sell as a novelty but to highlight the conditions. Look at the convicts' faces, the pain and suffering in their expressions, and here—' she pointed to a group being marched back to the prison with two warders either side — 'the bland acceptance of their lives as though they have long ago given up on everything, while the prison officers look smug and self-righteous.'

'The prisoners had been convicted of a crime,' Ryga pointed out, thinking of Sebastian Conrad and his time in Portland Prison.

'Yes, but the conditions were appalling. You wouldn't keep an animal in the manner they were kept.'

'Things have improved in prisons since then. They no longer shave the prisoners' hair and routine cellular isolation has been abandoned.'

'I should think so too.'

But it was only two years ago that penal servitude, hard labour and flogging had been abolished, and not before time. He'd witnessed the last two in the prisoner of war camp in Germany, had experienced cellular isolation and, although he'd like to forget his experiences and shut down the images, pushing them away didn't work. Neither did endlessly talking about it. That only served to dredge it all back up again. Facing up to what had happened and accepting it, then moving on, was the only way. Easy to say, not so easy to do, especially for some people. He was lucky in that he hadn't suffered as much as many had done.

He moved his attention to two paintings of fishermen. 'That's Harold,' he said, surprised.

'Yes, and Oswald and Billy.'

One painting was of the three men on the shore mending their nets, and the other was of them on their vessel in a stormy sea. Both illustrated their gruelling lives, but there was a hint of something in their eyes that made him pause.

'What do you see, Ryga?'

'I'm not sure,' he said, hesitating. 'A sort of contentment, perhaps?' he offered a little diffidently.

'And you'd be right. They're proud of their work and they're saying, "This is my life, I'm a free man with only the sea as my companion and my enemy, and if she wants me she can have me."'

'Did your aunt go to sea with them to capture that?' He pointed to the one of the vessel at sea and the fishermen hauling their catch.

'Of course. I have her sketches of these and some of her other paintings, not all of which ended up as oils.' She paused for a moment as if she had recalled something, but whatever it was she shook it off and continued brightly, 'There are several of her paintings exhibited in art galleries around the world and owned by private collectors.'

'Why don't you paint?'

'Because I'm hopeless at it.'

She moved away, and he followed her through the kitchen and into her darkroom, where she switched on the light. 'But I'm good at this,' she added, running a hand through her fair hair.

He agreed with her. His eyes travelled to the photographs spread out on the bench, but it was the ones of Conrad's parlour that instantly drew his eye. It was as though he was seeing the place for the first time and it made him shudder inwardly.

She must have sensed it. 'There's a darkness about it, isn't there? Difficult to say what exactly, aside there being a body of a man in the room, but in these two pictures Conrad is not in view and yet there's still something soiled about it.'

'Not soiled,' he answered. 'More despairing. An emptiness.'

She flashed him a surprised glance that turned to one of thoughtfulness and approval. As he gazed down at the pictures he wondered if the emptiness was inside him and not the room, and perhaps she knew that. It was as though this shabby, untidy, second-hand existence was all there was. As if everything they had been through during six years of war, all the austerity and suffering since and the empty promises of what would come after victory had come to this — just more of the same of what they'd had before.

Mentally he shook himself. There had been some positive changes, such as in health care. It just took time, and people were weary and impatient of waiting. Eva Paisley was a damn good photographer.

'Does anything else strike you about the room?' he asked, not looking at her but at the pictures taken from the doorway of the shop, the scullery, the stairs and behind the victim. 'Aside from what you said when we were there about Conrad being a man oblivious to his surroundings, possibly because he was too mean or not bothered about how he lived.'

'Which still stands, or the latter does. I don't actually think he was mean, just not bothered about having money. In fact, it's hard to see what he was interested in. There doesn't seem to be anything in that room, or the house, to indicate he was passionate about anything, not even his jewellery in that tawdry little shop — the items are dusty and laid out any old how. There was no pride in the man. Look at the pictures of the bedroom.' She spread them out. 'There's nothing there of his personality. There are no pictures, records, magazines, newspapers, ornaments. Just some shabby clothes hanging over a chair and a pair of worn boots.'

Ryga had missed the boots. He wondered if it was worth sending those to the analyst to see if they could pick up any traces from the soles that might have put Conrad in Church Ope Cove. Even if they did, though, it wouldn't help them find Conrad's killer.

She said, 'I can see a smugness about him, even in death. It's as if he's hugging a secret to himself.'

Ryga eyed her dubiously. 'Surely that's just your imagination?'

'Is it? Maybe.' After a moment, she continued, 'He's sitting back in that chair with his eyes wide open, so if he was drugged maybe he regained consciousness just before he was stabbed, or perhaps he was drugged with something that immobilized him but kept him awake.'

'What could do that?' Ryga asked.

'A nerve drug of some kind, something that can paralyse a person. Curare, for example. It causes paralysis, starting with the face and proceeding to the chest within minutes. The victim turns blue. He could have been blue before the signs of lividity spread to his face, turning him that blue-ish-purple colour. Hemlock is another one. It acts in a similar way, although death can be slower. Socrates was killed by hemlock in 399 BC. He was condemned to die for "impiety" and "corrupting the young". According to Plato he walked about until his legs felt heavy, then lay down until the paralysis reached his chest and then died. Conrad could have been given hemlock in a drink.'

'You seem to know a lot about it.'

'Pru knew her plants. And I've seen death many times in all sorts of forms, as you probably have.' She eyed him steadily.

Was she inviting him to confide his past? He wasn't going to. He said, 'I've sent the dregs that were left in the cup on the table off to our analysts.'

'If he was drugged, the pathologist might pick it up. Who's doing the post-mortem?'

Ryga told her. 'He did the post-mortem on the body in the cove. Wakefield claims Conrad was murdered in the same way.'

'But he didn't pick up any signs of poisoning?'

'No. I'll ask him if he can check on that.' He gathered up the photographs. 'These are a great help, Miss Paisley.'

She rolled her eyes and pushed back her hair. 'Oh, for heaven's sake, Ryga, call me Eva.'

'Eva.'

She smiled. 'And your Christian name is?'

'Alun, but you can call me Ryga.'

She laughed. He liked it and, as she showed him to the door, he thought he wanted her to continue calling him Ryga. It sounded good from her and somehow fitted.

'Do you have any leads as to who the killer is?'

'We have plenty of questions, which I hope will give us some leads.'

Her expression told him she'd acknowledged his evasiveness. 'Well, you know where to find me if you need my help again.'

'I sincerely hope I don't,' he said, and then realized that sounded rude. 'I meant I hope we don't need you for any more of this kind of photography.'

'Me too. Do you want a lift back to the station?'

Ryga admired the neat little sports car, but before he could answer, her telephone rang. She tossed an irritated glance over her shoulder, then crossed smartly to it. He waited.

'It's for you, Ryga. Sergeant Daniels.'

He took the receiver from her with a slightly quickening heartbeat. He hoped this might be news that could give them a breakthrough. Tactfully, she left him. He heard her moving about in the kitchen.

'The beat constable on Cameron Street has just reported in, skipper. He'd been speaking to a group of boys larking around down the end of the road, telling them to get off home and that it's too late for them to be out, especially with school tomorrow. They were all excited about the murder, asking him questions about it, as you can imagine, then one of the boys said he knew who had done old man Conrad in.'

Ryga could hear the excitement in the sergeant's voice and his own pulse picked up a beat or two.

'At first PC Jenkins thought the lad was just boasting, saying it to make himself look big in the eyes of his friends and told him so. Then the boy said he'd seen a car driving slowly down the road. It parked around the corner facing the seafront but the man who got out walked back and went into Conrad's shop. PC Jenkins took more interest in what the boy was saying then, although he didn't let on to the lad. The boy, Ron Chasely, was out early. He does a paper round and delivers to some of the boarding houses and small guest houses just off the seafront. They like their papers early — it was just after six a.m. on Wednesday.'

'But that's the morning the body was found in Church Ope Cove, not when Conrad was killed.'

'Yes. But Ron got the make of the car and the registration number because he collects them and he's hellbent on being a mechanic or racing driver when he grows up. The make and registration number match that of a vehicle we're very anxious to find, skipper. A Jaguar XK120 sports car.'

'James Legg!' At last they had a firm connection between the two men. 'Has Ron seen it again?'

'No.'

'Why would Legg visit Conrad?'

'He might have wanted to buy a watch or piece of jewellery,' Daniels said, tongue-in-cheek.

'At six in the morning! He checked out of the hotel just before six and then drove straight to Weymouth and to Conrad's house. Why?'

'To get something valued? Diamonds, perhaps, stolen from the dead man.'

'Possibly, but not the cufflinks, which he missed.'

'Maybe he didn't notice them.'

'He would have done if he had undressed and dressed him.'

'Perhaps the dead man did that himself. The clothes had been left for him.'

'Yes, in John Penn's Bath. Get off home, Daniels, unless anything else has come in?'

'Nothing positive, all negatives. No one had anything to add to what the landlord of The Cove Inn and the fishermen told you.'

'A breakthrough?' Eva asked, returning.

'Maybe.' For now he didn't want to tell her because she had been seen heading in the same direction as James Legg on Tuesday night, half an hour after him if the night porter was correct. Crawley hadn't said that Legg was carrying anything, but then Ryga hadn't asked him that question and Legg could have gone to John Penn's Bath earlier in the day with a holdall containing a change of clothes. Legg met the victim and gave him the clothes and identity papers in exchange for some diamonds. But they were disturbed when they heard someone coming. Eva Paisley. Legg and the victim hastily descended to the cove, where Legg killed him, unaware that the victim was wearing diamond cufflinks. Perhaps Legg had promised that a boat would come to meet the victim.

Again, Ryga considered the idea that the pinstriped man could be a crook, a man on the run, although that didn't fit with him having a pint of beer in a crowded pub. But then he had probably counted on no one from around here recognizing him. He could even be a foreigner. Dutch, perhaps, from Amsterdam, who had known Abramowski, Conrad and Legg. Legg then cleared out early and called at Conrad's to tell him the deed had been done and handed over the diamonds the victim had given him in return for securing a new identity and an alleged safe passage abroad.

When Ryga showed Conrad the cufflinks, he had recognized them and couldn't resist contacting Legg to tell him about them. Legg had realized that Conrad could give him away. And the diamonds he had given Conrad as his share of the spoil from the victim were still on the premises. Legg returned Saturday night, parked some distance away this time, killed Conrad and took the diamonds.

Ryga consulted his watch. It was just after eight. He wanted to have another talk with the night porter. The ride in Eva's sports car would have to wait.

CHAPTER NINETEEN

Ryga found Crawley behind the reception desk. He asked if Legg had been carrying anything when he had seen him crossing the lawns on Tuesday night.

'No, sir.' Crawley looked at him as though he was a little touched.

'Was he wearing a coat?'

'No, just his suit.'

'Did you see him return?'

'Not across the gardens if that's what you mean. As I told you before, I opened the front door to him.'

Legg could have deposited the holdall of clothes at John Penn's Bath earlier in the day and then brought it and the victim's duffel bag back with him and put them in his car before ringing the bell to be let back into the hotel. 'How many guest rooms overlook the sea?'

'Four. One in the round turret, another in the square tower, one sandwiched between them and another just above the dining room, but it doesn't have such good sea views.'

'Were any of them occupied that night?'

Crawley consulted the register. 'Mr Legg was in the round turret. The one next to him was vacant, as was the one above the dining room. Mr and Mrs Waverley are in the square tower.' Ryga recalled they had arrived on Friday. 'And Mr and Mrs Farringdon are in a suite the other side of the hotel.'

'I'll talk to Mr and Mrs Waverley.'

'They're in the lounge. I don't think Mr Dington will be very happy about you bothering them.'

'Then we won't tell him.'

Ryga found the couple, who were in their early sixties, listening to a play on the wireless. He apologized for the intrusion, showed his credentials and said he was investigating the death of a man found in the cove. They had of course heard of it but said they couldn't help in any way and looked affronted he had ever thought they might. They didn't invite him to sit. They looked a nervous, frigid pair, as though they might dissolve if anything unpleasant wafted their way. He wondered how they could have survived the war — the sound of the siren must have been enough to send them into a blue funk. But maybe he was being unkind and their nerves were shattered because of their wartime experiences. Besides, what did it matter? It had nothing to do with him or his investigation. They both declared they hadn't seen or heard anyone moving about and by ten o'clock they had retired to bed and were asleep. He believed them.

He returned to Crawley and asked for the keys to Legg's room. It was vacant. No one had been booked into it since Legg. Once inside, he gazed around. It was a large room comfortably furnished with a double bed, double wardrobe and matching chest of drawers, and a dressing table. It also gave on to a bathroom and toilet. He crossed to the windows and stared out over the gardens to the sea, but it was dark and there was no moon. He turned his attention back to the room, flicked on the electric light and began a methodical search, not sure what he was looking for but perhaps Legg had left something behind that might tell him more about the man or where he had gone.

There was nothing. The room had obviously been cleaned since Legg's departure.

Downstairs, he asked Crawley if any staff lived in.

'Aside from Miss Maudley and Mr Dington there's only the cook.'

Crawley escorted Ryga to the kitchen, where he introduced the cook, a lean man in his early fifties sitting at a table in a kitchen that was quiet with no evidence of any meals being cooked and only a small, neat woman in her forties washing up at a giant sink.

'We only do teas and a light supper on Sunday evenings,' the cook explained, gesturing Ryga into a seat across the table. 'And there are only a few guests staying in the hotel so we're hardly rushed off our feet.'

Crawley left them after introducing the woman as Mrs Flaxley, who came in to help in the kitchen for breakfasts and evenings. Ryga thought he heard her say under her breath, 'Skivvy, more like.'

He asked the cook if he had seen anyone in the grounds Tuesday night.

'I was in here until ten, then went up to my room, read for a while, listened to the wireless and went to sleep. Sorry I can't help you.'

Ryga looked across to the woman at the sink. 'What time did you leave on Tuesday?'

She turned and rested her back against the stone sink while wiping her hands in her apron. 'Just after eleven. I didn't see anyone, not unless you count Mrs Shepherd.'

Ryga wasn't sure he had heard her correctly. 'Sonia Shepherd from The Quarryman's Arms?'

'Yes. She was heading through Wakeham just as I turned out of the rear entrance.'

'Are you sure it was her?' Ryga felt a little disturbed by this new piece of information.

'Of course I am.'

He didn't much like the sound of this. His mind positively hummed with thoughts. Why should Sonia have left the pub? Why leave her son alone there? Did she have a lover she was calling on and it was too risky to let him into the pub? But after ten thirty closing time no one would have seen him. The conversation he had overheard on his first night here broke into his whirling head: *Why should it be him? . . . Well, I say good riddance if it is . . . Nasty piece of work.*

'What does your husband do for a living?' he asked Mrs Flaxley.

'He's a quarryman, why?'

'Does he drink in The Quarryman's Arms?'

She looked at him askance. 'Course he does.'

'Did you tell him you had seen Mrs Shepherd?'

'I don't know. I might have done.'

He took a slow, thoughtful walk back to the pub. First Crawley had seen Eva Paisley and now Mrs Flaxley reported having seen Sonia Shepherd. Mrs Shepherd had said nothing about being out that night. Maybe she didn't think it important. But surely she would have done given the discovery of the body in the cove the next day. She probably considered it had nothing to do with the murder. But she was certainly anxious and troubled about something. Perhaps she was nervous that her nocturnal movements would become known to the village and therefore the fact that she had a lover. Perhaps the lover was married and they had to meet in secret, out-of-the-way places. Or perhaps he didn't want to compromise her by being seen going into the pub at night and causing a lot of gossip. Ryga hoped it was something like that rather than being involved in murder, but he felt deeply troubled by what he had learned.

The pub was open though quiet given that it was Sunday evening. Sonia Shepherd met him in the parlour as though she'd been looking out for him. He wondered if Mrs Flaxley had telephoned her from the hotel to tell her she had mentioned seeing her on Tuesday night. There was no sign of Steven. He must be in his bedroom.

'Is it true that Sebastian Conrad is dead?' she asked with concern.

'Yes. Did you know him?'

'Everyone knows him. Knew him,' she corrected. 'Many of us have had to resort to him over the last ten years.'

'Including you?'

'Yes. Only the once though during the war. Do you think whoever killed him killed that man in the cove?'

'It looks likely.'

Her skin paled. She hesitated. A man's voice called out 'Shop' and she hurried out to serve him.

Ryga put the kettle on and sliced a large piece of bread off the loaf on the table.

On her return she offered to make him a sandwich. He said he could do that himself but she wouldn't hear of it. He silently willed her to tell him what she had been doing on Tuesday night, but she said nothing. She made a pot of tea and a cheese sandwich and got called to the bar again, where she stayed.

Ryga finished his snack and washed up. Then he entered the bar, where he sat before the fire and drank a half pint of bitter, watching her when she wasn't looking his way. He could see that something was eating into her — her movements were jerky, her expression troubled, and she looked even more tired than before. Several times, when their eyes met, she looked as though she wanted to speak, then she'd be asked for another drink or would turn away to wash some glasses.

He could confront her with what Mrs Flaxley had said but he didn't want to, yet. Perhaps because part of him didn't want to think she was involved. Could she have killed the man in the cove? Could she have taken a knife from here and stabbed him in cold blood in the neck? He shuddered to think it, but he knew that his job was to think the unthinkable and the worst in people. Could she and Eva be in league? Had Eva gone to meet Sonia that night and not Legg? Could Sonia have bought that pinstriped suit, tie and those shoes from a second-hand shop in Weymouth, taken them to the victim and watched him change? Was the victim in fact Sonia Shepherd's husband, who hadn't died at Dunkirk, and she had assisted James Legg, her lover, in getting away, possibly with Eva's help? Or perhaps Eva had witnessed this and was remaining silent for Sonia's sake.

He took his thoughts to bed and went to sleep with them, while something nagged at the back of his mind, something he had heard or seen that day that he felt was important to the investigation. What with Conrad's death and Mrs Flaxley's new information there was much to consider, but whatever it was gnawing away at the back of his mind refused to surface.

It was five a.m. when he woke with a start. That elusive thought had suddenly broken through. Previously he'd told himself that two people knew what went on in a village, the milkman and the postman, and he'd spoken with both, but he'd been wrong — there were three. The newspaper boy. In Weymouth, Ron Chasely had seen Legg's Jaguar in the early hours of Wednesday morning parked close to Conrad's shop because he had to deliver the papers to the hotels and guest houses. The Pennsylvania Castle Hotel must also like their newspapers delivered early. Ned, the milkman, had mentioned the paperboy, Trevor, on the day he'd been concerned about Prudence Paisley.

Ryga lay there in the silence of the house, letting his mind run on. Maybe the paperboy had seen Legg's Jaguar leave the hotel. But they already knew it had. There was probably no point in questioning the boy, but then again there was no point in ignoring the idea now that it had broken through his subconscious. Trevor could have witnessed something. And Ryga liked to be thorough.

He flung off the bedclothes and quickly and quietly washed before hurrying out into the dark, windy September morning. The weather felt as though it was on the turn. It had finally tired of summer and was hustling in autumn. Newsagents opened very early to take delivery of the newspapers and at 5.45 a.m. Ryga was inside the cramped little shop asking a small, dark, busy-looking middle-aged man with a sunny face and a Birmingham accent what time the paperboy who delivered to the hotel arrived. Six o'clock was the answer. Ryga didn't have long to wait.

Trevor was a small, lively boy with bright, intelligent eyes and a quick brain. Ryga thought he'd either end up a criminal or a very wealthy businessman. He sincerely hoped the latter. The boy was keen to help the Scotland Yard detective and Ryga could see he was mentally calculating how he'd relay this to his school chums.

'What time did you deliver newspapers to The Pennsylvania Castle Hotel on Wednesday morning?'

'Just after six o'clock, same as usual. They're my first stop then I work my way back.'

'See anyone?'

'The man in that Jaguar was coming out of the drive as I started my round back a few minutes later.'

'Anyone else?'

'Ned, the milkman, was down the street ahead of me and Mrs Shepherd was knocking on Miss Paisley's door.'

Ryga stared at the child, dumbstruck. Was this a lie? But no, it couldn't be. Why would the boy lie? He had no reason to. Ryga's stomach churned. 'Are you certain?'

Trevor nodded.

Ryga was glad the newsagent was busy and some distance away. He drew Trevor further outside. He didn't want to alert the child that he was deeply interested in this information or that it might be significant. 'Could it have been another morning you saw them?' he said airily.

'No, it was the same day that I saw the Jaguar leave, Wednesday morning. The day Miss Paisley found the body on the beach.'

Trevor clearly didn't think anything suspicious about the two women meeting up.

'I saw Mrs Shepherd go into Miss Paisley's house.'

'Did you see anyone else out and about at that time?'

'Mr Rivers on his bike. He was going to work.'

'Does Miss Paisley take a newspaper?'

'Yes, *The Times*. I pushed it through her door.'

'Did you see or speak to her?'

'No.'

'And did you see Mrs Shepherd return to The Quarryman's Arms?

'No.'

'Thank you, Trevor.' Ryga gave him a half a crown. Trevor looked as though his birthday had arrived.

Instead of returning to The Quarryman's Arms, Ryga walked down to the cove, only glancing across at Eva's cottage before turning into the lane. He postponed his thoughts until he had reached the shore and seated himself on a large boulder, watching the sun rise and the seagulls swooping and dipping over the sea as it washed onto the stones. He considered what he had learned last night from Mrs Flaxley and this morning from the paperboy. Sonia Shepherd had left the pub on Tuesday night and had been seen heading in the direction of the hotel just after eleven. Legg had been seen by Crawley walking towards John Penn's Bath just before eleven and Eva shortly before eleven thirty. The next morning Sonia had been out early and, if Trevor was telling the truth, which Ryga was certain he was, Sonia had visited Eva. Soon after, Eva had claimed to find the body. It was obvious the two women had colluded over that, but had they also conspired to kill the victim? Had they actually gone through with it? But if so there would have been no need for Sonia to be out and about on Wednesday morning. In fact, it would have been far safer for her to have stayed inside the pub and just let Eva make the discovery.

That left him with another equally terrible idea — that Sonia had killed the man and then confessed to Eva, who had helped her cover it up. And there was only one reason he could think of as to why Sonia had done such a dreadful thing. It was as he had previously considered, only now he had an even stronger reason to believe it. The dead man in the cove was her husband and James Legg was her lover. No one had claimed to recognize Sam Shepherd because they were all protecting Sonia. Legg had cleared out as soon as he had discovered Sonia had killed her husband. Perhaps he'd been scared, or perhaps when he discovered the truth he didn't want anything more to do with her. He'd probably been leading her on to begin with.

This left Ryga with two questions: why had Legg called on Conrad, and who had killed Conrad? Surely not Sonia Shepherd? She'd admitted she knew him, but then so did a lot of people.

There were too many questions he needed the answers to before he tackled Sonia Shepherd. He rose and hastened to the police station, where he settled himself to a day of obtaining them.

CHAPTER TWENTY

Monday

The man at the War Office said he would call Ryga back as soon as he had the information Ryga required. He gave no indication of when that might be but Ryga stressed the urgency of it. He had the impression that wouldn't make the slightest bit of difference to the clerk, who sounded as though he was suffering from dyspepsia. Inspector Crispin, who entered his office just as Ryga replaced the receiver, looked as though he was. Something was eating him. He was tired and his skin was drawn taut across his sallow face.

Ryga was glad Crispin hadn't heard him ask about Sam Shepherd. Not because he thought Crispin would go running to Sonia but he preferred to keep this new information close to his chest for the time being. He hadn't even told Sergeant Daniels, who was overseeing the inquiries into Conrad's murder in Weymouth.

He brought Crispin up to speed with the events of the weekend — the description that Harold and Bert of The Cove Inn had given him of the victim, Conrad's death, and the fact that James Legg's Jaguar had been seen in the vicinity. If Legg's prints were on file then hopefully they would pick them up from Conrad's house and be able to identify who he really was.

Crispin listened in silence as Ryga spoke, his back ramrod stiff. Ryga watched for reactions in the steel-grey eyes. Crispin was good at masking his emotions but Ryga thought he detected something. Was it resentment at not being involved in the investigation? It certainly wasn't anything as strong as anger but then maybe that went inside. He wondered if Crispin was as cold as he appeared. What would crack this iceberg of a man who had shown no emotion except disapproval when speaking of Eva Paisley?

Crispin picked up a piece of paper from his in tray, clearly indicating he had no further interest in or intention of discussing the matter. He'd shown a lack of professional curiosity about the two murders, which was strange to say the least. Ryga was curious about the man. But from his manner he knew he would get nothing from him. He made a mental note to ask Sergeant Braybourne about Inspector Crispin.

He picked up the telephone and rang the hospital. Wakefield had left a message at the desk to say he had completed the post-mortem and was in surgery that morning. Ryga hoped he might catch him before then. He was in luck.

'There's not much I can tell you, Inspector. It was as I said in the mortuary — death was caused by a stab to the neck, resulting in internal haemorrhage, the same as your man in Church Ope Cove. Death would have been almost instantaneous.'

'Caused by the same weapon?'

'Yes, or a similar one. A sharp, smooth-bladed, single-edged knife. I can't find any evidence he was drugged but I've sent tissue samples over to our lab.'

'It's been suggested he could have been given curare or hemlock.' Ryga caught Crispin's quick glance before he scowled and returned his attention to his paperwork.

'The killer would need to have been very knowledgeable to administer the right levels,' Wakefield said. 'Curare is derived from certain South American jungle vines and is widely used by natives to tip their arrows. It quickly paralyses and kills the victim but has no effect if taken by mouth.'

So they could rule that out.

'The hemlock plant grows wild all over Europe and North America. It is similar to curare in that it causes paralysis of the muscles although the effects are somewhat slower. It would take about half an hour for the symptoms to appear and several hours for the victim to die of paralysis of the lungs.'

'Both Conrad and the Church Ope Cove victim were dead for several hours before their bodies were found.'

'I didn't find any evidence of either curare or hemlock in the liver or blood of either man, but their tissue might yield some results. I'll get some samples from the Church Ope Cove victim over to our lab too. I'll ask them to test for any drug. It could be something from Africa or Brazil — places where tribal drugs can be manufactured from exotic plants.'

And pink diamonds were mined in Brazil. Then there were the aboriginals in Australia where, according to Conrad, pink diamonds were also mined. Perhaps their killer had been living there with the man in Church Ope Cove and had gleaned knowledge of such a drug, bringing that and the means to use it with him to England. If that was so then his killer couldn't be Sonia Shepherd. But she, like Eva, might know about hemlock. He felt cold inside.

Wakefield confirmed that Conrad had been in fairly good physical health considering his age and his background of hard labour at the prison. 'There was some heart muscle deterioration but nothing that would have carried him off immediately,' he said. 'Oh, and I've heard back from the dentist. There are no identification markers on the Church Ope Cove victim's dentures. I'm told this isn't unusual — dental laboratories rarely provide it. The dentures, though, are of a very high quality and made fairly recently, certainly within the last five years.'

Ryga replaced the receiver and tried to concentrate on reading through what Crispin's officers had amassed, including statements from some of the customers in The Cove Inn who had been interviewed late yesterday afternoon and evening. But he found himself distracted by Crispin's presence. Not that the man actually said anything or was hostile towards him in his body language, but Ryga sensed it. He also felt stifled being confined to the office. He had been used to being out on the Thames when he had first joined the River Police and had loved it. It was only on his promotion to inspector, his transfer to the Metropolitan Police and being ensconced in the criminal investigation department in New Scotland Yard that he'd realized how much he missed that freedom. Admittedly his investigations had taken him out and about in London, for which he was grateful. Now he began to wonder if he was cut out to stay in London. He glanced at Crispin, who had his nose buried in some paperwork. Would he want his job?

No. Ryga enjoyed the plainclothes role of criminal investigations. There was a vacancy for an inspector in CID in Weymouth but Ryga liked the challenge of the big cases and he wasn't certain that settling in Weymouth would provide that. There was a small but growing feeling of restlessness within him that he'd noticed lately, a desire to get out, explore and push the boundaries both intellectually and geographically.

Picking up his hat and shrugging on his coat, he nodded a goodbye to Crispin and made his way out. He couldn't sit here all day pushing paper around the desk and waiting for the telephone to ring or a report to come in. In the lobby, noting there was no one about, he addressed Sergeant Braybourne. In a quiet, confiding voice laced with concern, he said, 'Inspector Crispin doesn't look too well.'

'He's probably had one of his attacks. No one is to mention it though, sir. He gets very angry if we do.'

'Attacks? I'm sorry to hear that. What kind?'

'Asthma.'

'Poor man.'

'Precisely, sir.'

Ryga got his meaning. Crispin wanted no one's sympathy, pitying looks or understanding. It explained why he had been exempt from conscription and why he hadn't become a police officer in London like his father. The smog would probably have killed him, as it had many others.

He told Sergeant Braybourne that if anyone wanted him he would be at the naval base talking, he hoped, to the commander. It took him a long time and many explanations to several people before he got to the right man, who, after calling on more people, finally confirmed that no small boats had been sighted heading in the direction of Church Ope Cove from Weymouth and the east, or from the English Channel on Tuesday night and the early hours of Wednesday. The commander said he would ensure the victim's photograph was posted on all mess noticeboards and give orders for anyone recognizing the man to report in. Ryga was convinced they wouldn't get any answers from that quarter, but it had to be covered nonetheless.

He found a steamy little café just off Chesil Cove, where he ordered fish and chips and a mug of tea and let his mind return to Eva Paisley. There was no sign of Harold, his crew or his boat on the beach, so he was obviously out fishing. Maybe Eva had gone with them. Had she really come here on Saturday to ask Harold if she could take photographs of him and his crew? She must have done, because she hadn't come to silence Harold over the victim's apparel — not unless Harold had fabricated that in order to lead him in a false direction and that would mean the landlord and the whole blessed pub were involved in the conspiracy, and he just couldn't see that. Then there was Sonia Shepherd and her trips to The Pennsylvania Castle Hotel on Tuesday night and to Eva on Wednesday morning.

A message from Sergeant Jacobs was waiting for him on his return. Ryga eagerly returned the call from the desk behind Braybourne, which Daniels had previously occupied.

'None of the tailors in Savile Row recognize the description of James Legg but Wrexleys recognized the victim's suit,'

Jacobs said victoriously and still with some amazement in his voice. 'They made it for a customer in 1937, a Mr Frank Hunt, a wealthy business magnate who died in 1942. Mr Hunt left a widow who died in 1946 and didn't have any children, so it looks as though the clothes were given away or ended up in a second-hand clothes shop or pawnbrokers. We could look for relatives who might know what happened to the clothes, including that suit, but in eight years it could have changed hands many times so that could take for ever and a day. But before you get too disheartened, sir, we've had another piece of news that might cheer you up. Brighton Police have telephoned. The Jaguar is registered there and the owner is not James Legg or Joel Laycock, it's Mrs Bridget Norman, a widow. The car wasn't reported stolen so it looks as though Legg took it with her permission.'

'But he didn't take her to The Pennsylvania Castle Hotel, so where did he tell her he was going?'

'Maybe by now he's back with her in Brighton.'

'If he's our killer, he's cleared out. I'll telephone Brighton and ask them to send someone to interview Mrs Norman. If Legg is there I'll get them to take him in for questioning and not to let him go until I get there.'

Ryga rang and asked for the inspector in CID. He relayed the outline of the investigation and gave a description of Legg, including the information that, according to the night porter at the hotel, Legg had one shoulder slightly lower than the other while mentally noting that Ron, the Weymouth paperboy, hadn't mentioned that when he'd seen him enter Conrad's shop. Maybe he simply hadn't noticed or hadn't thought much of it. 'If Legg's not there, find out all you can about him.' Ryga relayed the telephone number of the station. Then he rang Daniels at Weymouth and gave him the latest news. Next Ryga telephoned Eva, but there was no answer.

There was also the diamond merchant to hear from and Ryga hoped that his chief would get that information today. He waited as patiently as he could in Crispin's office, thankful when the inspector left. Ryga didn't know where he went or why and he wasn't going to ask because it wasn't his business. Brighton might not come back to him until later that day.

The War Office telephoned and confirmed that Sam Shepherd had died during the evacuation from the beach at Dunkirk. The boat that he and several other servicemen had been evacuated on had got into trouble on the crossing from France and had sunk in the English Channel.

'That's all we have,' the clerk said. 'It was chaotic at the time.'

After yet another cup of tea had been placed on his desk — Ryga had lost count of how many he'd drunk — Brighton rang back. It was just before four thirty.

'Looks as though Legg has legged it!' came the smart announcement. 'There's been no sign of him since the Sunday before last, when he took off from Mrs Norman's in a Jaguar sports car that she had bought for herself, but really it was a present to him.'

Ryga gave a low whistle. He wondered if Legg, or whatever his real name was, had a driver's licence.

'He said he had a business meeting in London last Monday to discuss various investments.'

'Really!' Ryga said sceptically.

'Exactly,' Inspector Frampton replied. 'The description fits, although she didn't make any comment on him having one shoulder slightly lower than the other.'

Was Crawley the night porter lying? Had he really seen Legg head for John Penn's Bath? If he had fabricated the tale then why? Because he didn't like Legg and wanted to get him into trouble? But why should he do that? It was fact that Eva Paisley and Sonia Shepherd had both been seen that night, and that the body had ended up in the cove. He brought his attention back to Frampton.

'Legg didn't say where he was staying or who he was meeting,' Frampton went on. 'Mrs Norman expected him back Monday night. When he didn't come she thought he must have stayed in town. He didn't telephone her, but then she said he never did. She was very nervous, and I finally managed to extract from her the fact that she had given him several thousand pounds. Her husband was a clothing manufacturer, made a great deal of money out of army uniforms during the war, invested it in property and land and made even more. He died two years ago, shortly after the couple retired to Brighton. Legg has been courting her for six months. She said he was staying at the Grand Hotel.'

And that was expensive. 'Was he?'

'No. Not by that name anyway, and neither the manager, doorman nor receptionist recognized the description. My guess is he was staying at a much smaller hotel or boarding house, or he could have rented a furnished room. Do you want us to make enquiries?'

'Please.' Legg was clearly a con artist, an embezzler and a fraudster, but was he a killer? 'Did she give him any jewellery?'

'Yes, she bought him a signet ring with a diamond in the centre of it, several tiepins — one again with a diamond — and cufflinks as well as clothes.'

'Diamond cufflinks?'

'She says not.'

Was it possible that after checking out early from The Pennsylvania Castle Hotel, Legg had taken the jewellery Mrs Norman had given him to Conrad to sell? But that threw up several questions. Why come to Portland? Why was he staying at The Pennsylvania Castle Hotel? How did he know Conrad? And why, if he wanted to sell the jewellery, didn't he stay in Weymouth or simply take the jewellery there and go on his travels?

Because he had a rendezvous here. But with whom? The man in the cove, a woman from The Quarryman Arms, or a war photographer?

Frampton said he would telephone if they had any new information. The pub wouldn't be open yet, which suited him because it was time he confronted Sonia Shepherd with what he knew before she got called away to attend to customers. He asked Sergeant Braybourne if a car was available to drop him off at The Quarryman's Arms. The car wasn't being used by Inspector Crispin and Braybourne found a young constable to drive him there.

Ryga found Sonia in the parlour but she wasn't alone. Sitting beside her at the table was Eva Paisley. Ryga felt no surprise. Eva glanced up at him with pleading in her eyes — not for herself, he thought, but for Sonia, whose whole appearance was one of dejection and despair. His heart went out to her and his stomach knotted at the thought that she might have killed a man and Eva might have assisted her. Could he really put these two women's necks in a noose?

Yes, if they had cold-bloodedly planned to kill two men and connived to deceive him. He took a mental deep breath and steeled himself to the possibility that he was looking at two murderers.

CHAPTER TWENTY-ONE

'You know, don't you?' Sonia said, anguish in her voice.

'That your husband wasn't killed at Dunkirk as the War Office told me but was murdered last Tuesday night in Church Ope Cove by either you or Miss Paisley, or by both of you?'

Her aghast expression told him instantly that he had got it wrong. Thank God. He hadn't really believed it but he had to be certain. Mentally he breathed a sigh of relief.

Her skin blanched. Her knuckles whitened as she pressed her hands together to stop them from shaking. Eva looked set to speak but Sonia got there first. 'No, Eva, I have to tell him myself.'

Ryga could see this was costing her dearly. She was making a supreme effort. Eva nodded and took a deep breath while tossing Ryga a glance that said, 'Go easy.'

'I visited James Legg at John's Penn's Bath on Tuesday night because James Legg is my husband, Sam.'

Ryga's mind raced, putting this with what he knew. He sat down opposite Eva but didn't look at her. He kept his gaze fixed on Sonia at the head of the table, hoping that he showed nothing of what he felt — empathy.

Sonia continued, beseeching him with her dark, deep-set eyes to understand. 'I had no idea that Sam was still alive until he walked in here the Sunday before last after closing time.' Her voice broke. Eva made to stretch out a hand but Sonia, with an effort and a slight shake of her head, pulled herself up. Ryga could see that she wasn't faking her emotions. 'He'd changed a lot but not so much that I didn't recognize him.'

The shock of seeing the man she had believed dead for ten years must have been immense.

'I had been told that he had been taken off the beach at Dunkirk onto a small fishing vessel. The boat had got into trouble in heavy sea in the English Channel, just off the Isle of Wight. Everyone onboard had died. But Sam told me he had managed to grab a lifebelt and had somehow made it ashore to a secluded bay on the island. There he was helped by a woman, a widow, who lived alone in a house above the bay. I'm not sure exactly what happened.' She swallowed hard.

But Ryga knew she had guessed the ensuing scenario. So could he. Sam Shepherd had charmed the woman and had stolen from her. He had probably also stolen her late husband's papers or the money to buy new identity papers. Ryga wondered if he had also killed the widow. Was that where the man in the cove came into this? Was he a relative of the widow who had taken in Sam Shepherd? Had he tracked Sam down, confronted him and Sam had silenced him?

Sonia continued, 'Sam saw it as a good opportunity to start a new life. He certainly didn't want to go back to war. If anyone asked him why he wasn't in uniform, he said he had been invalided out.'

And Ryga could fill in the blanks. Sam Shepherd had travelled about Britain, managing to escape the worst of the bombing, and once his initial money had run out he had made friends with a new widow and then another, had charmed his way into their lives just as he'd done with Bridget Norman in Brighton. How many other lives had he wrecked? Ryga wondered. He had lived well, he'd had suits and shoes made especially for him — until the Sunday before last, when he had arrived here and his luck seemed to have run out. Or had it? Ryga had speculated that Sam aka Legg was here for a reason, and it was the reason he came back to: because one of his many victims' relatives had been after him and had eventually found him.

'Did the man in the cove ask your husband to come here?'

'I don't know.' But he saw her glance at Eva. 'Sam told me he was sick of England and that he wanted to go to America, where the real money and opportunities were. He said that if he could get enough money together he would take me and Steven with him. We could make a fresh start, forget the dreary war and all the empty promises that had been made to us about what it was going to be like afterwards. I wouldn't need to be a pub landlady.'

'Did you believe him?' Ryga asked quietly.

'I'd like to have done. But I knew what he was like before he was called up, and although now he had lovely clothes and was staying at The Pennsylvania Castle Hotel, I could see that he hadn't changed. If he hadn't been called up when he was, the brewery were about to bring charges against him for theft. I made the money good and they said I could stay on.'

'Generous of them,' Eva finally chimed in caustically. 'They didn't have much choice with all the men being called up. And with Portland being a target for German bombers they would have been hard pressed to find anyone to take on the pub. Sonia was doing them a favour, not the other way round.'

'I knew that he must be in trouble for him to have resorted coming to me. I told him that I didn't want to go to America, that my home with Steven was here. He could go without us. It wouldn't cost him as much. He looked as though he had done well for himself — surely he could raise the money. But he said he couldn't and that if I didn't get him some money he would have no alternative but to come and live with me in the pub. I said that people would recognize him and he smirked and said that might not be a bad thing, he'd be a hero. I could actually see that he was warming to the idea.' Her hands shook and she pressed them tightly together as though to stop them. She held Ryga's gaze and continued. 'He said he would claim to have lost his memory after being wounded and had made a new life for himself until his memory had slowly come back to him piece by piece. He said he had everything he needed here, drink, warmth, a son and a bed . . .'

Ryga flashed a look at Eva, whose expression was a mixture of fury and sorrow. Ryga knew full well what Legg had meant. He could read between the lines as well as Eva could. He found himself tense at the thought of Legg forcing himself on Sonia. Had he done so that Sunday night?

Sonia cleared her throat. 'I told him the brewery would have to be informed. He didn't see a problem with that — as I was the licensee there would be no change and I knew full well what he meant by that. I would do all the work while he would drink the profits, act the hero and go off whenever he pleased. My life was bad enough with him before he went to France — it would be worse if he stayed. I knew they were threats and that he didn't really want to stay here but he would if I couldn't give him money. He said I could take it from the till and he knew that I had some jewellery of my mother's. I had to get enough money, then he would leave us alone.'

Eva said, 'Until he ran out again and came back for more.'

Ryga's thoughts exactly. But why come here when his charm on widows had worked so well before?

'He wouldn't come back if he went to America,' Sonia insisted. Maybe she didn't really believe that, though, because her voice lacked real conviction. 'I had my mother's gold watch, a brooch and her wedding ring, and some small savings. I took them to Sam on Tuesday night. We'd arranged to meet at John Penn's Bath at eleven but I got held up by one of the customers so I didn't get there until about eleven ten.'

Ryga addressed Eva. 'You knew this?'

'No. I went there, as I told you, to do some moonlight photography and heard voices. I didn't lie to you, Ryga. I didn't see them.'

He eyed her sternly.

Sonia said, 'I just wanted him out of our lives. Besides, I didn't know that he had done anything criminal.'

'There's desertion,' said Ryga.

She looked down at her hands and back up at him. 'Yes. If the police got hold of Sam he would have to stay in England, and even if he went to prison he would come out back to us. Everyone would know the shame of his past and mine. They might think that I had known all along that Sam hadn't drowned. They'd prosecute me for taking my war widow's pension and they'd ask me to repay all the money I've been given. I can't do that — I haven't got it. I would go to prison and Steven would have to go into a children's home.' She shuddered violently. Ryga could see she was desperately trying not to cry. And he was desperately fighting the desire to sweep her in his arms and hold her tight. If he got hold of Sam Shepherd, he'd break his legs!

He said, 'The courts would be fully sympathetic. They wouldn't send you to prison.'

'But I can't repay that money and the brewery would throw me out. I didn't know what to do, so I gave him what he wanted. Please don't find him, Inspector. Please let him get out of the country.'

'You know I can't do that.'

Eva interjected, 'Oh, for heaven's sake, Ryga, act like a human being and not a policeman.'

'But I am a policeman and I like to think I'm also human.'

'You wouldn't even bother to go after Sam if you were the latter,' she snapped.

'I would if he killed a man.'

'You mean Conrad.'

'And the man on the beach.' His gaze swivelled on Sonia. 'And you know that because you went to the cove on Wednesday morning.'

Her face was harrowed and she looked as though she had aged years in the minutes he had been there. He continued, 'Someone saw you enter Miss Paisley's house Wednesday morning at approximately six a.m.'

'I didn't know what to do. I was frantic with worry. I couldn't sleep. I rose early and went down to the cove to think. Then I saw the body. I thought it must be Sam although I didn't know why I thought that, except that possibly someone had caught up with his criminal ways. Then when I saw it was a stranger I thought, "My God, Sam's killed him." There was only one person I could turn to. Eva.'

Ryga's eyes swept to Eva. 'You agreed with Sonia that you would make the discovery of the body half an hour later. You should have told me. Withholding information is a serious offence.'

'If I thought for a moment that Sonia had been involved in murder I would have done, but she hasn't anything to do with the man in the pinstriped suit,' Eva said.

'How do you know that?' Ryga asked, holding her steady and confident gaze.

'Because I have.'

CHAPTER TWENTY-TWO

A loud thudding broke the taut silence. A man's voice shouted, 'Hey, Sonia, have you run dry? We're gagging of thirst out here.'

She dashed Ryga a nervous glance. 'Can I open up?'

After a moment he nodded, and with an expression of relief she rose. She paused and looked at Eva, confused. She made to speak but the banging on the door came again and she left.

Eva scraped back her chair. 'Let's walk back to my house. There's something I need to show you, unless you intend to take me in for questioning.'

They stepped out into the dank September evening. He wondered if he should formally caution her and take her to the police station. But he felt that it would be wrong to do so. Chief Constable Ambrose would say he was being blinded by Eva Paisley's charm. Maybe he was, but he simply didn't want to believe she was a killer. And he was curious as to what she meant when she said she had 'something to show him'. He also knew he would get more from her at her house than in an interview room at the police station. He was glad to get away from the pub and the image of Sonia's drawn face.

'Sonia doesn't know about my involvement with the dead man in the cove, if you can call it involvement. I believe that man in the pinstriped suit was coming to see me,' Eva continued.

He stared at her, stunned and annoyed that she hadn't told him this at the start.

'I was to meet him at John Penn's Bath that night, Tuesday.'

It got worse.

'I know what you're going to say and you're right, I should have told you right at the start, but I didn't know you then. You could have been another Superintendent Meredith, or worse, Inspector Crispin.'

He stifled a smile at mention of the latter. He didn't know the former, but from Sergeant Daniels' account of when Meredith had first arrived on the scene — that he had been short with her and had said that the death of a man was hardly the subject for holiday snaps — he could see what Eva meant. Either or both men would have treated her patronizingly and possibly even refused to take her crime photographs seriously. They could have ignored the pictures totally, which would have been a dreadful waste. And they could have arrested her. But perhaps he was being uncharitable to his police colleagues. He felt flattered she viewed him differently, but perhaps flattery was her intention so that she could manipulate him into believing her.

She continued, 'Besides, I didn't know the dead man was the same man I was supposed to meet until today. I'm still not certain of it, but I'd gone to Sonia's to tell her about it and to say that we had to tell you the truth about Sam.' She paused and studied him to see if he believed her.

'Go on.'

'When Sonia knocked on my door Wednesday morning and told me about the body and about Sam turning up, we both thought that Sam must have killed the pinstripe-suited man. We thought the victim must have finally caught up with Sam for some past wrongdoing, but instead of killing Sam out of revenge, or because they were both involved in some kind of criminal activity and had fallen out, it had been the other way around and Sam had got the better of the other man.

'When you showed me the cufflinks and I saw they were diamonds, it didn't ring true from what I'd heard about Sam that he wouldn't have spotted them and therefore stolen them. And neither did the body being laid out neatly like it was sound the sort of thing Sam Shepherd would have done. I thought if Sam had killed him, he'd have just left his body as it had fallen. Then Harold told me about the dead man being dressed differently and I began to wonder if it might be the same man who'd telephoned me. That didn't mean that Sam hadn't killed him and that they weren't involved in some kind of crooked deal, and yes, Sam could have redressed the victim in one of his older suits and shoes in order to hide the dead man's identity, and just not seen the cufflinks, but I thought if the dead man in the cove was the man who had telephoned me to arrange a meeting, then why had he said he had something important to tell me in connection with my aunt? And what did that have to do with Sam Shepherd?'

Ryga flashed her a bewildered look.

'I know, it seemed crazy to me too,' she went on. 'I asked him what it was but he wouldn't say over the telephone, and when I asked him how he had known where to find me he said he knew I'd be at my aunt's house because of her death.'

'How did he know that?'

'I didn't get a chance to ask him. There was an obituary on her in some of the newspapers and in the culture magazines. Pru was an internationally acclaimed artist.'

'And you, her niece, a well-known photographer. The articles would have mentioned you.'

'Some of them certainly would have done, but they wouldn't have said I'd be at Pru's house. I suppose he could have guessed. I know he didn't enquire at my London apartment because the porter says no one has been around asking after me or my whereabouts. And he hasn't told anyone I'm away.'

Ryga was puzzled.

She continued, 'He refused to come to the house and said he'd meet me at John Penn's Bath at eleven thirty Tuesday night.'

'Didn't you think that strange?'

'Of course I did. I suggested we meet earlier in the day and somewhere more public but he was very insistent.'

'Your life could have been in danger,' Ryga said, then wished he hadn't when she gave him a withering look, but it contained no hostility.

'It wouldn't be the first time,' she said, not unkindly. 'I took a risk. It's what you, I, and others sometimes have to do. When I approached John Penn's Bath on Tuesday night I heard voices, one of which I instantly recognized as Sonia's. The other was a man's that I didn't recognize. I quickly stepped back but they were too engrossed in discussion to have heard my approach. I didn't know then that the man with Sonia was her husband. I'd never met him — still haven't,' she added, 'and like everyone else, including Sonia, we all believed he'd been killed at Dunkirk. Initially it crossed my mind that he must be the man who had telephoned me, but I dismissed that because why would he be with Sonia? So I thought it must be Sonia's lover and that he was married, hence the clandestine meeting.'

The same thought as Ryga.

'I surmised that because my rendezvous point had been taken over by someone else, my man would call me the next day to rearrange, but Sonia knocked on my door instead.' Eva fell silent as they walked past two women talking on their doorsteps. The sound of children playing came from inside one of the houses.

When they were out of earshot, Ryga said, 'Why did Sonia come to you?'

'Pru and Sonia were good friends. When Sonia was left alone to run the pub with a baby, Pru helped her all she could. She knew that Sam Shepherd was a bully and had knocked Sonia about before he went away to war. I had met Sonia several times when I'd stayed with Pru. We became friends. Plus, I was an outsider and Sonia didn't know who else to turn to, and don't say she should have gone straight to the police, because she couldn't. Not only was her husband a deserter and a cheat but she also thought he was a murderer.'

'He might still be.'

'I know.'

There was a moment's silence.

'Sam Shepherd was seen entering Conrad's shop early on Wednesday morning,' Ryga continued, 'so either he knew Conrad or Sonia told him where to take the jewellery.'

'I think it must be the former. He'd probably have known Conrad from before the war. But I can't think why Sam Shepherd would kill Conrad.'

'Unless Shepherd, Conrad and the pinstripe-suited man were all involved in a jewellery heist and Sam Shepherd got greedy.'

She frowned and pushed back her hair. 'Which means the dead man in Church Ope Cove is not the same man who telephoned me. But if he isn't then why hasn't he been in touch again?'

'Maybe he changed his mind. Perhaps the police presence has scared him off because he has something to hide or be afraid of.'

Eva unlocked her cottage door and stepped inside. Ryga, removing his hat, followed suit. It was dim and Eva switched on the lights. Several illuminated the paintings. The room was as before — comfortable, lived in, with what he thought was the essence of Prudence Paisley still inside it. He wondered what Eva's apartment was like. On the table to Ryga's right were two large cardboard folders and several sketches spread across them.

Eva shrugged off her leather jacket and threw it over the back of an armchair. 'Drink?' she asked, crossing to a cabinet by the wireless. 'Whisky? Sherry? I haven't got any beer.'

'Neither, thank you.'

'Don't mind if I do?' She poured herself a shot of whisky and swallowed it quickly. 'Take a look at these.'

He followed her to the table where the sketches were spread out.

'There's one missing,' she said.

He eyed her, baffled, not seeing where this was leading.

'I think it's important because I believe it's connected to our dead man in the cove. It was you who triggered the idea yesterday when you were looking at the paintings of the convicts.' She took a deep breath. 'I'll explain. A month ago, I photographed Pru's sketches for a book I was pulling together for her of her work. But there was one sketch I photographed that she quickly snatched away and said, "Not that one." I asked her why and she said it wasn't good enough, but although I could see that wasn't the real reason I didn't press her. It was her book after all. I remember it being a sketch of two convicts, one lying on the shore and a warder standing over him. I didn't think anything more about it until you and I began talking about the paintings and discussing how the prisoners had been involved in hard labour. We looked at their faces in those pictures on the wall and I thought of the dead man's face and his hands — labourer's hands. The more I thought about it the more unsettled I became, so yesterday I went through all her sketches and couldn't find the one of the two convicts.'

'Maybe she destroyed it after you'd discussed it to prevent you or anyone else finding it again and it being photographed, if she really was ashamed of it.'

'I'm certain that's not it, and I'll tell you why. I drove up to London today to look out the photographs I'd taken of the sketches. I found that one and the negative.' She reached into the envelope on the table and extracted a medium-sized black-and-white photograph. 'What do you see?' Her voice was now filled with excitement.

It was a photograph of a rough but evocative sketch of two convicts, one hunched on the shore under the sharp protuberance of the cliff on the coast between Church Ope Cove and the lighthouse where Ryga had walked on Saturday, and the other lying face down on the shore. The sketch was dated 14 April 1920. The prisoners must have been very young men but the face of the hunched convict was lined and worn down by the weather and hard labour and with something else etched into it that Ryga knew was despair. He felt his stomach knot as it reminded him of the faces he'd seen around him in the prisoner of war camp for four long years, growing more despairing by the day until those last months when they all realized the end was in sight. But even that had come with a new fear — that they'd be killed before they could be liberated.

He pushed the memories aside and focused wholeheartedly on the photograph.

'Here, take this.' Eva handed over the magnifying glass. 'Look at the figures behind the rock to the left of the picture, on the shore.'

Although it wasn't totally clear, Ryga saw that in contrast to the hardened, world-weary prisoner peered the faces of two boys, their expressions excited, youthful, laughing. No, mocking. It made him feel nauseous. The convicts were the boys' entertainment, or so Prudence Paisley had interpreted it. Perhaps she was wrong, or he was, because their entertainment couldn't have been the prostrate convict on the shore. He peered more closely then glanced up at Eva.

There was a gleam of excitement in her blue eyes. 'Tell me?'

'I could be wrong, but there is a strong resemblance in one of those boys to the man—'

'In the cove, yes. The same shape of face and that broad brow. We could be mistaken, but look at the prison officer.'

Ryga again peered through the magnifying glass, this time at the man standing over the convict, whose expression was smug, superior and cruel.

'My God, it's Crawley, the night porter at The Pennsylvania Castle Hotel.'

'It is. So why would he want to steal that original sketch and kill Pru?'

'You believe your aunt's death was suspicious?'

'You bet I do now. Did she really get up in the night to go to the toilet or to fetch a drink because she couldn't sleep? Or did a noise wake her, an intruder? All the locals knew where she kept her key — most people around here keep theirs in the same place. Easy enough for someone to enter the cottage. I was told her death was due to a coronary. She'd been under the doctor and had an irregular heartbeat. Inspector Crispin was called in but the doctor deemed it to be from natural causes. That was the end of it. There wasn't a post-mortem. Yes, it's possible she could have suffered a heart attack brought on by shock at finding someone in the house. Or perhaps she was killed by some method that neither Crispin nor the doctor noticed or looked for. That sketch is missing. A mysterious caller told me he had something to tell me about my aunt, and now it appears that person is also dead. Look, Ryga, I have no idea why or what happened but there has to be a connection. Pru, as you can see from her paintings, was renowned for her candid scenes in all their harsh reality. That scene—' Eva stabbed at the photograph — 'existed. It happened, she captured it, and she didn't want it to appear in her collection. I'd like to know why.'

Ryga put on his hat. 'Then let's go and ask Crawley.'

CHAPTER TWENTY-THREE

'The date, the fourteenth of April, 1920. Mean anything to you?'

'Eh?' Crawley's eyes darted to Eva and back to Ryga. They were alone in the hotel reception. Music emanated from the radio in the lounge.

'No. Why should it?'

'I would have thought it would have been ingrained on your mind but then perhaps you thought the death of a prisoner insignificant.' Ryga didn't know for certain the prisoner was dead. He might have slipped and fallen from the cliff edge while working and been badly injured — a thought that he had expressed to Eva on their way here. He'd also told her to let him lead the interview and to say nothing about the fact she had photographed the sketch, nor to mention the two boys who were in it. He'd play it by ear depending on Crawley's responses. They needed all the information they could get and this could be leading them down a blind alley. Even bringing her along was highly irregular, but it did concern her and he found he valued her assessment of the man and the situation.

'I haven't a clue what you're talking about,' Crawley said.

Oh, but he had. Ryga could see it is his shifting, wary eyes, and he knew full well that Eva would too. 'You know precisely what I am talking about,' Ryga said, 'and I suggest you get your memory back very quickly, Mr Crawley, otherwise I'll have to take you to the station to—'

'No!' He sniffed and glanced nervously around the reception hall. They still had the place to themselves. He lowered his voice. 'It was years ago. Why do you want to know about it? It was just . . .'

'Another convict,' Eva said coldly. 'And no one of any consequence.'

'I didn't mean that. I meant . . .'

'Yes?' Ryga prompted when Crawley dried up.

'I can't talk here and now.'

'Fine. Then let's go—'

'No. All right, I'll tell you.' Crawley held up his hands in capitulation.

Ryga could feel Eva's tension and excitement beside him. Crawley's eyes swivelled around the lounge as though looking for an escape, or perhaps he was making sure no one was within earshot. He removed a handkerchief from his trouser pocket, wiped his brow and replaced it, all actions designed, Ryga thought, to give him time to compose his thoughts or to decide how much to tell them. Or perhaps even to think of a lie.

After a moment, he began in a slightly shaky voice, 'It was a very hot day, unusual for April. I was detailed to take a work party of two convicts to the shore, below part of the quarry that wasn't being used, to collect some rocks, stones, shells and driftwood for the governor's wife's new beach-themed garden. I left a pushcart on the track above the shore. There was a steep descent down to the small bay. I escorted the prisoners down there and shackled them while I, er, left to take a toilet break.' He darted a glance at Eva.

'But something went wrong,' Ryga prompted.

Crawley swallowed hard. 'When I came back I found one of them dead.'

And that's what Prudence Paisley had captured in her sketch. Ryga didn't look at Eva. He wondered if the same thoughts as his were running through her head.

'I didn't know how I was going to explain it. But as it happened no one seemed at all interested anyway. I unshackled them and, with the other convict, climbed back up the path. I chained him to the cart and ran to get help. A police officer telephoned the hospital and returned to the cove with me. He confirmed the other convict was dead, then we waited until the ambulance turned up and they got the body onto a stretcher and the four of us carried it up the track to the cart. The ambulance took the body to the naval hospital mortuary and I took the other convict back to the prison.'

'Didn't he tell you what had happened?'

'He didn't say a word, not then or afterwards. He looked ill. The shock of seeing his fellow convict drop down dead before him with a heart seizure must have been too much.'

'Is that how he died?'

'Must have been — there wasn't a mark on him. There hadn't been a fight or anything like that.'

'Was there a post-mortem?'

Crawley shrugged. 'If there was, no one told me about it.'

'And what did you tell the prison governor about why you weren't with them?'

Crawley shifted uneasily and straightened the register. 'I didn't mention it. The other convict wasn't going to say anything because he knew no one would listen to him anyway. He seemed to have lost his power of speech and everyone just thought—'

'That one dead convict didn't amount to much anyway,' Eva said with bitterness.

Ryga flashed her glance. She glared back at him, then her angry expression eased and she exhaled.

'Who were the convicts?' Ryga asked.

'I've forgotten their names.'

Eva snorted with disgust. 'I'd have thought they would have stuck in your mind.'

'Well, they didn't. A lot has happened in the years since, including a ruddy great war where lots of people died,' he snapped. After a moment, though, he resumed more calmly, 'The other convict died twenty-four hours later.'

'How?' Ryga asked, his mind racing.

'He was found dead in his cell. They said the shock must have killed him.'

Convenient. 'How long did you leave them alone on the shore?'

'Five minutes, maybe ten at the most.'

That was clearly a lie. Ryga simply raised his eyebrows and peered hard at Crawley until his eyes dropped. Coolly, he said, 'Did you know that Prudence Paisley was there?'

Crawley's head shot up and dashed troubled glances between Ryga and Eva. His face was now a picture of misery.

'I see that you did.' Ryga wondered if Eva had drawn the same conclusion. Crawley had sneaked off to meet Prudence Paisley.

'Did you also know that she sketched the scene?' And it had taken some nerve for her to do that and some callousness, he thought, but was it any different from what her niece did? Eva had taken and still took pictures of bodies. Prudence probably reasoned she could do nothing for the dead prisoner, but she had seen the boys, so why not go down and offer to assist Crawley so as to shield them from the horror of death? Why say nothing about this event over the years? The answer was because she was also shielding Crawley and perhaps her own reputation.

'But she couldn't have done.' Crawley's eyes widened and his lip trembled, and it didn't appear as though he was faking it. Maybe this was the first he knew of any sketch.

'Why not?' Eva asked.

He shifted and looked away. 'Because when I left her she was returning to Easton.'

Confirmation that they'd had an assignation. Eva was looking incredulous. Ryga could see that she found it difficult to believe that her aunt and this man had been lovers.

'You saw her go?' Ryga asked before Eva could speak.

'Well, no. I had to get back.'

'She followed you and found you down on the shore. Didn't she ask you about the dead man?'

'She never said a word about it to me or anyone else that I know.'

But had she, and recently, which had set in motion this murder spree?

'Were you married in 1920, Mr Crawley?'

His face flushed. That was a 'yes' then.

Eva said, 'You mean that you and Pru were having an affair.'

Ryga didn't think Crawley could go any redder but he did, then his eyes searched the reception hall furtively as though his wife might suddenly appear as a ghost to accuse him of adultery. 'I would have married her if—'

'You hadn't already been married,' Eva finished for him. 'I've heard that one before.'

Ryga wondered where and how many times. He thrust the thought aside. 'Why didn't you marry her after your wife died . . . When was that?'

'In 1934. Pru wasn't interested then. In fact, it only, well . . . it fizzled out before it had even started. We were just two lonely people attracted to each other. Her husband had been killed in the Great War and my wife was an invalid.' He coughed and made a great study of the backs of his hands.

Ryga wasn't here to judge his morals and he didn't care whether the affair had continued or not, but he wondered from the sketch if Prudence had suddenly seen a different side to the man she had just made love to and didn't like what she saw. She'd abruptly broken off any liaison between them. He was certain Eva was thinking along the same lines. 'Was there anyone else on the shore?'

'I would have said if there had been.'

'Are you sure?'

'It was just me and the two convicts. I swear it. Where is that sketch?' he asked.

'In a safe place,' Ryga lied.

Eva remained silent. Ryga wondered if the boys in the sketch had been an artist's imagination or interpretation — innocence and guilt. But whose guilt? Crawley's at leaving the prisoners unattended or Prudence's at making love to a married man? And where did innocence come into it, if not that of the boys? If he thought of Crawley's expression in the painting, maybe he had the answer — Prudence's bitterness at her own innocence for believing Crawley would leave his wife for her.

'If the names of the dead prisoners come back to you, telephone the police station and leave a message for me.'

Crawley quickly assured him that he would but Ryga didn't believe that for a minute. He caught the man's expression of relief as he turned to leave, then swung back. 'Who was the police officer who accompanied you back to the shore?'

'I—' He was about to say he didn't know but saw that any admission of failing memory on that score wouldn't wash. 'It was PC Daneman.'

Outside, Eva turned to Ryga. 'Do you believe him?'

'To a degree.'

'I find it incredible that Aunt Pru would have had an affair with him.'

'They were both young. And maybe "affair" is too strong a word. She was lonely as Crawley said, and maybe he capitalized on that.'

'You mean a fling, or a one night — or day — stand.' She took a deep breath. 'You're right, Ryga, it could be possible.'

They walked towards the car. Eva continued, 'Pru followed him back to the work party probably intending to sketch it. She'd have taken her sketching pad and pencils with her as a cover for their meeting in case anyone saw them together. I don't know what she saw in Crawley. But then what did Sonia ever see in a bully like Sam Shepherd?'

'You think Crawley was a bully?'

'You've seen his face in the sketch and his posture.'

'Your aunt could have exaggerated that. Maybe he told her after he'd made love to her that he had to end the affair. They rowed, she was furious, followed him and sketched him how she then saw him.'

'But why didn't she report the death of the prisoner?'

'Because she'd have to admit she was there with him.'

'So she pushed it away and got on with her life. Perhaps she didn't even know the prisoner was dead.'

'She must have witnessed Crawley testing for a pulse and marching the other prisoner back up to the clifftop. It's possible she thought Crawley had killed him.'

Pausing by the car, Eva's forehead creased in thought.

'Crawley could have tried to see her afterwards to make sure she said nothing. He might have asked for one last meeting,' Ryga added.

'Which she refused.'

'Crawley was just glad that no further questions were asked about the convicts' deaths. No one wanted to stir up trouble and no one was going to put themselves out for a couple of criminals. But they weren't the only ones at the scene. Those two boys. Unless they are the result of your aunt's artistic licence and we're mistaken about the similarity between one of them and the dead man in the cove. The camera might not lie but the artist's paintbrush or pencil can and does.'

'So too can the camera, or rather the person behind it.'

'But if they're real why didn't *they* speak out?' Ryga posed.

'They could have been told to keep quiet?'

'Or were too scared to come forward. Crawley doesn't seem to know they were there.'

'Perhaps they weren't local but were on holiday. Was it Easter?'

Ryga said he would check that. 'Why else would boys stay silent?' he mused, then answered his own question as he climbed into the car. 'Because they were up to no good.'

'But what could they have been doing there? There was nothing to steal or wreck.'

'Spying on the convicts? Taunting them was probably fair game in 1920.'

'But you think it was more than that, don't you?' She swivelled round to face him.

'It's unusual that both convicts died within twenty-four hours of each other and both apparently of natural causes.'

'Poison? One or both of the boys gave the convicts a poisoned drink while Crawley was away. But why the devil would they do that?'

'For a dare? Out of curiosity?' Ryga shrugged. 'In order to do so though they would have needed to have come prepared, which makes it premeditated murder.'

'But surely they didn't intend to murder the convicts?'

'Perhaps they thought it was a game and the poison or chemical they gave the convicts would only make them sick.'

'How could they have known the work party would be there?'

'Three ways,' Ryga promptly replied. 'One, your aunt told them — yes, unlikely if she had a secret rendezvous with Crawley, which she did. Two, Crawley told them, again unlikely if he was to meet your aunt, but he could have mentioned it casually to one or both boys. Three, they heard of it from someone else within the prison. If they did, one or both boys could have been related to a warder there. How old would they be now? Early to mid-forties?'

'About Sam Shepherd's age. You think he could be the other boy in the sketch?'

Ryga knew that wouldn't have escaped Eva. 'Was he living on Portland then? Was he related to anyone at the prison or did he know Crawley?'

'You'll need to ask Sonia.'

Ryga said he would.

'Shepherd certainly knew Aunt Pru when he was working at The Quarryman's Arms before the war, because she gave him a dressing down for hitting Sonia. Could Pru have known he was returning?' Eva posed. 'And she threatened to reveal the sketch, which showed him as a boy. Until then he'd had no idea it existed. He knew where she lived, returned, killed her and stole the sketch.'

'Then he came back to blackmail the other child in the sketch.'

'The man in the pinstriped suit. But—'

'I know what you're going to say — he wasn't wealthy, or at least not according to the way he was dressed both when Harold and the landlord of The Cove Inn saw him, and in a suit that was too small for him when he was killed, but there were the diamond cufflinks, and his shirt, tie and underwear were of the best quality. Perhaps he donned that suit to fool Shepherd into thinking he didn't have much money or maybe he met Shepherd dressed in the clothes Harold saw him wearing and Shepherd changed him after killing him in order to hide his identity. Perhaps he returned with other diamonds as payment to Shepherd for his silence and for the sketch, only Shepherd took the diamonds, kept the sketch and then took the diamonds to Conrad.'

'Why didn't Crawley recognize James Legg as Sam Shepherd?' Eva asked.

'Perhaps because he, like everyone else, believed Shepherd was dead. Perhaps he's not very good at remembering faces, although he said he was. Or perhaps he did recognize Shepherd but was paid to keep quiet.' Or was threatened into keeping quiet, Ryga added to himself. 'He didn't ask us why we were enquiring about that sketch now. And he seemed genuinely shocked there was a sketch.'

'Could have been an act.'

'Maybe, and if it was then it throws up another possibility. Crawley could be the killer. In 1920 he stole poison from the prison medical officer and poisoned both prisoners to silence them for either his affair with your aunt or for some other fiddle he was involved in. Your aunt knew he had killed those men after she'd followed him back to the cliff edge and saw him down on the shore. She then ditched him after she had discovered the truth. And perhaps she never spoke out because of Mrs Crawley. Your aunt could have been protecting her all those years and then, when she died, thought it not worth raking it all up. But a few weeks ago, she had a change of heart and told Crawley and showed him the sketch. Or he could have found it by chance while visiting her. Perhaps she had left it out by mistake after you had photographed the others.'

'But he'd hardly be likely to get in touch with either of the boys, if he knew where they were, and risk being exposed as a killer.'

'No. So it's far more likely that *if* Sam Shepherd is one of those boys, then he recognized Crawley at the hotel and decided on a spot of blackmail. That would be motive enough for Crawley to want to silence him. And Crawley couldn't take the risk that Shepherd hadn't said anything to the other boy. Crawley contacted the other boy, killed him, undressed and dressed him, then killed Shepherd and dumped his body in the undergrowth. Or perhaps he managed to get Shepherd's body into the Jaguar. Crawley could have driven that Jaguar to Conrad's shop and pawned the jewellery Sonia gave her husband, then ditched the car somewhere.'

'Can you really see him doing that?'

'People can be deceptive. And he could be desperate.'

'I'll enlarge the photograph I took of the sketch and focus in on the children, and I'll run you off some prints so you can ask around to try and identify the boys, but I need to return to my apartment in London for the equipment. I'll drive up there tonight. I should have something for you tomorrow.'

'We're already checking out prison records for Sebastian Conrad's background but I'll ask Sergeant Jacobs if he can get me anything on the prisoner who died on the fourteenth April 1920 and the one twenty-four hours after that, although I'm not sure that will give us much. But Conrad was at the same prison as those dead convicts — perhaps he suspected something about their deaths but kept quiet because he was going to be released shortly. On his return to England from Amsterdam it wasn't worth rocking the boat, so he continued to keep quiet about it until recently, when one of those boys on the shore returned, and Conrad thought *he'd* go in for a spot of blackmail.'

'And ended up dead. I'll drop you back to The Quarryman's Arms,' Eva said, starting the car.

'No, I'll walk from your cottage.'

His head was spinning and he needed time to think, especially as he had a delicate conversation with Sonia to come. Tomorrow he would take another look around Conrad's seedy little shop.

Eva drew up outside her cottage.

'Eva, promise me you won't go off investigating on your own.'

'On two conditions.'

He raised his eyebrows.

'If you discover anything significant or the identity of either of those boys before I return, you tell me. Here's my London telephone number.' She reached into her jacket pocket and handed him a card. There were an awful lot of initials after her name.

'And the second?'

'I'll save that for another time.'

CHAPTER TWENTY-FOUR

It being Monday, The Quarryman's Arms was quiet, but Ryga knew he wouldn't be able to speak to Sonia until the pub closed. He didn't go to the bar — he spent some time in his room then made his way to the parlour and found her waiting for him. It was just after 10.15 p.m. and she had already closed up.

She offered him a drink. He accepted a cup of tea and they both remained silent while she made it. She looked exhausted. Not surprisingly. She'd been through a lot, and a dark, menacing cloud of what the future held hung over her. Had Crawley killed Shepherd? Would she be free of him?

After she had poured his tea and sat down, Ryga said, 'Tell me about Sam. Was he raised here on Portland?'

'Yes. His family lived in Castletown. His father worked for the dockyard and then Folly Pier Waterworks.'

Ryga hadn't heard of it. His expression made her elaborate.

'Oh, it's not there anymore. It was built mainly to serve the prison — you can see the ruins and the empty reservoirs just near the coast at East Weare on the east of the island. He worked in the boiler house until they closed the waterworks in 1920 because of an outbreak of typhoid which killed several prisoners who had drunk the water.'

The deaths of the two prisoners was hardly likely to concern the prison authorities if they had a number of inmates dying of typhoid.

'By the time the prison became a borstal in 1921, most of the old waterworks had gone but they used the reservoir tanks as swimming pools for the borstal boys until one of them sadly died in a swimming accident there in 1933. Sam's family left Portland after his father lost his job and he was given a new one at the waterworks serving Weymouth. He died in 1929. Sam's mother died in 1923.'

'Did you know Sam when he was a boy?'

'No. I'm five years younger than him. Besides, we didn't go to the same school. He lived in Castletown and I lived here. He was eleven when the family moved to Weymouth.'

'When did you meet him?'

'It was December 1937. He was standing in for the regular drayman, who had gone into hospital for an operation. I was behind the bar. I'd left my job in a dress shop in Weymouth because of Dad's health. My mother had died four years before. I was practically running the place. Sam was charming, handsome, fun. Then my father died suddenly in March 1938. Sam proposed and said that we could run the pub together. The brewery agreed. We got married in June 1938 and Steven was born in March 1939. But Sam changed once we were married. Oh, to the outside world he was still the genial host, but he was lazy, cruel and hateful.'

'And you were frightened of him.'

'Yes, but there was nothing I could do about it. If I spoke out he made sure that I felt the back of his hand — not where it would show to the customers and the brewery, he made sure of that — and I would keep my arms covered. I can't tell you what a relief it was, Mr Ryga, when he got called up just before Christmas in 1939. He tried to get out of it but he couldn't. He was fit and able and he didn't have a reserved occupation. I knew he would have to come home on leave but I hoped that it wouldn't be too often. Neither of us expected him to go to France and so quickly.'

And Ryga knew the reason for that was because the army was so desperately short of men after having suffered serious cutbacks in the years before the war. It wasn't really until the first half of 1939 when it became clearer that appeasement was failing that the military budget was increased, a limited form of conscription was introduced and spending on new equipment was made. The British Expeditionary Force was then greatly increased during the 'Phoney War' between September 1939 and May 1940, when the numbers in France to repel German offences swelled to nearly half a million men. Sam Shepherd was one of them.

'The thought of Sam with Steven terrifies me. I haven't told Steven about his father or that he has come back. I'll have to, though. What will he think? Will he believe me when I tell him what his father is really like? If the other boys know his father is a coward, a deserter and a crook, they'll make Steven's life hell on earth. He's a sensitive child and clever, but not all the other boys understand that.'

Reading between the lines, Ryga guessed that Steven was bullied and perhaps that was what caused his nightmares. It was stupid to offer pointless platitudes because he knew as well as she did that it was going to be incredibly difficult for her whichever way this turned out. Would she stay here? he wondered. Perhaps she would be better off making a fresh start somewhere. Perhaps Eva would help her.

He asked if she had a photograph of Sam as a young boy. 'No. I'm not sure he had one, and as you probably have seen, I don't have one of him.' She waved her arm about the room. 'The ones I did have I destroyed when they told me he was dead.' That was understandable given her experiences.

'Did you see any pictures of him as a child?' Ryga persisted, but she shook her head.

When Ryga got the enlarged photograph from Eva he would show it to Sonia to see if she recognized one of the boys in it as being her husband. He asked if she had anything in the house that Sam had touched on his visit there the Sunday before last that she hadn't cleaned or washed up, or anything he had given her at their rendezvous. Her eyes flew to the framed photograph on the mantelshelf of Steven as a baby. Of course, he should have guessed.

'Would you mind if I dust it for fingerprints and take yours for elimination purposes?'

'No, of course not.'

'I might also need Steven's in case he's touched the frame but don't worry, I can do that tomorrow if necessary and I'll make out that I'm demonstrating to him how it's done. There's no need for him to know anything else.' *Yet.*

She looked reassured at this and Ryga set off to his room to fetch his murder case. Half an hour later he had the prints he needed. Sonia's were on the frame — he was glad she hadn't decided to wipe it clean in a symbolic act of trying to obliterate her husband — and there was only one further set of prints. 'I don't need Steven's prints,' he said. She looked relieved. He asked her for a description of the jewellery she had given Sam and jotted it down in his notebook.

'What are you going to do now?' she asked.

'We have a call out for Mr Shepherd.' He refused to say *your husband*. Although she was technically married to him, the marriage was over and he certainly didn't think she deserved to be reunited with him. 'I'll also circulate a description of this jewellery, but I want to see if I can find it in Conrad's shop first.'

'Do you think Sam killed Sebastian Conrad?'

'If he did then your jewellery won't be there. He'll have taken it with him to sell elsewhere.'

'And the man in the cove? Did Sam kill him?'

'He might have done.' Ryga wasn't going to say that Sam might also be dead.

She took a breath and pulled herself up. 'What did Eva mean when she said she knew that dead man?'

'She thinks he knew her late aunt. More than that I can't say at the moment.'

She looked puzzled but nodded solemnly.

Ryga spent another restless night. He could not help thinking that across the narrow landing, just a few steps away, Sonia Shepherd lay awake, troubled and upset. He could almost hear her breathing although he knew that was his imagination. Part of him longed to comfort her but he knew that was out of the question. He felt desperately sorry for her, but were his feelings more than that? How much more? Was he falling in love with her? And what were his feelings for Eva Paisley?

He turned over, irritated with himself, and tried to sleep. He counted sheep. He thought of the sea, of waves rhythmically washing on the shore, but that only brought him back to the myriad of questions whirling around his head about the dead man in the pinstriped suit. He tried to shut his mind to everything but it refused to cooperate. Then he willed himself to stay awake because the pretence eliminated the one great obstacle to sleep — the fear that he wouldn't be able to. Usually it worked, but not this time. His mind was too active. He refused to put on the light and look at the clock. Its slow tick seemed to grow louder with each second but perhaps it was that which eventually made him sleep. It wasn't for long, or at least it didn't feel like it.

He switched on the light and saw that it was six o'clock. Good, he could get up. He washed, shaved and dressed, making as little noise as possible for fear of disturbing Sonia. She didn't show but he got the sense she was awake and perhaps waiting for him to leave the house before rising.

Carrying his murder case, he caught the train from Easton to Weymouth and stopped off at the police station, where he gave instructions for the fingerprints he'd taken last night to be checked against the ones taken from Conrad's shop. Then, collecting the key for the latter, he made for Cameron Street and was pleased to see that a constable was at the other end of it doing his rounds.

PC Wiley drew level with Ryga. 'Nothing to report, sir,' he said. 'No further sightings of Legg, the Jaguar, or anyone else seen entering the shop since last week.'

Ryga explained why he was there and asked the constable to help him search Conrad's shop. It was daylight but the overcast morning, which threatened rain, made the dim interior even gloomier. Ryga flicked on the electric light. The bulb was unshaded but so thick with dust that it did little to illuminate the dreary room. Ryga gave instructions for Wiley to search the two cabinets closest to the door, after telling him what he was looking for, while he addressed those on the counter. There were three low-level ones with sloping glass covering the contents.

It didn't take him long to spot Sonia's jewellery. He told Wiley he could stop searching and removed the jewellery after making sure to don his gloves. He dusted the items for prints but got nothing but smudges as he'd expected. He put the jewellery into one of his evidence bags and placed it in his case. 'This means that Sam Shepherd, aka James Legg, didn't kill Conrad. He sold the jewellery then left.'

'Unless he's clever enough to work out that's what we'd believe and he killed Conrad before leaving.'

'The timing's wrong for that, but he could have returned.' Conrad must have paid Sam Shepherd for Sonia's jewellery, which meant that Conrad had had cash in the house. The fact that neither he nor Daniels had found any could mean he'd paid it all out for Sonia's jewellery or that Shepherd had stolen it when he returned to kill Conrad. Or perhaps another person had taken it after stabbing Conrad in the neck, if there had been any left to steal.

Ryga locked up and returned to Weymouth police station. He telephoned the Yard and asked Sergeant Jacobs to instigate enquiries about the two dead prisoners with the Prison Commission. The question he toyed with the most was how the killer knew the sketch existed and that it was still in Prudence Paisley's possession. He came back to the fact that Crawley could have seen it on visiting Prudence for some reason. Perhaps they had recently resumed a relationship. She'd had the sketches out on the table just as Eva had done yesterday and idly Crawley had looked at them while Prudence was upstairs or in the kitchen or garden. He'd been startled to see the one of him with the convicts and he'd also seen the two boys. He had recognized them and suddenly been fearful they would tell the authorities about his part in the deaths of those convicts. If that was the case then Crawley was a damn good actor and cunning and clever enough to keep quiet about the two boys.

He postponed all his thoughts and questions and tucked into a cooked breakfast. Once he was done, he pushed away his empty plate and drank his tea. He was glad to see Sergeant Daniels enter and beckoned him over. Ryga brought him up to date with his interview with Crawley and the discovery of the missing sketch.

After listening in silence, Daniels said, 'Crawley could have killed Conrad because Conrad knew what had happened in 1920, but I can't see him keeping quiet about it all these years, certainly not since he returned to Weymouth in 1938. He'd have bled Crawley dry.'

But would he when he seemed so disinterested in money? 'If that's the case,' Ryga said, 'then Conrad didn't know about the sketch and the boys until recently.'

An officer was heading towards him. 'Message from the Yard, sir.' He handed Ryga a piece of paper.

After thanking him, Ryga read it. 'The report's come in from the Hatton Garden expert. He's confirmed what Conrad told us — they are pink diamonds, mined in Australia. What's more, he claims they were cut by Abramowski.'

Daniels looked surprised. 'Why didn't Conrad tell us that? He must have recognized the cut.'

'He did and I think he knew from it who the dead man in the cove was. And he knew who the killer was.'

'Crawley?'

'I'm not sure. I can't see where he fits in with the diamonds, but I'd like to talk to him about Sebastian Conrad. First, though, we've got an inquest to attend.'

CHAPTER TWENTY-FIVE

Tuesday

The inquest went as planned. The coroner opened and adjourned it after hearing brief details from Inspector Crispin on the discovery of the body in the cove and Captain Surgeon Wakefield's report on the post-mortems of the two victims. Ryga told how he had found the body of Sebastian Conrad but in agreement with the coroner beforehand, a thin, bald man in his late fifties, he didn't mention Eva Paisley's part in that but told him privately she was instrumental in helping them pursue their investigation, not as a suspect, he hastened to add. The information on Sam Shepherd aka James Legg was also shared with the coroner but not raised in court on the grounds that Ryga said it might jeopardize his investigation, especially given that Sandy Mountfort was in court.

The coroner agreed to give Ryga another two weeks. Ryga hoped he wouldn't need it. Outside, Mountfort collared Ryga, as he had fully expected on seeing him in the thankfully small crowd. Crispin took Wakefield aside, and the two men along with Sergeant Daniels entered the police station, leaving Ryga to handle the journalist. He did so politely and apologetically, saying he would let him know as soon as he had more on the case. Mountfort looked sceptical, as any newspaper man would. Ryga had been surprised and relieved that none of the national press had shown up. Mountfort told him he was acting as special correspondent for the *Daily Wire* working on space rates and was feeding them the story in addition to working for the local newspaper so the other press didn't think they would get much more out of it.

'Not worth them sending someone down from Fleet Street,' Mountfort added grumpily before going off to write up the latest.

Inside the station Ryga found that Daniels had brought both Crispin and Wakefield up to date with the latest development of the missing sketch and the death of the two prisoners.

Crispin said, 'I can't see how that can possibly have anything to do with these recent deaths.'

'It might if one of those boys is the body in the cove and the other is Sam Shepherd,' Ryga replied. 'Crawley might be able to identify them for us. Or he might be the killer, having eliminated them and Sebastian Conrad, and before them Prudence Paisley.'

'Mrs Paisley's death was from natural causes. There was nothing the slightest bit suspicious about it. I *was* on the scene, Inspector Ryga,' Crispin said. He didn't have to add that he thought Ryga was getting carried away with Eva Paisley. Ryga could see it in his expression and hear it in his voice.

'It's just something that needs following up,' Ryga replied.

'Like those tissue samples I sent to the lab,' added Wakefield. 'I'll chase them up and call you as soon as I have any information.'

'Do you want a lift back to the hospital?' Daniels asked.

'No, I'll walk.'

Ryga addressed Daniels. 'Let's have that chat with Crawley.'

It was mid-afternoon and raining when Ryga knocked on the door of a small house on the outskirts of Southwell.

'Not more questions,' Crawley grumbled.

'Can we come in?' Ryga stepped forward.

'Looks as though you already have.'

Ryga and Daniels entered the narrow hallway, which smelled of fried food and cigarette smoke. Crawley led them to a small, cluttered and dusty room. Beyond it was the kitchen. Ryga noted the photograph on the mantelshelf of a thin, dark-haired woman in her thirties with a sullen expression, probably Crawley's late wife. Two worn and faded beige floral-patterned armchairs straddled the unlit fire. Crawley, wearing patched brown trousers and slippers, pulled a much-darned maroon woollen cardigan around his chest, covering a striped pyjama top and the vest beneath it, which showed at the open neck. The air in the chill room was filled with tension. The rain beat against the window and the rising wind whistled down the chimney. Somewhere a dog was whining as though desperate to be let in out of the storm.

'There's nothing more I can tell you about that body in the cove or those convicts who died.' Crawley reached for a packet of cigarettes on the mantelpiece.

'Then perhaps you can tell us why you killed Prudence Paisley.'

Crawley's hand froze in the act of extracting a cigarette. His eyes widened. He pushed a podgy hand through his thinning white hair. 'You're nuts. Why the blazes would I want to kill Pru? No one killed her — she died of natural causes.'

'Why is your expression in that sketch one of gloating arrogance?'

'How the hell do I know?' Crawley sat down heavily. 'I haven't seen it.'

'Then I'll tell you. It's because she discovered that you had killed those two convicts.'

Crawley shook his head slowly and sadly. 'You're scraping the barrel, Inspector. I've told you what happened. I had nothing to do with their deaths. Why would I want to kill them? It was my job to look after them.'

'And you failed.'

'I didn't know one of them would keel over.'

'You neglected them and you were sacked from your job.' It was a stab in the dark but Ryga could see that he was right.

'They did me a favour. I got a much better one working on the farm. I hated being stuck inside at the prison, but then I'd had no choice — my father got me the job. He was a warder there before me and you follow in your father's footsteps, don't you?'

Crawley was right. His father had been a merchant seaman and it was therefore the only job for him until the war had intervened. He had loved the sea and being on and around it but he had never liked being away at sea. Maybe the war had done him a favour because without it he would never have met George Simmonds in the prisoner of war camp, who had encouraged him to study, question, analyse, think and go into the police. And he'd made sure to put in a recommendation for him, which had enabled him to get his discharge from the merchant navy and join the Thames River Police.

He brought his mind back to Crawley, who gestured him into the sagging armchair opposite. Ryga perched on the edge while Daniels took the hard-backed chair by the gate-legged table against the wall. Working on a farm, Crawley would know about weed killer and other poisons that could have been used on the pinstripe-suited man and Conrad.

'Has the name of those two prisoners who died come back to you?'

'After spending all night thinking about them, yes. Kelsey and Gordons.' Crawley lit his cigarette.

'What do you know of them?'

'Nothing.'

Ryga eyed him pointedly.

'Only that they were both inside for violent armed robbery and assault. We had a lot of prisoners. It was a big place. And it was chaos in the prison at the time. The governor was in a right flap. Prisoners were dropping like flies because of the typhoid.'

Ryga recalled Sonia's words about Sam Shepherd's father having worked in the boiler house at the waterworks until it was closed because of the fatal outbreak of typhoid.

Crawley said, 'The governor didn't want to know about Kelsey's death. There was nothing that could be done for him. The priority was the sick men and there were a couple of doctors and some nurses in the prison trying to treat them even though for some it was hopeless. When Gordons got worse he was just one of several sick men. He died before the doctors could reach him. Once the waterworks closed down the typhoid stopped.'

'Did they vaccinate the prisoners?' Ryga knew that the vaccine, although fairly new in 1920, had been successfully given to soldiers, and since then had been developed further.

'I don't know. I didn't get vaccinated. I got the sack. Still, as I said, I was best out of it.'

'And neither Kelsey nor Gordons exhibited any of the symptoms of typhoid poisoning — high temperature, headaches, muscles aches, stomach pains?'

'They might have done. They didn't say. They didn't look feverish and they would have had muscle pains anyway from the hard labour.'

Was it just a coincidence that the men had died during the outbreak? Had they somehow contracted it without showing symptoms or had there been signs and Crawley and his fellow prisoner officers were just too busy and perhaps too callous to have seen and acknowledged them?

He had a few more questions to put to Crawley. 'What do you remember about Sebastian Conrad?'

Crawley looked surprised for a moment. 'Kept his nose clean, in with the governor.'

'How was that?'

'He was good with his hands and knew a lot about jewellery. Turned out a few pieces of jewellery in the prison for the governor's wife and others.'

Could he have made those cufflinks? Ryga wondered. 'Do you drive a car?'

'No. I don't have a licence.'

'Do you have a motorcycle?'

'No. The only transport I have is these.' He hit his legs. 'And a bicycle.'

But the fact he didn't have transport or a licence didn't mean that he couldn't drive. He could have used a car he had garaged somewhere to drive to Conrad's shop and kill him. He could have an accomplice with a vehicle or he could have used Shepherd's Jaguar.

'Were you at the hotel all Saturday night?'

'Of course I was.'

'Did anyone see you?'

'No. Hang on, Mr Dington came down to the kitchen. He wanted a glass of milk for his indigestion.'

'What time was this?'

'Just after three. He stayed talking for a while then went back up to bed.'

That still gave Crawley time to get to Weymouth by car, kill Conrad and return. Ryga wondered if anyone had seen or heard a car in the early hours of Sunday.

'Ned, the milkman, came round just before five, and I chatted to him for a while.'

The time window was narrowing. Ryga studied Crawley carefully. They would confirm this with Dington and Ned. And Ryga would ask Inspector Crispin's officers if any of them had seen a vehicle in the early hours of the morning, perhaps even a motorcycle.

Ryga rose and took his leave, noting the relief cross Crawley's face. In the car, he said to Daniels, 'I want you to keep an eye on him. If he leaves the house, follow him, even if it's only to go to work. I'll drop you off around the corner.'

Ryga then drove to the hospital and asked to see Captain Surgeon Wakefield. He was told he'd have to wait for an hour but a message had been sent to the surgeon, who was operating. Ryga decided to take a walk outside despite the rain. Anything was better than waiting inside a hospital. He hated the smell of death and disinfectant.

When he returned he was greeted by a haggard Wakefield, who beckoned him into an office and offered him a cup of coffee. Ryga accepted. They had the room to themselves and with a coffee in front of him Ryga took the seat opposite Wakefield across a table scattered with newspapers and magazines.

'I'm sorry but there's no result on the tissue samples yet,' Wakefield said wearily.

Ryga surmised the operation hadn't gone too well. He felt bad for disturbing the surgeon. 'I haven't come about them. What do you know about typhoid?'

Wakefield looked surprised but answered, 'A fair bit actually. It was my father's area of specialism — infectious diseases. He was a doctor at the London School of Tropical Medicine. Typhoid is a nasty, highly contagious and often fatal disease. I hope you're not expecting an outbreak.'

'It's come up in the course of my enquiries.'

'Really! Well, I can tell you now that neither the man in the pinstriped suit nor Sebastian Conrad died of typhoid poisoning. There was no internal bleeding, no tissue or organ damage to indicate it, and as far as I'm aware neither man exhibited the symptoms.'

'Which would be?' Ryga knew what they were — he'd mentioned them to Crawley — but he was keen to know if he had missed something significant.

'High temperature, stomach pain, constipation or diarrhoea.'

'Could someone have it without knowing?'

'They could carry it without being aware they were doing so. Some people who survive typhoid fever without being treated can carry the Salmonella typhi bacteria. It continues to live in the carrier's body and can be spread in faeces or urine. If the carrier handles food after going to the toilet without washing his hands then he can infect others who eat that food, but the carrier doesn't have any noticeable symptoms of the condition.'

'That's a frightening thought.'

‘Yes. After eating food or drinking fluid contaminated with the Salmonella typhi bacteria, the bacteria moves into the digestive system and quickly multiplies. Left untreated, it can get into the bloodstream and spread to other areas of the body. The typhoid fever gets worse during the weeks after infection and it can kill.’

‘Weeks then, not hours?’

‘Yes, unless the sick person has some other underlying medical condition that accelerates it, but you’d still be looking at days rather than hours after being infected with it.’

So neither Kelsey nor Gordons had typhoid poisoning, but Ryga hadn’t really thought they had.

‘I’m curious — how has this come up in your investigations, or can’t you say?’ asked Wakefield.

‘It’s connected to something that happened at the prison during Conrad’s time there.’

‘Ah, and when those two prisoners died, the ones in the sketch that Sergeant Daniels told me and Inspector Crispin about.’

‘Yes, but they didn’t die of typhoid poisoning. They didn’t show any symptoms and their deaths were fairly rapid. Both were put down to heart failure.’

‘A convenient let-out clause. We all die of heart failure.’

‘Quite. There was no post-mortem.’

Wakefield looked thoughtful and took a sip of coffee. ‘So you’re looking for a means that could have caused heart failure or sudden death.’

‘The first man died rapidly, yes — the second man twenty-four hours later.’

‘And you’re thinking the same method of poisoning could have been used on the man in the pinstriped suit and Sebastian Conrad, before they were stabbed?’

‘Possibly.’

Wakefield sat back and ran a hand through his hair. ‘We spoke about curare and hemlock before as a means of paralysing a victim before death. Curare quickly paralyses and kills the victim but not if administered by mouth, so the convict would need to have been given it intravenously.'

'He was in a work party when he died.'

'We'll rule that out then. Hemlock, though, is a possibility. The first convict could have died within half an hour if given a sufficiently heavy dose in a drink. Does that fit with what you know?'

'Yes.' Ryga knew that Crawley must have been with Prudence Paisley for much longer than the ten minutes he had claimed.

'The second man could possibly have had less hemlock to drink, enough to kill him, but it would have been slower to take effect, and therefore he died later. Hemlock can't be detected during a post-mortem and it's practically impossible to find even on analysis of tissue samples, which, if the man in the cove and Conrad were given it, the stabbing in the neck was just window dressing designed to make us believe they'd been stabbed, but why disguise a poison that is practically impossible to find anyway?'

Ryga had a reason but he wasn't going to reveal it. The killer of those two convicts hadn't wanted their deaths connected with the recent ones and poison was the connection.

Returning to the station, he found a message waiting for him from Eva to say that she was back at her aunt's cottage. She didn't need to say more than that. There was also a message from Weymouth police station asking him to phone. In Crispin's empty office he did so.

'A police constable has identified the man fitting the description of your victim, wearing a donkey jacket and a Breton cap, carrying a sailor's duffel bag,' the sergeant said when he came on the line. 'He caught the ferry from Weymouth Quay to Portland on Tuesday morning. The porter at Weymouth Quay railway station remembers the man getting off a Paddington train. He thought the man was sailing on the Channel Island ferry but a crew member on the ferry to Portland remembers him boarding.'

From Paddington it was likely the man had come into the Port of London but from where — Australia, Europe, America? As previously discussed with Sergeant Jacobs, if the man had been a passenger on a liner it would be almost impossible to track him down, but if he was a passenger onboard a cargo ship, or crew, then even given the number of ships that docked it might be possible to discover who he was and where he had come from.

That wouldn't answer why he had been killed, though, or by whom, but Ryga felt he was getting closer to that. If the pinstriped man was one of the boys in that sketch, he had returned to Portland for a reason — to retrieve and destroy the sketch so that no one would place him at the scene where the convict had died. But that begged three more questions. Why return now? How could he have known about the sketch? And, knowing about it, why would he think he was in danger of being discovered as being involved in the murder of two convicts over thirty years ago? If he had left well alone he would still be alive and no one would have known a thing about the convicts' deaths.

As Ryga drove to Wakeham and Eva's cottage, his thoughts ran on. If the man in the Breton cap had got off a boat that had docked in London on Sunday or Monday over a week ago then he wasn't Prudence Paisley's killer. He had come here to possibly warn her that she was in danger, not knowing about her death, but why travel all this way when he could have telephoned her from London or from where he had originated? Maybe he didn't trust the exchange. Or perhaps he had visited Prudence earlier, before her death, and seen the sketch, realized its potential significance and told the other boy, now a man, about it. Then, when he had heard of Prudence Paisley's death, he decided to return to tell her niece, Eva, what he knew.

As Ryga drew up outside Eva's door there were many gaps and lots of loose ends gnawing away at the back of his mind, but perhaps if the photograph was now enlarged he'd have some chance of plugging those gaps and identifying not only the victim but also his murderer.

CHAPTER TWENTY-SIX

'He most definitely is the man in the pinstriped suit,' Eva said the moment she opened the door.

'You're sure?'

'See for yourself.' She led him to the table, where she had already switched on the bright Anglepoise light and focused it on the picture. Ryga placed his hat beside the photograph. She had done an excellent job of enlarging it so that the two boys' features were now crystal clear. He examined the picture closely. The boy Eva was pointing to was older than Ryga had first thought. He looked to be twelve, or maybe thirteen. He had a square jawline, prominent brow and wide mouth. She was right — even though the life lines hadn't yet been etched on that face, it was indeed the man found dead in the cove.

He turned his attention to the other boy, wishing he had a photograph of Sam Shepherd as a youngster. Was it him? The picture was black and white but despite that he got the impression of fair hair or possibly light auburn because Pru had sketched the other boy with much darker hair. The fairer boy's face was sharp featured with a narrow, thinner mouth and a slightly cunning or maybe sour look about him. He expressed that view to Eva.

'I agree. And if you look carefully, I would say he is the leader of the two. Even though he is younger, he's sitting slightly more forward than the other child. He has prime position behind that rock and his chin is higher. His lips are stretched in almost a sneer or a gesture of defiance, as though he's smug about something, while the other boy looks more serious and troubled.'

Ryga wondered if that was just preconception talking because they both knew the convict had died and in suspicious circumstances. 'Could they have witnessed Crawley giving the convict a poisoned drink?'

'If so then the boys had a hold over him. Did they use that knowledge, though? Crawley doesn't look as though he has much money for blackmail.'

'It might have been a fortune to two adolescents.' Ryga relayed what Crawley had told him and Daniels, adding that Daniels was keeping watch on Crawley's cottage.

'Poor man. I hope he's found a sheltered spot to do so, otherwise he'll be soaked to the skin by now.'

'An occupational hazard,' Ryga said with a smile, then continued more seriously. 'But maybe it's the other way around and Crawley found he could blackmail those boys, now men, because *they* poisoned the convicts. He only realized what they had done after he saw that sketch here at your aunt's. He recognized them, made contact with one or both of them, and when the man in the cove didn't play ball he killed him, perhaps even as a warning to the other man to pay up. And if that other man isn't Sam Shepherd, and Crawley didn't eliminate him too then, as I suggested earlier, Crawley's chances of staying alive look pretty slim.' Ryga picked up the photograph and his hat. He glanced at his watch. 'Crawley should be at work at the hotel, and that means Daniels would have followed him there.'

Driving the Wolsely, Ryga told Eva about the inquest, his subsequent interview with Wakefield, and about the possibility of hemlock poisoning.

'How would the boys know about hemlock?' Eva turned into the hotel drive. 'And how would they know how much to use, or even how to use it and its effects? It sounds much more likely to have been Crawley.'

Ryga agreed as he pulled up at the hotel entrance. A bedraggled, sodden Daniels stepped out of the bushes and squelched his way onto the back seat. The rain beat against the car roof and windows.

'He didn't leave the house until he came here for work and no one visited him,' Daniels said.

Ryga swivelled round and handed Daniels the enlarged photograph. 'Ring any bells?'

Daniels shone his torch down on the picture and gave a start. 'That's the man in the cove,' he said, pointing to the boy both Ryga and Eva had identified. 'The other one looks familiar but I can't say why,' he added, puzzled. 'There's something about him . . .' His words trailed off. Ryga had felt the same but couldn't say what had struck a chord with him. He took the photograph back, tucked it into the inside pocket of his raincoat and climbed out of the car. Eva followed suit. She didn't ask if she could accompany them and Ryga didn't think of not allowing her to. He valued her judgement. If Daniels was curious about this unusual police procedure he made no comment.

Crawley looked up from behind his station and gave a start before annoyance crossed his round features. Ryga apologized for disturbing him again and said they needed his help in identifying the two boys on the shore on the day the convict had died.

'What two boys? What are you talking about?' Crawley said.

'If you wouldn't mind taking a close look at this photograph of Prudence Paisley's sketch, which Miss Paisley here has been good enough to enlarge for us.'

Crawley reached for his spectacles with shaking hands. He took a while to put them on and pick up the picture as though scared of what he might see rather than deliberately stalling for time. Ryga watched him carefully and knew that both Eva and Daniels were doing the same. Crawley looked up, mystified. His gaze swivelled from Ryga to Eva and then back to Ryga.

'I had no idea he was there. He never said a word and neither did his father,' Crawley said.

He? 'You recognize them?' Ryga asked while hiding his excitement. He sensed Eva's and Daniels' tension.

'Only the one. Him.' Crawley pointed to the boy that both Ryga and Eva had identified as the dead man in Church Ope Cove. Ryga felt himself holding his breath. 'That's Leslie Burrows. What the devil was he doing there?'

'Who is Leslie Burrows?' Ryga asked, relieved and delighted that they now had a name. He hoped that it would lead him much closer to solving the case.

'Leslie was the son of Roy Burrows, a prison warder. He and I worked together.'

'In 1920 when that picture was taken?' Eva interjected.

'Yes. The lad was to follow in his father's footsteps, like you do, as I said earlier to Mr Ryga. He was a good boy, steady, quiet. I wondered if he were cut out for the job but as it turned out he never took it up.' Crawley frowned as his mind went back thirty years and Ryga could see he was recalling what had happened. Nobody spoke. Sounds of low conversation came from the dining room as a door opened and closed. Ryga hoped they weren't going to be disturbed.

After a moment, Crawley continued. 'He ran away to sea. Never came back, never wrote to his parents. Broke his mother's heart. Leslie was an only child and the light of her life. She died a few years afterwards and Reg went to pieces, followed her to her grave eighteen months later. Very sad.'

But Leslie Burrows had returned and now he too had joined his dead parents.

Ryga said, 'Do you know why he ran away to sea?'

'Didn't want to go into the prison service. Marjorie Burrows blamed her husband for driving her boy away by insisting that he did, and then guilt and sorrow killed Reg after she was gone.'

That wasn't why Leslie had run away. He had been frightened by what he had witnessed. And what had happened to the other child? Ryga asked Crawley again if he recognized him. He swore blind he didn't. 'Is it Sam Shepherd?' Ryga pressed.

'No idea.'

Was that the truth? 'You didn't know Sam when he was a child?'

'I barely knew him as a man, only from what I saw of him in The Quarryman's Arms before he was conscripted.'

Sonia had told him that Sam had left Portland when he was a child of ten so Crawley was possibly telling the truth. But there might still be someone around who would recognize him, someone good with faces, and he knew who that might be.

There seemed nothing more to be gleaned from Crawley for the moment. If he had seen Leslie Burrows at the hotel or around the cove he certainly hadn't recognized him, unless of course he was lying. Outside, in the shelter of the car, Ryga asked Daniels to resume his watch. 'I think he's telling the truth when he says he doesn't recognize the other boy but his memory might come back to him and he might think he can capitalize on it. Or he might unwittingly tell the killer he's seen the sketch. If he does it's likely he could be the next victim. If anyone approaches the hotel, watch them. See if Crawley comes out to meet them or talks to any visitors who are not guests. Don't confront them, though. Just take down what details you can.'

Daniels climbed out. Ryga said he would drop Eva back at her cottage. He was heading back to Portland police station. 'I need to get PC Daneman's address,' he explained. 'He's the officer Crawley says returned with him to the shore to confirm that the convict was dead. The boys would have left by then but Daneman's patch was the Grove and he might very well recognize these two boys and be able to tell us more about Leslie Burrows. I think it highly likely now, based on what Crawley said, that Burrows ran away to sea and ended up working in a diamond mine, possibly in Australia, until he was in a position to help himself to some valuable pink diamonds. If he'd had an ounce of intelligence he'd have known that Amsterdam was the centre of the diamond-cutting world and maybe he'd even heard of Abramowski.'

'He took the diamonds to Amsterdam,' Eva continued for him. 'Where he met Sebastian Conrad. Would Conrad have recognized him? He was a convict, Leslie's father a prison warder.'

'Possibly. Or perhaps as they got talking about the past they made the connection. Abramowski cut the diamonds and took some as payment for his services but because Hitler was up to his nasty tricks and Abramowski was a Polish Jew and Conrad probably also a Jew, although we have no confirmation of that, they needed to get out of Europe. Leslie Burrows assisted them in getting a passage. He'd probably worked onboard ships for some time before ending up in Australia.'

'Would he have returned with them?'

'Say he did. Abramowski died on the voyage, either of severe seasickness, as was the official cause of death, or of poison.'

'Administered by Leslie Burrows, who had used it once before on the two convicts.'

'But as you said earlier, how would he have known about hemlock as a child and how to use it?'

'Maybe it wasn't hemlock,' Eva said. 'You mentioned the possibility of Crawley taking some poison from the prison medical officer. Well, perhaps Leslie Burrows' father was given some medicine, which taken in small doses was safe but in larger doses could kill, and the boy stole it from his father.'

Ryga considered this as he drew up outside the cottage. 'Why didn't he also poison Conrad in 1938 on that journey back to England?'

'Perhaps he tried but Conrad recovered. Or perhaps Conrad was happy with his haul and content to return to Weymouth and set up shop, while Burrows, after reaching London, decided to take off again by boat to Australia or

America . . .' Her words drifted away. Ryga could see she was rapidly thinking. 'Of course!' she exclaimed. 'I should have thought of it earlier. How slow of me.' She swivelled to look at him, her face radiant. 'Leslie Burrows went to America, to Pennsylvania.'

'Because he'd heard about it as a boy, William Penn being the grandson of John Penn, and the man who founded Pennsylvania,' Ryga added, recalling the postman's amazement that a Scotland Yard detective hadn't known such an important fact. 'His sons, Thomas and Richard, also owned the Pennsylvania state.' *Makes you think, doesn't it?* Well, it didn't then but it did now.

Eva continued, 'Aunt Pru exhibited at the Pennsylvania Academy of Fine Arts in Philadelphia two months before her death. She was there in person. She *must* have met Burrows. That's where he must have settled. Or perhaps on reading about the exhibition he decided he had to visit it because the paintings would be of his home.'

'Would she have recognized him after all these years?'

'We did and we're not artists, or at least you aren't to the best of my knowledge, but Pru would have seen instantly that here before her as a man was one of the boys behind that rock. But did he identify the other boy to her?' Eva frowned, then her expression cleared. 'He must have done, and Pru must have made contact with that other boy on her return, which is why she was killed. And don't say she wasn't or that we don't know that for certain because it's pretty obvious she was. It confirms this boy, or rather man as he is now, is living locally.'

'Not necessarily. Maybe he came to Portland after learning of the sketch. But why would she tell this other boy about the sketch and about Leslie Burrows if she believed they had killed the prisoners and put herself at risk?'

'That wouldn't have scared her,' Eva dismissed. 'Maybe she wanted them to own up to it after all these years. Or perhaps Burrows told her they were innocent and therefore Crawley had killed the prisoners. She could have asked

Burrows to return to testify against Crawley. Pru could have urged Crawley to own up, only Crawley, after learning about the boys being there on that day, contacted them and decided to eliminate them and Aunt Pru.'

'Then the other boy could still be Sam Shepherd and Crawley has also dispensed with him, as I mentioned before. And now Crawley thinks he's in the clear.'

'I'll put a trunk call through to the Pennsylvania Academy of Fine Arts. It's about four p.m. there. I'll speak to the curator of Pru's exhibition and get a guest list. I'll also ask if they have any staff who fit Leslie Burrows' description in case he was an employee and not a guest. I doubt if he would have used his own name.'

Ryga agreed. He said he would return to her after his interview with the constable. He drove as fast as he could to the police station, where he obtained Daneman's address. He lived in a police house at Easton not far from Eva's cottage. Crispin had gone off duty so there had been no need to explain why he wanted the address, for which Ryga was thankful. With a great sense of urgency he made for the police house, hoping that Daneman was blessed with a good memory for names and faces.

CHAPTER TWENTY-SEVEN

Ryga was shown into an ice-cold, immaculately tidy front room that smelled of polish and disinfectant by a woman with equally immaculate hair, neat appearance, and a no-nonsense expression. She smelled of carbolic soap. When she ushered in her husband a couple of minutes later — a large man with a weathered face — he instantly said, 'Let's go somewhere warmer.'

Ryga agreed with alacrity. As Daneman led him into a warm middle parlour with a roaring coal fire, Mrs Daneman gave her husband a withering look. 'Can't have an inspector of Scotland Yard catching pneumonia, Mother,' he said cheerfully. 'I'm sure the inspector would like a cup of tea.'

'That would be most welcome if it's not too much trouble, Mrs Daneman.'

She melted. Her smile was broad and warm. 'Not at all, Inspector. Let me take your hat and coat, I'll hang them up for you.'

He obliged and off she went to the kitchen with one last censuring look at her husband. Daneman switched off the radio and gestured Ryga into the seat by the fire, which popped and crackled alarmingly. Ryga was glad to see the guard in front of it. He didn't want to end up with scorched trousers like the rug in places before it.

Daneman reached for a pipe on the mantelshelf. 'Do you mind, sir?'

'Go ahead.'

'Can I offer you a smoke?'

Ryga shook his head and waited for Daneman to get his pipe going before he retrieved the photograph from his jacket pocket. 'I want you to look very carefully at this picture and tell me if you recognize either boy.'

Daneman studied the sketch. Ryga could hear the rattle of crockery from the kitchen.

'That's Leslie Burrows,' Daneman declared with certainty and slightly triumphantly, as though he'd passed a test. He was pointing at the same boy Crawley had identified. Neither man had recognized Burrows from the picture of the dead man in the newspaper, and in Daneman's case from the police photographs circulated, but perhaps that was because they'd completely forgotten all about the boy.

'What do you remember about him?' he asked.

'Quiet lad, ran away to sea, couldn't bear the thought of working in the prison with his dad.'

That was what Crawley had said. 'How do you know that?'

'He left a note for his parents, short and not so sweet. "Gone to sea, don't try to find me."'

'And did they try?'

'His father did. He asked at Weymouth Quay but nobody remembered taking on Leslie Burrows or seeing him board a ship. Neither did they see him at the railway or bus stations. Roy, his father, asked me to look into it but there was nothing I could do.'

Ryga wasn't convinced of that but he let it go. 'Is the other boy Sam Shepherd?'

'Good Lord, no. Shepherd was a miserly, scrappy little thing, face like a ferret and lazy. Cunning, too.'

'You're certain that it's not him?'

'Positive. I had to clip him around the ear once or twice for getting into trouble, stealing and answering back. I was a young constable when he and his family upped and left for Weymouth. It was a bad day when he returned and Sonia Miles fell in love with him. I hoped she'd never marry him but she did, against her dad's wishes, but he could see he could do nothing to dissuade her and he was ill. They married very quickly after he died. Shepherd was bone idle — left all the hard work to Sonia once her father died. Turned out true to form, though I shouldn't say that, seeing as he was killed at Dunkirk.'

'He wasn't.'

Daneman froze with the pipe halfway to his mouth. The kettle in the kitchen started whistling but was cut off in its prime.

Ryga said, 'He came back from Dunkirk and he's been living off rich widows ever since.'

'Well, what do you know! True to type, eh? Does Sonia know?'

'She does now, and I don't need to tell you, Constable, that this goes no further than this room.'

He nodded solemnly.

Ryga continued, 'We thought that Shepherd might be the body in the cove but it isn't him.' But could Shepherd be the killer and not Crawley? Ryga recalled what Wakefield and he had discussed about the means of death — that they were looking for a killer who could kill silently and swiftly, one trained to do so. Shepherd had been in the army. 'Was Shepherd friendly with Leslie Burrows?'

Before the constable could answer Mrs Daneman appeared with the teapot and the best china. She poured them both tea and put the plate of three Rich Tea biscuits between them on a small table close to her husband. He smiled his thanks while Ryga expressed his and she left.

'I don't know if you'd call it friendly but they were at school together,' Daneman resumed. 'Until Shepherd left the area when he was eleven. He was a bully. He bullied Burrows and encouraged some of the other lads to do the same. But that changed when Leslie took up with that other boy.'

'What other boy?' Ryga asked.

'The one in the picture with him.'

Ryga could have embraced and shaken him. Why hadn't he said so straight away? He curbed his impatience by sipping his tea and almost scalding his mouth. 'You know who he is?'

'No,' came the disappointing reply. 'He wasn't a local boy. He'd come to Portland for the sea air on account of poor health — a weak chest. Not surprising living in London, all that smoke and smog, begging your pardon, Inspector.'

'I agree with you,' Ryga rejoined while his thoughts flashed to Inspector Crispin, who suffered from asthma and had lived in London with his father, a police officer.

'He was a fair-haired boy, spoke nicely, clever. Not sure why he took to Leslie but Leslie went everywhere with him while he was here, which if I recall correctly wasn't long. Leslie worshipped him. First real friend the lad ever had.'

'Didn't the other boys bully this stranger?'

'No, because as I said he wasn't here long. He didn't go to the school. It was Easter and the school holiday.'

'Then how did Leslie Burrows meet him?'

'Through the prison. Leslie Burrows would come up to the prison to meet his father from work and the other lad was staying there, with the governor and his wife. I don't think he was related to them but was the son of a friend of the governor's.'

At last the pieces were beginning to fit. But Ryga wasn't sure he liked them much.

'Leslie ran away from home before the other boy left but not long before. Now what was his name? It's not like me to forget it.'

'Maybe it will come back to you,' Ryga said, silently willing it to do so.

'I must have heard Leslie talking about him. Leslie was a bit slow on the uptake, not backward, you understand, but he seemed to think a lot, was withdrawn, and the other boy was an outsider, so I guess it was natural for them to join up.'

'If Leslie was shy and withdrawn was it true to character for him to run away to sea?'

Daneman shrugged.

'Did he take any money?'

'Some coins his mother had put away in the jar on the mantelshelf. They wouldn't have got him very far.'

But they had done, eventually, because Ryga believed that Leslie Burrows had reached Australia. He might have been a stowaway on that first boat or perhaps the master had taken him on no questions asked and by the time the alarm was raised the ship had sailed.

Daneman drew thoughtfully and solemnly on his pipe, which made a hissing, bubbling noise.

'Did you interview Leslie's friend, this boy?' asked Ryga.

'No. By the time I got round to it he'd already gone back to London.'

Ryga recalled what Crawley had said about Conrad making jewellery for the governor's wife. Had Conrad met this boy? Had he known his name and what had happened to him thirty years later? It was possible because Conrad had been murdered. Ryga could ask the prison authorities for the name of the governor and his wife and contact them to get the boy's name, but that would all take time and there was a chance that the governor and his wife had passed away or wouldn't be able to recall it.

'And you still don't know his name?' Ryga asked with some desperation.

Daneman's face screwed up with concentration. He put down his pipe. 'It might come to me in a moment.'

Ryga sincerely hoped so. Maybe Daneman needed more prodding. 'You remember being summoned by Crawley to visit the shore where a prisoner had been taken ill and died?'

'Yes. Crawley was in a right state, not surprising really. He'd only left the prisoners for a few minutes, and when he came back one of them was stone-cold dead. Lying on his stomach with his fellow inmate struck dumb in horror.'

'Was there anyone else on that shore? Did you hear or see anyone?'

'No. Least not on the shore.'

Ryga's ears pricked up.

'Leslie and his friend were on the cliff path. They saw me looking up at them and skedaddled off.' Daneman picked up a biscuit and vigorously dunked it in his tea before putting half of it in his mouth. He dunked the second half of the biscuit, saying, 'Funny thing is, that was the last I saw of Leslie. I never thought of that before. But now that you mention it, I don't think anyone except maybe his parents saw him again from that day to this.'

'They have. And recently,' Ryga said. 'Leslie Burrows is the dead man found in Church Ope Cove.'

Daneman paused with his biscuit in his hand, which slowly plopped into the tea. 'You don't say. Well, well. Leslie came back home. And you think Sam Shepherd could have killed him? Can't see why Shepherd should, unless Leslie recognized him and it was to stop Leslie telling anyone Shepherd was alive and a deserter.'

'Leslie Burrows had diamonds.'

Daneman's eyes widened and he gave a soft whistle. 'Then Shepherd could be your man. I wouldn't put it past him to rob a dead man, and yes, I would say he was capable of killing. But I'd swear that isn't Shepherd in the picture but the other boy. If you don't mind me asking, sir, where did that picture come from?'

'It's part of a sketch executed by Prudence Paisley.'

'Ah, Mrs Paisley,' he said fondly. 'A very spirited lady.'

'This,' Ryga said, handing over the full photograph, 'is a photograph of the original. It was sketched the day the prisoner died in the cove.'

'That's Crawley.' He looked up, bewildered. 'But this means those boys were actually on that shore when the prisoner died.'

'It does.'

'I thought they'd just come along the cliff path by chance. Crawley never said they were there.'

'He claims he didn't know.'

'The other prisoner never mentioned them either.'

'He probably didn't want to get them into trouble.'

Had he mentioned them to Crawley, though, and had Crawley told him to keep quiet? Perhaps the other prisoner had also mentioned them when he was back in his cell and dying. But no one was listening and maybe they thought he had killed his fellow prisoner.

There came the rattle of some pans from the kitchen. Ryga was certain Mrs Daneman had been listening. 'Did your wife know Leslie Burrows?'

'We weren't married then, but yes, she knew the Burrows family. Mary's father was also a prison officer.'

Then he should have included her in the conversation, Ryga thought. 'Perhaps she'll remember the other boy's name.'

Daneman didn't look so sure but he crossed to the kitchen and called her in. Ryga rose and quickly explained that he was making enquiries about Leslie Burrows and his friend in 1920. She looked at him steadily and didn't question his reasons, either because she was a very good policeman's wife or she had heard every word of their conversation.

'This is the boy.' He showed her the enlarged photograph. 'Can you remember his name?'

'Only that it was Chris. I heard Leslie call out to him.'

'As in Christian or Christopher?'

She shrugged.

'Your father didn't mention the boy staying with the governor and his wife at Easter 1920?'

'If he did, I didn't take any notice. I'm sorry I can't help you, Inspector.'

But perhaps she had, although it was possible Mrs Daneman had misheard Leslie. It could be a nickname or it could have been a shortened version of a surname. He asked PC Daneman if the boy reminded him of anyone he had seen around the island, or anyone he knew. Daneman's face screwed up for several seconds as he scrutinized the picture. After a few moments of sucking on his pipe he said, 'Now you come to mention it, he does look familiar, but I can't say why or who he reminds me of.'

Ryga drove back to Eva's, his mind full of what he had learned. He was searching for a boy who had lived in London in 1920, whose father had known the prison governor. Did that make him someone connected with the Prison Commission, a civil servant, or perhaps a police officer? Crispin's father had been a London policeman. And Sergeant Braybourne had told him that Crispin suffered from asthma. Had Crispin been sent to Portland in the hope that the sea air would cure it?

What had been the treatment for asthma in 1920? Ryga had had a suspect a couple of years ago suffering from the ailment and they'd had to call in the police doctor. He racked his brain recalling what he had said. There was some kind of drug that was used in an electric nebulizer. Epinephrine, that was it, but the doctor had given them a lecture on the cures through the ages and one now came to him — the plant belladonna, commonly known as deadly nightshade, which, although it had medicinal qualities could also be poisonous and induce paralysis, coma and respiratory failure. The doctor had claimed it was an old asthma remedy from India that had become popular in the late 1800s and involved inhaling the smoke of stramonium, lobelia and belladonna.

Could Crispin have killed Burrows and Conrad? Ryga didn't like to think so but he knew it was possible. Crispin had a position and a career to protect. And although Daneman couldn't positively identify the boy as being Crispin, that was because he had only seen the boy a few times at most and way back in 1920.

As Ryga pulled up outside the cottage he thought of Crispin's narrow features studying him across the desk in his office and those of the boy in the sketch. Daneman was right — there was definitely something familiar about the child. The son of a police officer would have heard about his father's cases, which could have included death by poisoning. He had been a clever child, maybe even carried with him a contempt for convicts possibly gained from his father, and had been curious enough to see if the poison he had heard mentioned really did kill.

Ryga took a deep breath and climbed out. He knew that he would have to get evidence to prove this because Crispin would never confess to it. Ryga wasn't sure he would be able to get it. Not unless he caught Crispin in the act of trying to silence Crawley.

You follow in your father's footsteps, don't you? The words taunted Ryga as he made to knock on Eva's door but it swung open before he could do so. Her expression told him that she had managed to speak to someone at the Pennsylvania Academy of Fine Art and that she had some news to impart.

'Leslie Burrows arrived in Philadelphia, Pennsylvania in November 1938 and set up home there. Or at least a rich Englishman called Luke Bordon did. He'd made his wealth abroad in diamond mining and had a passion for art. He became a benefactor of the academy. A quiet, thoughtful single man and a very generous benefactor. He was at Aunt Pru's exhibition. In fact, he was one of the major sponsors. He left America a month ago to come to England. He said it was unlikely he would return. Did he know he might be killed?'

'If he contacted the other boy, yes. PC Daneman says it isn't Sam Shepherd. Perhaps Leslie Burrows thought it was time to confess what he and the other boy had done in 1920 and realized he'd have to pay the price for it. The post-mortem showed he was suffering from an incurable disease so had nothing to lose. I think it was Burrows' intention to confess everything to you at John Penn's Bath but Burrows saw Sam and Sonia in the meeting place. He might even have seen you arrive and leave. He went down to the shore, but his killer had followed him to John Penn's Bath and then to the shore. Or perhaps Burrows had already arranged to meet him in the cove later that night after he told you everything. He might even have written a confession intending to give it to you in the event of anything happening to him, which his killer took from the body. If Burrows knew or suspected your aunt had been killed then he must have known he could also be killed.'

'Maybe he thought he could get the better of the other man in a fight.'

If he remembered him as being weedy and suffering from asthma then yes, thought Ryga. 'If I'm not mistaken,' he said, 'Crawley is also in danger, because I believe he recognized the other boy. I've just learned that the boy was staying with the prison governor and his wife for the Easter holidays because London didn't suit his health. Once Crawley recognized Leslie Burrows in the picture he knew the identity of the other child, and he's made contact with him. Bring your camera. I think Crawley may have agreed a rendezvous with the killer and I know where that will be.'

'John Penn's Bath.'

'Yes.'

CHAPTER TWENTY-EIGHT

It was just after eleven thirty when Crawley emerged from the rear of the hotel and headed across the gardens towards the trees. Ryga could easily make out his bulky figure in the light of a weak and fleeting moon and from the torch Crawley was carrying.

Keeping his own torch low, Ryga led Eva and Daniels across the gardens, staying well behind Crawley and urging the others to be silent. Ryga's pulse was racing, as he knew theirs must be. In the dim light he glimpsed Eva's expression. It was as he expected — serious, focused, alert. Her lean body moved stealthily, silently and with great agility. She was like a cat, he thought. She made Daniels for all his fitness look clumsy — him too, probably. This was not exactly child's play for her but nowhere near as deadly as the photographic assignments she'd been engaged upon. And if she was determined to pursue her career as a war photographer, which he had no doubt she was, then soon she would be embroiled in the bitter conflict in Korea. His gut twisted at the thought but he hastily pushed it aside. This was neither the time nor the place to consider such things. Although she was a civilian and he was ultimately responsible for her safety and well-being he had total confidence in her, and that was a reassuring thought. He knew she was capable of handling herself.

Thankfully the rain had ceased but the ground was soggy. Although this hampered their progress it also helped to muffle their movements. The trees and bushes dripped water onto them. He had rung Portland police station from Eva's cottage to request assistance. The duty sergeant had promised it and Ryga had urged silence and stealth. He'd also learned that Inspector Crispin was not on the premises. Ryga hadn't expected him to be. He would have gone off duty hours ago. But would the duty sergeant call his senior officer and tell him what was on the cards? Ryga knew he would. Crispin would have left explicit instructions to be kept fully briefed on the Yard man's orders.

He gestured at them to halt as they came within hearing distance, slightly to the left of the ruin where Ryga had previously noted there was good cover. Crawley was standing over the bath, shining his torch into it. Ryga couldn't see into the bath. He knew, though, that the killer was already there.

Crawley made his way down and as he did Ryga gestured to Eva and Daniels to move forward, one each side, but with extreme caution. The sound of a twig breaking would alert the two men and ruin everything, although it would take them a moment to climb out of the hole.

Ryga held his breath and sensed his companions were doing the same. They were close enough now to hear the conversation and Ryga could see the two men.

'Well, what is it you want, dragging me out here in the middle of the night?' came the terse demand.

Crawley said, 'I know what happened in 1920 on the shore with that convict. Don't worry, I haven't said anything to Inspector Ryga. I told him I didn't know who you were. They have a picture of a sketch that Prudence Paisley did of the convicts and me, with you and Leslie Burrows in it. I told them I recognized Burrows but not you. I didn't tell them that you and Leslie Burrows poisoned those men.'

'I don't know what you're talking about.'

'The police will be interested when I tell them that you killed Leslie Burrows because he'd returned to Portland.'

'What do you want?' came the harsh reply, all pretence of innocence gone.

'A gratuity, then I'll clear out. I'm sick of this place — the weather plays havoc with my rheumatism. I'd like to go somewhere warmer and drier, Spain maybe. You can afford it.'

'It will take me some time to get the money.'

'I can wait a couple of days.'

Foolish, thought Ryga. Crawley would be dead by then, or would have been if they hadn't got here.

'All right. I'll meet you here in two days with the money.' He turned to leave but as he did he pushed up against Crawley, dislodging the torch. In a flash Ryga could see what was about to happen — it had been the same with Leslie Burrows. As Crawley bent instinctively to pick up the torch the killer's hand went into his pocket, but before he could stab the syringe into Crawley's neck, Ryga was on him.

The killer fell to the ground with Ryga on top of him. The syringe shot across the ground and within seconds Ryga had the man's hands behind his back and the handcuffs on him. He hauled him up as Eva took a picture.

'Good work, Ryga, I've got a fabulous one of you launching yourself on him.'

'I hope you're not going to sell it to the newspapers,' Ryga said, dreading the thought.

'No, this is for my private collection.' She smiled. He returned it.

'What the blazes is going on? I haven't done anything,' Crawley protested as Daniels clipped handcuffs on him too.

'Withholding vital information will do for a start,' Ryga said. He caught the sounds of footsteps heading through the undergrowth. It was good timing. Ryga, removing his handkerchief from his raincoat pocket, picked up the syringe.

Two police constables came into view and beside them, with his customary deep scowl on his lean face, was Inspector Crispin. Crispin wasn't the only man to have followed in his father's footsteps. He wasn't the only man who had lived in London in 1920. And neither was he the only man who knew about poisons. The man safely handcuffed and staring at Ryga with a calm self-assurance was the other.

Captain Surgeon Kit Wakefield.

CHAPTER TWENTY-NINE

Wednesday

It was just after 7.30 a.m. when Ryga was dropped off outside Eva's cottage. The door opened even before he had climbed out of the car. She looked as tired as he felt and he guessed she had hardly slept — perhaps she hadn't even gone to bed. He certainly hadn't. He'd spent the night in an interview room with Captain Surgeon Christopher Wakefield, Wakefield having adopted the nickname Kit on joining the navy, he'd said. Wakefield had filled in the gaps in Ryga's investigation, not that there were many, but Wakefield had seemed glad to oblige. He didn't seem at all disturbed that he would face a capital charge. But then with his arrogance — or was it vanity? Maybe they amounted to the same thing — Wakefield probably believed he would get off entirely.

'Coffee and breakfast,' Eva said on greeting him, and led Ryga through to the kitchen. She didn't ply him with questions. In fact, she didn't speak at all, for which he was profoundly grateful. It wasn't that he needed to gather his thoughts, just that he was very hungry and tired. The coffee and food would help to recharge the batteries.

As he watched her fry a mackerel, his thoughts flitted between the slender, fair Eva to the dark-haired, more curvaceous Sonia Shepherd. Two women so different in looks and personality, the former forthright, confident, comfortable in her own skin, professional with a successful career and a taste for danger. The latter was gregarious on the surface, but Ryga knew that was an act performed for the customers of The Quarryman's Arms for the sake of her and her son's survival. Sonia was as strong and determined as Eva, but behind the show of confidence was a deep insecurity and an emptiness that resonated within him. His feelings for both women were confused and because of that he was irritated with himself. Soon both of them would be out of his life and the small stab of regret inside him told him he was sorry for that. Eva was off to Korea and Sonia was married to Sam Shepherd, who would be located by the police at some stage, so what he wanted was neither here nor there. Later today he was returning to London.

He brought his mind back to Wakefield as Eva placed the plate of fish and a cup of coffee in front of him. She took the seat opposite with a coffee of her own and let him eat his breakfast. Only when he had finished did she finally speak.

'Did Wakefield kill Pru?'

'Yes.'

'How?'

'The same way he killed Burrows and Conrad, only with Pru he didn't disguise it with a knife wound because that would have created an investigation and he had to make it look like natural causes. He injected her, Burrows and Conrad with a massive dose of insulin — the same method he was going to use on Crawley. It was easy enough for him to get insulin from the hospital and, as you probably know, an overdose causes insulin shock, resulting in rapid heartbeat, shallow breathing, coma and death. He then stabbed both Burrows and Conrad in the neck to disguise the injection mark, and of course, being a doctor, he knew exactly where to strike to prevent external bleeding. He didn't know then that he would be called upon to conduct the post-mortems. That was an added bonus for him. Even so, a large dose of insulin is very difficult to detect. In fact, it's practically impossible, so Wakefield told me, unless the tissue is injected into mice and the mice produce all the symptoms of an insulin overdose.'

'He's tested that?'

'He didn't admit to that but he's had ample opportunity in his career to do so. With your aunt he took a chance that the doctor wouldn't find the needle mark in her neck, but then he wouldn't have been looking for it. There was no evidence of a break-in, nothing stolen. Prudence Paisley just collapsed and died, and as you said, there wasn't even a post-mortem.'

Eva sipped her coffee. 'And the prisoners? How did they die? Wakefield couldn't have had access to insulin then. He was only a child.'

'No, but his father was a doctor at the London School of Tropical Medicine, so he would have known about it and other poisons. However, with the convicts he used aconite.'

'From the plant monkshood or wolfsbane. Now why didn't I think of that?' she said. 'It's a very common cottage garden plant. Its leaves look like parsley and its roots like horseradish, and contains a poison if taken by mouth.'

'Yes. The governor's wife was redesigning her garden, as Crawley told us, hence the convict work party to the shore to collect items for her new beach-themed garden. She needed to move some plants to make way for this, which included monkshood. The time to transplant them is spring, so she thought April was ideal. She showed the young Wakefield how to carefully tease the fragile roots apart and replant the crowns just below the soil surface, while giving him a lecture on how poisonous the plants were.' Ryga recalled how Wakefield had relayed this coolly, clinically. 'Wakefield was intrigued by this. He telephoned his father to ask him about it and was told that a large dose, if taken by mouth, could kill almost immediately. It is absorbed through the gastrointestinal tract and affects the central nervous system, paralysing the muscles, including the heart muscles.'

'So he dug up some of the plant and put it in what?'

'Not a drink, as I previously thought, but in some Dundee cake the prison governor's wife had made. Leslie Burrows offered the prisoners a piece of cake each, not knowing that Wakefield had mixed the crumbling pieces with aconite.'

'And to them it must have seemed like a wonderful charitable act, not to mention a luxury.'

'Yes. Wakefield, ever curious, had altered the doses. One piece of cake contained a huge amount of the plant, the other less so. One killed the prisoner almost immediately while the other man took longer to die. His symptoms would have been a burning and tingling in the mouth, followed by numbness in the tongue, throat and face.'

'Thereby silencing him. No wonder the poor soul never said a word. He couldn't.'

'And he'd probably have vomited in his cell before his respiratory muscles became paralysed and then his heart muscles. The only post-mortem signs are those of asphyxia, but of course there was no post-mortem in their case.'

'And Wakefield's father never suspected?'

'Wakefield said not but I'm not so sure. He had been sent to stay with the prison governor and his wife for the Easter holidays by his father, for his health according to Wakefield. The London smog was making him a sickly child. He could have stayed at his boarding school in Surrey but his father thought it was unsuitable and withdrew him.'

'Why?'

'I only have Wakefield's version and what I've inferred from his personality and what happened with those convicts. He was a very inquisitive and highly intelligent ten-year-old. He thought those at his school beneath him and didn't endear himself to them.'

'He was bullied.'

'Possibly, or he was the bully and had caused some problems with the other boys at the school. When he arrived on Portland he recognized someone being bullied — Leslie Burrows. Wakefield cultivated him. Burrows became Wakefield's slave. He'd do anything for his new friend. Wakefield told Burrows to give the convicts the cake once Crawley was out of sight. Burrows always believed he had killed the convicts, and he had, but only because he had been tricked. He had no idea the cake contained a lethal poison. When he saw what happened he got very frightened and ran away to sea. Wakefield said his father heard about the typhoid outbreak and whisked him away from Portland, and he went into the navy, which gave him discipline. He trained to become a doctor, satisfying his intellect and enquiring mind.'

'With such an obvious disregard for human life it makes you wonder why he became a doctor.'

'I asked him that. He looked at me as though I was stupid. He said it was always the clinical challenge that excited him, the analysis of the condition, the diagnosis, then the experimentation of the treatment, and outcome. It didn't seem to matter to him whether patients lived or died. He'd have been far more suited to pathology, cutting up dead bodies than treating live ones. He lacks compassion and, to his mind, even back in 1920 as a child, the prisoners were expendable. They were human guinea pigs.'

'Much like the Nazis,' Eva muttered.

There was a brief silence between them before Ryga spoke. 'Wakefield knew the prisoners would be going on the work party because Leslie Burrows had heard about it from his father. Wakefield thought it was the ideal opportunity to try out his experiment.' Ryga had shuddered inside when Wakefield had said this in the police station, evenly and in a matter-of-fact manner. The Chief Constable had sucked in his breath and his body had become rigid. 'The boys went to the bay and hid themselves behind the rocks.'

'How did they know Crawley would leave the prisoners?'

'They didn't. Wakefield said that one of them would have decoyed him away but when he went of his own accord they took their chance. When Burrows saw what happened he broke down and became a risk to Wakefield. He gave Burrows what money he had—'

'Enabling him to say Burrows had stolen it if he needed to.'

'Yes. But he never did because he also left shortly afterwards. Burrows told Wakefield on the shore in Church Ope Cove that he had stowed away on a boat in Weymouth and had managed to work his way to London, where, as we said, he eventually ended up in Australia. But he told Wakefield no more than that.'

'Probably didn't get the chance.'

'No. The rest, as I believe we already worked out, is that Burrows ended up working in a diamond mine and stole diamonds as a means of escaping poverty and hard labour. He took them to Amsterdam, contacted Abramowski and discovered that Conrad had been a prisoner at the time of the typhoid outbreak. He probably asked him about Chris Wakefield and the two prisoners. Conrad wouldn't have known much, if anything, about them but the fact that Burrows had asked made Conrad curious and maybe he recognized or twigged who Burrows was. Burrows was certain to have adopted another name by then.'

'Not so slow or backward then.'

'He was never backward,' Ryga said. 'Just thoughtful. When he reached Weymouth in 1938 with Conrad, he learned that his parents were dead and that there was nothing for him on Portland, so he took off again for America with his diamonds.'

'And reinvented himself as Luke Bordon, a rich philanthropist with a love of art.'

'Wakefield was surprised and irked. I took great pleasure in telling him that. Wakefield thought Leslie Burrows was a poor fisherman or sailor, a man who had never got out of his class.'

'Which was what Burrows wanted him to think, hence the sailor's clothes. And Wakefield changed some of the clothes, the suit and shoes, after he'd killed Burrows and stole Burrows' identity to stop you tracing him.'

'Yes, but he missed the cufflinks.'

'And the tie? Surely he'd have thought a man of Burrows' supposed class wouldn't be wearing a silk tie designed and made by Van Heusen of Pennsylvania? And the shirt was of good-quality cotton.'

'Wakefield thought Burrows had stolen the tie and got the shirt second hand. Seeing the vest and socks were silk must have made Wakefield wonder that day in the mortuary, but I didn't see any sign of surprise on Wakefield's face. He was very good at hiding his feelings, but then he doesn't seem to have any. He told me that he had been in a hurry to undress and redress the body in case anyone came, although it was the very early hours of Wednesday morning and there was little chance of them being disturbed. I think Burrows agreed to meet Wakefield in the cove, or even suggested it himself as their rendezvous point, because as I mentioned before it was his intention to have already relayed to you the truth about your aunt's death at your meeting at John Penn's Bath. But you hadn't shown up and two other people were there, so he went down into the cove to wait for Wakefield. Perhaps he thought he could get the better of Wakefield if he attempted anything. Burrows was strong and he'd learned how to handle himself in the intervening years. What he hadn't counted on was the insulin injection.

'The pinstriped suit and handmade shoes Wakefield got from a corpse in the mortuary, a man with no relatives. And he'd even pointed out the poor soul to me naked and on the slab!' *Sadly he died on the operating table, cardiac arrest during surgery. It can happen. No relatives and no mystery surrounding him.*

Eva sipped her coffee and sighed — not sorrowfully, thought Ryga, but at the evil mankind is capable of. But then she, like him, had seen a lot of it.

'He made sure there were no tailors' marks on the suit or the name of the shoemakers and both were second hand when the other corpse acquired them.'

'But—'

'How did he know they would fit? He didn't for certain, although he'd probably managed to extract a fair description of Burrows from your aunt. If the shoes hadn't fitted he'd probably have left Burrows barefoot but they did. He wasn't too worried, just as long as he left no identity on Burrows, and he wanted to confuse the picture as much as possible. He didn't count on Scotland Yard becoming involved. Or if we did, that we would get anywhere with the investigation.'

'He didn't bank on you then?'

Ryga smiled. Then continued more solemnly, 'I got the impression dressing the corpse in a dead man's clothes was something of a joke for Wakefield.'

'A damn sick one.'

'Yes. He took the duffel bag and rifled through it but there was nothing to indicate where Burrows had come from or what he had been doing in the intervening years. Not even his passport, which Burrows must have hidden or deposited somewhere.'

'At a bank in London, perhaps.'

'Possibly. Burrows was clever but sadly not clever enough to avoid being killed. Wakefield says he weighed down the duffel bag with rocks and ditched it in the sea.'

'And he thought he was safe until Conrad tracked him down. Did Conrad make the cufflinks for Burrows?'

'He must have done, and he recognized them when I showed them to him. He knew then that the dead man was definitely Leslie Burrows and he knew who Burrows' friend had been all those years ago. Either Burrows had told him or he remembered the name of the boy staying with the governor's wife. He had made jewellery for her, according to Crawley. It wasn't until he read the article by Sandy Mountfort in the newspaper that the man carrying out the post-mortem was Captain Surgeon Kit Wakefield that he suspected that Wakefield had killed Burrows. Conrad had the newspaper in the shop when Daniels and I first arrived but there was no sign of it when we returned to search the place. And it wasn't with the rubbish. Conrad got in touch with Wakefield via the hospital and said he had some information for him on the man found in Church Ope Cove that the police might be very interested in hearing.'

'What an idiot!' Eva scoffed. 'Did he really think Wakefield would let him live with that knowledge?'

Ryga shrugged. 'People can be very stupid and very greedy. Crawley was about to make the same mistake.'

Eva poured Ryga another coffee and herself one. She said, 'Burrows, on seeing that sketch in the exhibition, should have left well alone.'

'Maybe he would have done but for the fact that your aunt recognized him after all those years.'

'And Burrows saw in that sketch Wakefield's expression as Pru had interpreted it — gloating — and suddenly he saw how he had been used and deceived. Pru must have contacted Leslie Burrows on her return to England and told him where Wakefield was. She'd have got Wakefield's name from Burrows and she had contacts at the admiralty — she simply asked one of them to find out where Wakefield was. But how did she know he was in the navy?'

'She contacted the Prison Commission and asked for the names of the prison governor and his wife in 1920. She got their address — she probably told the commission she had a painting she'd like to give them — and visited them. A constable will call on Wilfred and Lillian Faye today. They live in Bookham, a village in Surrey, and they'll confirm what Wakefield's told us. He said your aunt told him she'd traced him via them. They told her that his father had put him into the navy and that he had trained as a doctor and had become a very good one. He'd earned himself a distinguished career during the war. All she had to do then was contact someone in the admiralty to ask where he was based. Your aunt also passed this information on to Leslie Burrows by telephone but then foolishly contacted Wakefield and told him she had something he might like to see from 1920.'

Eva shook her head sadly.

'When Wakefield visited your aunt earlier in the day on which he killed her he spun her a yarn about becoming a doctor so that he could atone for what he and Burrows had done all those years ago. By doing so he had saved many lives, which is fact. He acted as though he was consumed with remorse and said he would make it up to Burrows if he knew how to get in touch with him.'

Eva raised her eyebrows. 'Don't tell me Pru told him?'

'No. She said she would contact Burrows and pass on his name and contact details, which she obviously did. Wakefield had hoped to get the information from her but he couldn't physically hurt her for fear her death would look suspicious and be investigated. But he had seen the sketch and he knew where to find it after killing her. Your aunt told him nothing about Burrows' background but Burrows, having got the details from Pru, then read about her death and knew what must have happened. He came to England and made contact with Wakefield.'

Eva ran her hand through her hair. 'So when and how did Crawley track down Wakefield if he couldn't remember the boy's name?'

Ryga sat back and rubbed his temple. It had taken a while to get the truth out of Crawley but at last, through threats that he'd be charged as an accomplice to murder, he had coughed up. 'Oh, he remembered, but only after I showed him the enlarged photograph. He'd also read the same newspaper article as Conrad, where Mountfort had mentioned Wakefield. He did much the same as Conrad. He called the hospital and asked to speak to Wakefield about something that had happened in 1920 that had always troubled him. He didn't know for certain he had the right man. Wakefield came on the line and said he didn't know what he was talking about.'

'So Crawley enlightened him.'

'With a brief version of events.'

'And Wakefield suggested they meet.'

'Yes. So he knew he was right. You know the rest. Crawley should have come to the police. He withheld information and almost got himself killed in the process.'

'Poor Aunt Pru.' Eva shook her head sadly.

'I'm sorry.'

'She'd have liked to know the outcome. Thank you for catching her killer, Ryga. At least that is some kind of justice, which is more than many people get.'

'Yes,' Ryga answered. Wakefield had left a trail of deaths behind him and he had shown no remorse. He didn't seem to know how to feel it and was surprised it was expected of him. Ryga broke the short silence between them. 'Are you still going to Korea?'

'It's what I do, Ryga. I'm a war photographer.'

He nodded slowly.

'And you? Are you returning to London?'

'As soon as I've collected my things from the pub.'

'I'll drive you there.'

'No, I'll walk. The fresh air will help keep me awake.' He could sleep on the train.

He rose. She followed suit.

'Will the police still look for Sam Shepherd?' she asked.

'They have to.'

'Poor Sonia.' At the door, she said, 'Will you come back here?'

He knew what she meant by that. Would he continue to see Sonia?

'Perhaps. I don't know.' He held out his hand. She took it.

'Well, you know where to find me.'

My God, had he misjudged her last remark? Had she meant would he return to see her?

'I'll either be here, in London, or Korea, although that is a long way to come so I won't expect you. Good luck to you, Ryga.'

'And to you, Eva.'

She smiled. And her smile and parting words stayed with him all the way to London.

THE END

THE JOFFE BOOKS STORY

We began in 2014 when Jasper agreed to publish his mum's much-rejected romance novel and it became a bestseller.

Since then we've grown into the largest independent publisher in the UK. We're extremely proud to publish some of the very best writers in the world, including Joy Ellis, Faith Martin, Caro Ramsay, Helen Forrester, Simon Brett and Robert Goddard. Everyone at Joffe Books loves reading and we never forget that it all begins with the magic of an author telling a story.

We are proud to publish talented first-time authors, as well as established writers whose books we love introducing to a new generation of readers.

We have been shortlisted for Independent Publisher of the Year at the British Book Awards three times, in 2020, 2021 and 2022, and for the Diversity and Inclusivity Award at the Independent Publishing Awards in 2022.

We built this company with your help, and we love to hear from you, so please email us about absolutely anything bookish at feedback@joffebooks.com

If you want to receive free books every Friday and hear about all our new releases, join our mailing list: www.joffebooks.com/contact

And when you tell your friends about us, just remember: it's pronounced Joffe as in coffee or toffee!

ALSO BY PAULINE ROWSON

INSPECTOR RYGA
HISTORICAL MYSTERIES
Book 1: DEATH IN THE COVE

THE ART MARVIK MYSTERIES
Book 1: DEADLY WAVES
Book 2: DANGEROUS CARGO
Book 3: LOST VOYAGE
Book 4: FATAL DEPTHS

THE SOLENT MURDER MYSTERIES
Book 1: THE PORTSMOUTH MURDERS
Book 2: THE LANGSTONE HARBOUR MURDERS
Book 3: THE HORSEA MARINA MURDERS
Book 4: THE ROYAL HOTEL MURDERS
Book 5: THE ISLE OF WIGHT MURDERS
Book 6: THE PORTCHESTER CASTLE MURDERS
Book 7: THE CHALE BAY MURDERS
Book 8: THE FARLINGTON MARSH MURDERS
Book 9: THE OYSTER QUAYS MURDERS
Book 10: THE COWES WEEK MURDERS
Book 11: THE BOATHOUSE MURDERS
Book 12: THE THORNEY ISLAND MURDERS
Book 13: THE GUERNSEY FERRY MURDERS
Book 14: THE RAT ISLAND MURDERS
Book 15: THE LUCCOMBE BAY MURDERS
Book 16: THE SOUTH BINNESS MURDERS

Printed in Great Britain
by Amazon

42787435R00158